A PRIMARY DECISION

THE WORTHINGTON DESTINY ■ BOOK 3

A PRIMARY DECISION

A NOVEL

DR. KEVIN LEMAN
AND JEFF NESBIT

℞
Revell

a division of Baker Publishing Group
Grand Rapids, Michigan

© 2016 by Dr. Kevin Leman and Jeff Nesbit

Published by Revell
a division of Baker Publishing Group
P.O. Box 6287, Grand Rapids, MI 49516-6287
www.revellbooks.com

Printed in the United States of America

Library of Congress Cataloging-in-Publication Data
Names: Leman, Kevin, author. | Nesbit, Jeffrey Asher, author.
Title: A primary decision : a novel / Dr. Kevin Leman and Jeff Nesbit.
Description: Grand Rapids, MI : Revell, a division of Baker Publishing Group,
    [2016] | Series: The Worthington destiny ; book 3
Identifiers: LCCN 2016023544 | ISBN 9780800723309 (softcover)
Subjects: LCSH: Upper class families—Fiction. | Political campaigns—Fiction. |
    Ambition—Fiction. | Domestic fiction. | Political fiction. | GSAFD: Christian
    fiction.
Classification: LCC PS3612.E4455 P75 2016 | DDC 813/.6—dc23
LC record available at https://lccn.loc.gov/2016023544

"To those who are given much, much is required" is a paraphrase of Luke 12:48.

Edited by Ramona Cramer Tucker

16   17   18   19   20   21   22   7   6   5   4   3   2   1

///

To all those curious enough
to seek, question, and forge their own path in life.

And to those who choose to do the right thing,
no matter the consequences.

///

Glossary

AF: American Frontier
AG: Attorney General
DA: District Attorney
DHS: Department of Homeland Security
DOJ: Department of Justice
FBI: Federal Bureau of Investigation
GOP: Grand Old Party (Republican Party)
JC: Judiciary Committee
NGO: Non-governmental organization
NYPD: New York Police Department
RNC: Republican National Convention

1

RUSSELL SENATE OFFICE BUILDING
WASHINGTON, D.C.

Tension crackled in the air.

All eyes in the room swiveled toward attorney general nominee Sarah Worthington.

"You don't think it's an issue?" The dark eyes of Senate
Judiciary Committee Chair Phelps pierced Sarah with an ac-
cusatory glare. "That, should you be confirmed as the head
of the Department of Justice, that same department will be
prosecuting American Frontier? The very company for which
your brother is CEO? In one of the biggest oil disasters our
country has ever faced?"

It wasn't the first targeted barb she'd faced from the 18-
member committee during the all-day vetting session. Arrows
had flown from both majority and minority members inside
the dark wood–paneled room of the Russell Senate Office
Building.

Sarah didn't flinch. Steely gaze met steely gaze. "I believe I
have already answered that question from multiple venues in

the past eight hours, Mr. Chairman. But let me be even clearer. I will do the right thing always, no matter the cost to me personally." She lifted her chin. "Just like every member in my family has done in every venture they've been involved with. And that includes my brother Will at American Frontier."

She could have said much more. Her natural instinct was to defend her family from completely off-the-mark comments. But long ago she'd learned from Will that staying calm under fire and using fewer words was better. People had less ammunition for their arguments. From her other brother, Sean, she'd assimilated the masterful art of negotiation—seeing both sides of any situation. The members of the JC were merely doing their job. She'd already gone rounds with their questions not only about her work on past cases with the Department of Justice's Criminal Division, but also about her two brothers' recently aborted political runs—Will's for the Senate seat in New York, and Sean's for governor of New York.

But the intensity of questioning and the flash of cameras in the press gallery had built into what now threatened to be a migraine. Sarah was tired of sitting behind the same nine-by-twelve black-cloth table.

Tired of being grilled by senators who had to sit in the same room but didn't like each other. It was like watching adolescent boys trying to one-up each other on the playground by flexing their muscles.

Tired of the lukewarm water in the plastic pitchers next to her, since the ice had long ago melted.

The chairman gave a short, dismissive nod. "That concludes our business here today. Voting will proceed at the next session. We thank you for your time, Ms. Worthington."

Sarah swiftly gathered her papers and stashed them in her

briefcase. She was glad for the previous meetings with the legislative affairs staff at the White House to prepare her for the vetting process. The White House staff had warned her that the JC process would be ugly—that she'd likely receive vengeful challenges from surprise quarters. Her nomination by President Rich, whose tirades earned him increasingly wide enemies and fair-weather friends even within his Republican camp, and the fact she'd somehow vaulted over several rungs of Department of Justice leaders had raised suspicions in both Democrat and Republican wings. That she was a woman didn't help with the male old-timers on the JC, especially when only two of the previous 80-plus US attorney generals had been women. That she was from a well-known blue-blood family headlined often by the media notched up the controversy further.

The White House staff had assumed the threat of any weaknesses being exposed would scare Sarah. Instead that threat made her more determined to face down any bullies. She would not cave in. America needed strong, dependable leaders with courage, expertise, and long-range discernment. She had determined long ago to be in those ranks. The only questions had been exactly where and when.

From the earliest moment she could remember, her father, Bill Worthington, had drilled into her mind the mantra that continually drove her: "To those who are given much, much is required."

So, at the end of those prior meetings with the legislative affairs staff, she'd only said, "Let's get to work then. I do not intend to lose this."

Now the vetting session she'd prepared for was over. The Senate Judiciary Committee would call a vote at a later date. If that vote was in her favor, the matter would go to the Senate floor next. Then the full Senate vote would likely take a few weeks, even a month.

The long and short of it was, if she was confirmed, she'd be the new head of the Department of Justice and serve on the president's cabinet. She intended to use that power for good, no matter who she'd have to face off with.

Now, though, after the intensity of the grilling she'd just gone through with the JC, she knew the road ahead would likely be harder than she'd ever dreamed.

NEW YORK CITY

Will Worthington had felt conflicted all morning and into the afternoon during his high-powered Worthington Shares meetings. Sarah was taking a big step today. He was worried, and not only about her. Her being vetted as attorney general meant a lot of people would be digging deeply into the secrets of the Worthington family. Less than a year ago, that wouldn't have concerned him in the least. Now, well . . .

He checked the time. Hopefully she'd be out of the Judiciary Committee vetting session. He speed-dialed her cell and asked without preamble, "So, how did it go?"

She laughed. "Typical big brother, cutting to the chase." Then her voice sobered. "It was intense. Very intense."

Anxiety flickered again. "Anything in particular?"

There was a pause. "Nearly everything. I haven't had a chance to filter through any of it. I left the room only minutes ago. I'm not even in the limo yet."

He took a breath. It was now or never. He had to ask, even though he was certain what her response would be. "Sure you want to do this?"

"Why—you think I'm not up to it?" Her tone turned testy.

So, he gathered, it had been a much harder day than even his unconquerable sister had imagined.

"No, that's not it," he replied gently. "I learned the hard way never to underestimate my little sister."

"What is it then?" He didn't have to be standing next to her to picture her scowl and narrowed eyes.

He steeled himself to stay calm. It was something he'd learned well from their father. "Stay calm and you stay in control," Bill Worthington always said. "As soon as you lose your cool, you lose control and the other person gains it."

"This isn't just about you, you know," Will said. "They'll be digging a lot into our family too."

"You mean that crazy rumor that floats around about where Worthington money originally came from?" Her short laugh was sarcastic. "Seriously, Will."

"But they could care about the photos of Sean." He didn't need to say which photos.

"As far as public sentiment is concerned, that case is as dead and buried as the bomber," she said in the hushed but meaning-business tone she'd perfected when in a crowd. "Sandstrom's in jail. Nobody cares that some no-name blew a chunk out of a corporate building anymore."

"But you care, or you wouldn't still be digging," he shot back. "And it's still Sean's face on those photos. They could pop up anywhere, anytime. You know that. I know that. And Mom and Dad have no idea."

At that minute Drew, Will's right-hand man and mentor, caught Will's eye and pointed to his watch. Will nodded. They were already a couple of minutes late for a potential acquisitions meeting.

"We can talk later." He ended the call.

Apprehension prickled down his back. Trying to shake it off

so he could focus on the coming meeting, he walked briskly toward Drew. But the feeling of trouble on the horizon remained.

She has no idea just how deep and far this could go.

MAPUTO, MOZAMBIQUE

Sean Worthington had been in Maputo for several days checking out multiple potential NGOs. Since Mozambique had one of Africa's fastest-growing economies, small businesses were booming, especially in the medical and engineering fields. One of those businesses, Sean felt strongly, was poised on the edge of what could become phenomenal growth in caring for the medical needs of remote tribes in Africa.

He'd just spent the day going over the company's financials when he received a text from his *New York Times* reporter friend Jon Gillibrand.

Heard from your sis?

After two decades of reporting at the environment desk and then the science desk for the *Times*, Jon was a master at remembering details. More than that, he genuinely cared about people in every strata of society. Jon didn't care a whit that Sean was a Worthington or that he had more cash stashed in his closet for emergencies than Jon had in his entire savings account. Jon wasn't impressed by wealth or position. He was real and honorable. Such people were difficult to come by in the Worthingtons' complicated world.

Sean

Not yet. Probably still in the middle of the lions' den. I'll call her late tonight her time.

Jon
Ah, the traditional late-night wake-up call by
Sean Worthington.

Sean laughed. It had become a joke among his circle of friends.

Of course. Would it be any other way?

This time you might want to let her sleep. I've
covered the vetting process. It's intense.

Sean lifted an eyebrow. Jon was giving him advice about his sister? That was a new one.

Jon, Sarah, and DHS field agent Darcy Wiggins were still working together on the Polar Bear bombing case. Once those three had their teeth into an unsolved case, they didn't let go.

Many reporters were only after the hottest story of the day. But Jon had built a career not only on tracking details and evidence but also on the human element behind the news. Because his stories had the largest readership at the *Times*, they got the biggest hits digitally, and he'd been there for so many years his editors cut him some slack to work on the stories he wanted to write.

The Polar Bear Bomber had done a nosedive off a 30-story building in New York City, leaving a suicide note that succinctly explained his actions. The NYPD, Department of Homeland Security, FBI, and Department of Justice had heaved a sigh of relief at having one high-profile case officially off the books.

But Jon, Sarah, and Darcy remained convinced there was more to the bombing than met the eye, especially after they'd met a close friend of the bomber. They had continued to dig, meeting on their own time, usually at Sarah's penthouse in Greenwich Village.

Even though Sean himself had been implicated in the bombing through a shady setup, he had walked away mentally from any desire for revenge. But he knew his sister, whose strong sense of justice was ingrained in her DNA, would never give up until everyone involved was revealed and had received their due.

Sean grinned, remembering how the once-closed investigation had been hastily reopened after Eric Sandstrom's arrest. A simple hint in Jon's *Times* article that the DOJ might be looking again into the bombing had pressured Sarah's disgruntled boss, John Barnhill, to reopen the case within the hour. When the media frenzy again died down, the investigation quietly moved back to the dusty archives of the DOJ. But not for Sarah, Jon, and Darcy.

A thought struck Sean. Why was this particular bombing so important for Jon, who'd been entrenched in the news as a career? Was it merely his desire that justice be done for his friends the Worthingtons, who had been pawns in a high-level power struggle? And for the bomber, an emotionally unstable young man who needed help but instead had been used?

Sean pondered for a minute. He and Jon had just weathered the first major test of their friendship, when both became interested in Elizabeth, the third of their best-friends trio. In Sean's large circle of friends and acquaintances, the brilliant scientist, passionate in her views, was the only woman Sean had ever wanted to compete for. After a tense period between the friends, Jon had backed off, saying Elizabeth wasn't for him. He admitted Sean would be better for her.

Sean had been puzzled. Jon never backed off while pursuing anything he'd set his sights on. Then again, the straightforward Jon would never say something he didn't mean. So Sean had accepted him at his word.

But had Jon also backed off for another reason?

Another text flashed.

Jon
You still there?

Sean
Yup.

He had to say it.

So what's the sudden interest in my sister's well-being?

There was a full minute of text silence, then:

She's a good person. I care about her and what happens to her.

Sean snorted at such lame comments from the master of words. They could mean only one thing—Jon was in cover-up mode. Sean's instinct was confirmed a second later when Jon added:

I care about all of you Ws. Even you, when you're a pain in the neck. Which has been a lot lately.

Jon and my sister? Sean's stomach rumbled. He tucked away the question for future pondering—after he'd found the best local fare in Maputo.

Washington, D.C.

Light drizzle cooled Sarah's cheeks as she strode out the double doors of Washington's oldest United States Senate office building. The dampness and gray sky in the capital didn't bother her as much as the call from Will.

"This isn't just about you, you know," he'd said in his trademark tone that drove her crazy. It was the big-brother voice he'd used all his life to bend his siblings—and anyone else—to the way he wanted them to go. "They'll be digging a lot into our family too."

So he does think his baby sister can't do it—that such a big job is too big. Sarah rolled her eyes. Likely she'd get a call from their father soon too, questioning whether she was up to the challenge.

Sarah exhaled in annoyance. She was in her midthirties, for heaven's sake. Yet her family couldn't let her move on from her baby-of-the-family status, even with all she'd accomplished in her career. She had held her own for years in the tough world of the Department of Justice's Criminal Division. Still, all they could see was the little girl who used to twirl in pink princess garb, waving a bejeweled-star wand and singing off-key at the top of her lungs.

Sometimes she still felt like the puppy of the family. The one patted on the head and told "Good job" for being a cute decoration in the room. She chafed against their non-expectations, their belief that her major accomplishment in life would be finding a suitable marriage match so she could step into a role similar to her mother's.

Will was clearly the star of their family—even if his two most recent decisions had tarnished his brilliance a bit. His abrupt announcement that he was stepping away from the Senate race had stunned her family, derailing his straight-ahead trajectory. Then he'd chosen to take over the CEO position of American Frontier at its worst moment in history. Yet even with those startling decisions, her father hadn't been all over Will's case. In fact, Bill Worthington had been strangely reticent to step in—a character quality completely opposite of his usual behavior in his children's lives.

Bill still didn't take Sarah seriously, she felt. He didn't understand why she had taken the career track she did. It would have been easy for her to finish university as the social butterfly hub and to marry one of the blue-chip male admirers who eagerly trailed in her wake. But she hadn't wanted any of them.

Instead she'd chosen to get serious about law. A stint in pro bono work had given her a passion for assisting the underprivileged. One thing had led to another. She'd signed away her voting rights to Worthington Shares and started earning a salary, leaving her father scratching his head. With a generous trust fund, she didn't need the salary, he said. He didn't know she gave nearly all of it to charitable causes.

Her mother, who had spent her life making her family happy and smoothing their pathways in life, just wanted Sarah to be happy. And married, of course.

Her oldest brother was always in protective mode, poised to face down any giant on his sister's behalf. With that thought, some of her fiery temper about the phone call dissipated. Will was just being Will. He couldn't help it.

And her middle brother? Sean was off globe-trotting, doing his own thing as usual, but happier than she'd ever seen him. Likely that had everything to do with Elizabeth, the quirky scientist he'd fallen in love with.

But the entire Worthington family agreed on one thing. The AG appointment by the president of the US—and its timing—had stunned them. Even Sarah, who had quietly dreamed of attaining the position someday, had been shocked by her boss's sudden announcement that the president wanted her. Even now, she still wrestled with the motive behind the nomination.

How much, if anything, did the president's choice have to do with her relentless fight on behalf of the DOJ's Criminal Division to put the former CEO of American Frontier, Eric Sandstrom, behind bars?

Sandstrom had contributed in a big way to the president's first run at the White House and had promised significant funds toward his reelection campaign in the coming year. Was the president simply trying to clear a determined Worthington out of his way before she embarrassed him? Or had she truly earned the opportunity to become the nation's attorney general, even over those more qualified? Clearly, her boss, a veteran in the DOJ, had expected such an appointment to come to him.

Or did the sudden move have more to do with American Frontier and the story Jason Carson, Sandstrom's lackey, had leaked to the media? And with whatever behind-the-scenes deal Carson had made with the president to keep himself squeaky clean while Sandstrom went to jail? Those questions haunted Sarah in her waking hours.

Her thoughts flicked to the potential future. If she was confirmed as the chief People's Lawyer, she'd have considerable authority over the lives and well-being of every person in the United States through the large-scale decisions she'd be making. It was a job she took very seriously. Even more, she felt confident the skills she'd acquired through her work in the legal system and later through the Department of Justice would assist her in doing that job well.

But the past continued to tug at her. She would have to leave all of her individual cases at the DOJ behind. The candidate stepping into her job was more than competent. No worries there. The transition would be seamless. But Sarah's hands would be tied on the American Frontier and Polar Bear bombing investigation. The White House staff had strongly suggested she recuse herself from any cases involving AF, since her brother was now CEO. That meant she could no longer aggressively pursue the truth about the bombing with her contacts.

Thankfully, she could count on Darcy and Jon. They'd keep her in the loop on anything they discovered.

She paused momentarily outside the impressive white building to clear the day's tension. Her gaze swept the skyline of the city that housed the most powerful cogs in the wheels of America's government.

She recalled again Will's statement, "This isn't just about you, you know."

A shiver coursed through her. She was used to him abruptly ending phone calls. But his hesitancy unsettled her.

Sarah had never seen Will be hesitant about anything until he'd backed out of the New York Senate race. The reminder of Carson hanging around the shadows to the side of the stage when Will made his announcement still incensed her. It had been extremely frustrating for Sarah, who could wrestle the truth out of nearly anyone, not to be able to get immediate answers for why Carson was present. Will had remained close-mouthed until she'd at last learned about the photos through Jon's revelation.

Even after that debacle, life had turned out all right for Will. He now had his dream job—though not in the timing any of them would have expected—as the CEO of American Frontier.

His acceptance of the position had publicly pitted brother and sister against each other, keeping the media buzzing. Her job for the DOJ's Criminal Division was to sue the very company her brother was CEO for. But the Worthingtons attacked that problem the same way they did everything—head-on. The two siblings had shared a brief press conference. Their frank honesty and unified approach had taken the sting out of the media's coverage and caused both AF and the DOJ to come out looking stronger.

So why was Will hesitant now? Was he just worried about his baby sister as she stepped into her new position, afraid she couldn't take the daily heat? Or was something else going on? Will rarely backed away from confrontation.

With those quandaries, her attorney instinct and determination kicked into high gear. With cool, calm assessment, she again studied the landscape of D.C. This would soon be her town, her responsibility.

Spotting her limo, she strode confidently toward it.

2

Drew Simons, Will's mentor and trusted advisor, waited outside the boardroom.

"So?" Drew asked simply.

Will didn't have to explain. Drew just knew. He'd known all day Will was concerned about his sister's Judiciary Committee hearing. Will had found Drew's keen eyes on him often, evaluating him. "All she said was that it was intense. But she's not giving up."

Drew nodded.

Will scanned the hallway. It was empty. "Drew, by pursuing my dream, have I made it harder for my sister to pursue hers?"

"You're talking about the media having a field day?" Drew shrugged. "You've dealt with lots of those before. And you're already over the biggest hump."

The media firestorm had been fierce and extremely draining for Will when he assumed the CEO position of American Frontier. Drew had been a bulwark in that storm as Will navigated the tumultuous waters to pull the company back from the brink. Because of a shared press conference, Will and Sarah—the president's nominee for attorney general—had both emerged as solid voices of reason and shining examples of transparency in the public eye.

Now Sarah was in the most intense, final stage of the vetting process. Will's protective edge kicked in. He didn't want his little sister—or his family—to get hurt in the process.

"What if . . ." He spread his hands in a helpless gesture.

Drew looked him straight in the eyes. "You can allow what-ifs to control you. Or you can do what you do best. Move relentlessly ahead on the path you've been called to walk."

Will sighed. "But at what cost?"

"Everything good and worthy comes with a cost. You know that in business. The same is true in any arena of life." Drew paused. "I've said before that truth will always win out. Things that are hidden will be revealed. Will, are you sure you don't want to be in the driver's seat? Doesn't Sarah deserve to know . . . everything?"

"But Dad doesn't want—"

"I know he's worried about what his little girl will think if she finds out the truth. How she'll respond emotionally." Drew's keen blue-gray eyes fastened on Will's. "But she's far stronger than he or any of you think." A smile flickered. "And a lot smarter too."

A Secure Location

He was waiting for the call. When it came, he picked up immediately.

"Still on?" the authoritative voice on the other side of the secure line barked.

"Yes."

"Our job just got harder—and more dangerous."

"Indeed."

"But we can't back down now. Too much is at stake."

"Agreed."

There was no further response. Just a click as the man on the other line hung up.

WASHINGTON, D.C.

Sarah had barely stepped into her limo to head to the Ritz Carlton in Georgetown before the next call came. She didn't need her attorney instincts to predict the caller. Indeed it was Bill Worthington, checking in on his little girl.

"So how did your day go, princess?" he asked in the bass rumble that had been so intimidating in her childhood.

And there it was again. Her father could never think of her as anything other than the social butterfly of their home and, later, of Harvard. That Sarah was a formidable force in her own right didn't seem to enter his consciousness. She swallowed back her irritation.

"It was . . . intense." The instant she said the word, she was annoyed with herself. She'd used the same word with Will. Had the day completely stripped her of any creativity?

"It will only get tougher from here. Sure you're ready?"

She should have known better than to pick up the call when she was tired and already irritated with Will. Father and son were cut from the same cloth.

"Yes," she announced. "I'm ready. But I can't talk right now. I'll have to call you later."

"Okay, princess. Just know . . ." He hesitated. "I love you. I will always love you, no matter what happens. No matter what you decide."

"I know that," she said.

"All right then. We'll talk later."

She ended the call and sank back against the soft leather of the limo seat. She did know her father loved her. He loved all his kids and provided for them in every way possible. But when she was growing up, he hadn't really been present with them. Instead, he'd been present in meetings and travels for Worthington Shares. It had been her mother, Ava, who held down the family fort.

All that had seemed to change, though, when Sean went missing for a while. Perhaps it had been an early midlife crisis—a time for Sean to figure out who he was and where he was going. To find out how he really felt about Elizabeth. Or maybe Sean had just tired of the constant clash with their father and the way he focused on Will with laser-like regularity. Sean, elusive since childhood, had continued to sidestep any of Sarah's direct questions about his time away. It was most infuriating.

But after Sean's return, she'd seen a puzzling difference in his and their father's relationship. The two still didn't always agree. She didn't think they ever would. But there was now an attitude of respect, as if Sean had finally attained adult status in their father's eyes. Sarah had even glimpsed her father standing with his arm around Sean or patting him on the back for bringing a new NGO on board. The affection was groundbreaking between two men who had, for over three decades, either ignored each other or gone head-to-head.

There had never been a lack of affection between Sarah and her father. As the baby of the family and the only girl, she had claimed more than her share of his attention as a child. What she'd never had, though, was his respect. She couldn't seem to earn it, no matter what she did.

Even at Harvard Law, when she became editor of the prestigious *Law Review*, her father only said, "I'm glad you've finally found something to do that doesn't come with Visa receipts."

She had winced. Up until that point in her life, she'd thought nothing of flying to Beverly Hills or LA for some power shopping over a weekend and racking up five figures on the account her father covered. He'd never chided her for her rampant spending, other than to deliver an eye roll every once in a while.

But that comment had helped her focus on getting serious about life. Pro bono work every Saturday while she was in law school had firmed her resolve to do all she could to make the planet a better place to live. She became passionate about justice and people's rights, especially for those who didn't have the tools or means to fight for themselves.

At 24, she graduated from Harvard Law, took a position as an assistant DA in New York City, and worked there for nearly four years. Right after her twenty-eighth birthday, she took a career government position as the deputy assistant attorney general in the Department of Justice's Criminal Division. To do so, she'd given up all her legal obligations to Worthington Shares. Her father had been in India when she'd made it official. She'd had to fend off multiple apoplectic calls from him afterward.

When she'd finally chosen to face the music and pick up his call, a heated Bill Worthington said, "This makes no sense. You're not making sense. You know you don't have to work. Your mother never did. You're taken care of for the rest of your life. And you know that if you feel like you have to work, you can have almost any job you want at Worthington Shares. So why exactly are you doing this?"

"Because I need to do this. For me," she replied. She hadn't explained further, even when her father pressed her.

To be sure, there were times she wished she hadn't made that decision, but she never admitted it to her family. Nor did she let on to her father that there was any trouble in paradise, even on the nights she crawled home, exhausted both from the long hours and from trying to prove her worth as a human being, aside from being a Worthington.

She had a feeling, though, that somehow Drew knew. From time to time his eyes would linger on her, as if assessing how she was doing. He still did the same today, each time he saw her. But with Drew, she never felt censure, only that someone was carefully watching her back and would stand up for her as needed. It was a comforting thought.

John Barnhill, her boss, had been anti–blue blood from day one. She'd caught an earful of his diatribe against her to a co-worker on her first day of work. She'd arrived a quarter hour early and was waiting outside the door of his office.

"I don't like 'em, don't trust 'em, and don't want 'em working for me or anywhere in my vicinity," he'd railed.

He was caustic about people "like her" not wanting to get their hands dirty and was angry he was stuck with her. And as a political appointee in a Republican administration, he wasn't crazy about a woman from a high-profile Democrat family working for him, causing trouble. He'd made all that clear to her within an hour of her arrival.

His railings and drive to see her fail so he could get rid of her only made her more determined to work hard—harder than anyone else—to earn his respect. And through the years, she had. In spite of the rocky beginning, John Barnhill had grown to trust Sarah and her instincts, despite her family connections and wealth.

When John had been told the president wanted her as the next AG—a position John had his sights on himself—his respect for Sarah had kept him closemouthed. The only thing he'd said was, "Good luck with that can of worms." It was the closest he'd ever come to admitting publicly any whiff of discontent with the Republican president.

John Barnhill was a tough nut to crack, but she'd done it. Yet she still couldn't crack the toughest of all—her father. She thought of his words, "It will only get tougher from here. Sure you're ready?"

Now she murmured the words she most wished to hear from him: "I know you can do it. I believe in you."

Yes, she had her father's love. But she longed for his respect.

Sarah wasn't cut from the same cloth as her mother—happy just to be hitched to her husband's star, the glamorous woman by his side, the director of the family's activities, and the reigning present-day Jacqueline Kennedy in the circles of New York's rich and famous. Within Sarah was the drive to do more and be more. She had grown up with an intricate window into the strategy of corporate growth and how it was accomplished. She had seen firsthand how society worked—to the good and detriment of others. She'd rubbed shoulders with people of all occupations, circles, and income brackets in dozens of countries. Through her travels and work with the underprivileged, she'd developed a compassionate heart to help those in poor and difficult circumstances. Her passion to see justice and a safer world for all had propelled her into her current career of law.

But she wasn't naïve enough to think that the American justice system was perfect. She'd seen the brokenness of it. Such as the fact that government-paid workers could get away with only a hand slap and a lesser retirement after being caught in embezzling, extortion, and fraud. Or that Eric Sandstrom, the former CEO of the company now grappling with the worst oil fiasco in history, couldn't be prosecuted to the full extent of the law. As a result of his foolhardy actions in not pursuing the proper channels of research, millions of people and animals around the globe were being impacted by the oil seeping from the Arctic into the earth's ocean systems. As Chairman Phelps had rightfully said, it was an ecological disaster.

Sarah knew she should be satisfied. At least Sandstrom was behind bars. He hadn't walked off scot-free to vacation somewhere in the Galápagos Islands. But if she'd learned anything over her years at the DOJ, and from her friend Darcy, it was that many things weren't as they appeared. People's motives were usually self-seeking. Eric Sandstrom had been led like a lamb to the slaughter. He hadn't even attempted to fight his jail sentence.

Why had it been relatively easy? That question still bothered her.

Part of the mystery had already been revealed by the whistle-blower Jason Carson, painted in the media as a good guy whose conscience had prompted him to reveal the dirty dealings behind the scenes. The prominent headline had announced, "President Rich Scandal . . . $25 Million Payoff Revealed."

The truth? That the majority of President Rich's reelection campaign was based on a quid pro quo payoff—$25 million from Big Oil donated to his campaign in exchange for exclusive drilling rights in the Arctic. Sandstrom had been the hub of directing that payoff, with the majority of funds coming from AF.

Sarah frowned. Public accusations had flown since the release of that news. Will had his hands full untangling the continuing media mess.

But the complete answer was not yet revealed. Someone else— or multiple persons—had something big to hide. Darcy and Jon would keep digging until they found it, even if Sarah's hands were technically tied with her job transition. But she would still do everything in her power to reveal the dirty dealings behind the scenes.

Her eyes narrowed. *Even if it does go all the way to the top of the barrel. To the person who nominated me for this position.*

If there was one thing she'd learned from her father, it was to never give up. His persistence drove her crazy sometimes, but it had also left an impression on her like wet cement when she was young. That same character quality had hardened to flintlike determination as she grew older.

Especially now, with the welfare of an entire nation at risk, Sarah would never give up. She would always persist in doing the right thing.

3

///

Will held up a finger before he and Drew headed into their dinner meeting with AF's chairman of the board, Frank Stapleton. "I need to make a quick call."

"Laura." Drew nodded.

Whenever Will was troubled about anything in his family, he talked first to his wife, Laura. It was a fact of life Drew knew and understood.

Laura picked up on the second ring. After telling her about his short conversation with Sarah, he concluded, "I think she feels I don't believe she can do it. But you know that's not it at all."

"I know," Laura said. "But honestly, what else could she think? Will, you know you're going to have to tell her sometime."

"Drew says the same thing." He cast a wry glance at Drew standing a few feet away.

The enigmatic Drew clearly caught the message. A smile flickered across his normally impassive face.

"And he's right," she shot back. Then, in a gentler tone, she added, "But I know you've got to get your dad and mom on the same page first."

"So what do I do in the meanwhile? Sarah had a tough enough day without me—"

"I took care of it hours ago."

"What? You talked to her? Told her about Sean? Why I'm nervous about this appointment? But—"

"No," she inserted over his rapid-fire questions. "I ordered flowers. They should be in her hotel room by the time she gets there. The card says, 'We believe in you.'"

That was so Laura, anticipating what Sarah would be feeling. He sighed. "Thanks. How did you—"

"Nearly two decades of marriage to you, that's how. And I believe in you too. So quit stalling. Get to that meeting so you can get yourself home to me and the kids."

It was vintage Laura—straightforward, no-nonsense, taking care of matters. After their first summer together at Chautauqua, there had never been any doubt in Will's mind that she loved him or that she'd always be 100 percent in his court.

He laughed. "Yes, ma'am."

Funny how she was the only one who could order him around and get away with it.

***

WASHINGTON, D.C.

Now that Sarah was cozily settled into the Ritz Carlton in Georgetown and a few hours distanced from the Judiciary Committee grilling, she thought of all the things she could have said. For example, when Senator Hoyt had gone after Sarah's handling of the Martin Corp case in the DOJ's Criminal Division, Sarah would have given a million bucks to be able to say what was really in her head: "With all due respect, Senator, my methods may have been a bit off the books, but I closed that case in a year. A far better record than the three years you've been dealing with your state's mishandling of funds, especially in your office."

She grinned, thinking of the shock on the haughty senator's face. The trouble Sarah could have gotten in might have been worth it.

But she was a Worthington, after all. Everything she did, small or large, had inestimable consequences and leaked to the press. She didn't need to make unnecessary enemies. Even more, Thumper's motto, taught by his father in *Bambi*, still resonated with her: "If you can't say nothin' nice, don't say nothin' at all."

In the DOJ Sarah had realized how important it was to keep her mouth shut about many things, especially in her role at the Criminal Division, where letting information slip to the wrong person could end a career or let a bad guy go free.

Now, as she put together the clues of the growing mystery and thought of where she ultimately wanted to end up in her own career, she vowed to be even more careful about what she shared, and with whom.

NEW YORK CITY

"Watch your back," Laura had warned Will before she'd ended their call. She and Drew were the only ones besides Will who knew that Frank Stapleton, a former business mentor of Will's, couldn't be trusted. Stapleton was still chairman of the board at American Frontier, and Will, as CEO, was entrenched in working with him for now. As a GOP kingmaker and the head of City Capital, the wealthiest banking enterprise in the Western hemisphere, Stapleton was highly regarded by the board and had served on it for too many years to be ousted easily.

But Will knew where Stapleton really stood—with the highest force in the land, the president, even if that president didn't have the best interests of the country in mind. Stapleton had thought he could bend Will to his bidding by grooming him as a potential GOP candidate for the presidency. But when Will had decided to run for Senate, he'd run as a Democrat. With the president screaming to Stapleton that he didn't want a Worthington running against him in the next election, Stapleton had tried to dissuade Will in a friendly way from pursuing the race.

When that didn't work, Stapleton had played it dirty behind the scenes. He, Sandstrom, and President Spencer Rich had colluded—though Will couldn't yet prove it—to take Will out of any position of authority. First by undercutting him on the board of American Frontier, and then by ending his Senate bid early by setting up photos of Sean with the Polar Bear Bomber. It was ironic indeed that once Sandstrom was jailed and AF needed a new CEO, Stapleton had approached Will. Perhaps he thought he could control Will by baiting him with the prize he had wanted for years. But Will was no longer fooled by the seemingly straightforward good ol' boy. Knowledge was power, and now Will secretly held that power over his former mentor.

Still, Will had to watch his back.

When Will and Drew entered Eleven Madison Park, Stapleton was already seated at one of the restaurant's best tables, which was decorated with a stunning white-rose tree. He looked up, smiled, and got to his feet. After shaking their hands, he gestured toward their seats.

"Sit down, sit down." Stapleton leaned toward Will. "Things are going well. You've stepped into the CEO role even more easily than I thought."

Will bypassed the compliment. "We've made significant progress, but we have a long way to go."

"Well, on the surface, things are really looking up for AF. We've pulled the company back from the brink. You're doing a great job, Will," Stapleton said.

Will and Drew exchanged glances as Stapleton moved his napkin to his lap.

"What you see on the surface isn't always the truth," Will said. "We all know that."

"And how changeable things are," Drew added. "People certainly are."

Stapleton shifted uncomfortably and rearranged his napkin. "With you at the helm, the media is working for us again."

"Again," Will said, "we have a long way to go. We all know we can't completely clean up the oil spill. That's physically impossible. But we need to give it our best effort and figure out ways for it not to happen in the future."

"Because of the yelling ecologists?" Stapleton shrugged. "They always yell. And as you know, I really don't give a rat's tail about the polar bears or any of that save-the-whales business." He nodded to the waiter to refill his water goblet. Once the waiter had left, he continued. "What I do care about is the president's approval rating dropping over that quid pro quo nonsense."

Will raised a brow. "And that's what you think it is? Nonsense? Seems to me there was a fairly direct connection between the campaign donation and AF getting approval awfully fast to drill in the Arctic."

"None that can be proven," Stapleton shot back. "And that's what counts."

Will tilted his head. "None that can be proven *yet*. And that's what counts."

"What happened in the past has a way of circling around to the present and influencing the future," Drew stated.

Stapleton exhaled. "Well, I believe we can make our own path. Sometimes people don't know what to believe until we tell them what to believe. Then that becomes their reality. Like the fact Americans in general have turned the corner in feeling positive again about American Frontier. Sure, we've made some mistakes, but we've stated publicly that we're willing to do whatever we can to fix them. Frankly, that's all we can do." He eyed Will. "Still, it wouldn't hurt for someone of your stature to assure them again that we're doing all we can."

"You mean instead of saying that we've been able to clean up only a small percentage of the oil, but we're still working on making reparations in every area we can?" Will countered.

Stapleton spread his hands. "Look around you, Will. Nobody wants to hear the negative side, at least not for long. Think about the masses. They've got enough to deal with in their own lives. They need to know that companies like AF will provide gas to run their cars, to cook food, and to warm their houses. They don't need to know the nitty-gritty of what we can't fix."

Will narrowed his eyes. "In waging any media battle, I've always found that honest talk is best. So that's what I give them. And it's working thus far."

"Working for you," Stapleton said. "But not necessarily for the stockholders."

"Or for the president?" Drew added.

Stapleton frowned. "That too."

"We present the facts and don't hide anything," Will insisted. "That's the best and only way to go."

"Agreed," Drew put in quickly. "If there's nothing to hide, there's no fear of discovery." He caught Stapleton's gaze and held it. "We can forge ahead, no holds barred, to do all we can to solve the problem."

"You ready to order?" Stapleton boomed. "All this talk is making me hungry." He crooked his finger toward the waiter.

In that moment, Will's and Drew's eyes locked. Drew hid his smirk by taking a sip of water.

The rest of the dinner went smoothly. But Will noticed that although the usually voracious Stapleton made a great show of rearranging the poached lobster with escarole and almond on his plate, he didn't eat much.

When Stapleton took his leave, Will swiveled toward Drew. "Must have had indigestion."

"Indeed." Drew's eyes twinkled.

Will grinned all the way home. He couldn't wait to tell Laura.

4

MAPUTO, MOZAMBIQUE

Sean couldn't help himself. He called Sarah around midnight her time. He loved to get a rise out of his spunky sister.

"Figured you'd be settled in at the Ritz by now," he said with enough volume to wake her from her groggy state. "So?"

"So, what?" There was a fumbling sound, then, "Sean, do you know what time it is?"

"Of course I do. That's why I called. You know, tradition," he joked. Then, in all seriousness, he added, "You're going to make me ask, aren't you?"

"You bet."

He smiled. So the process might have been nasty, but his sister still had her spunk. She was okay. "How did it go?"

"Remember when I stepped on that lionfish when we were wading in the Pacific?"

"Couldn't forget it. I've never seen a dance like that before."

"And you never will again."

"That bad, huh?"

"Yup, that bad." She yawned. "But I certainly gave them a run for their money."

"Now that's my sister." He laughed.

"Used a few of your negotiation tactics, even," she added. "Worked like a charm."

"You're actually giving me some credit? Wow, you must have had a rough day."

"I always give credit, *when* and *if* credit is due, dear brother."

Yes, she was all right. She'd gone through one of the toughest days of her life, no doubt, but she'd kept her balance and sense of humor.

"That sounds like my sister." He paused. "I'm glad you're all right. Did they ask—"

"Anything about you or Will?" she finished. "Of course they did. But I gave them the same answer Will gives when he doesn't want to talk about aborting the Senate race. And I mentioned that you temporarily dabbled in the idea of running for governor of New York, but then the press made more of it than it was. I said both of my brothers were settled into their respective jobs, so they might as well stop hunting for any skeletons in the closet."

"What if they find out—"

"About the photos of you with the Polar Bear Bomber?" Again she finished his sentence. "Then we do what we Worthingtons do best. We answer the speculations with straightforward, truthful facts. People will choose what they believe. There's nothing we can do about that."

"But it might—"

"Sidetrack my AG position? Oh ye of little faith," she told him. "Give your sister a bit more credit than that."

"Always do," he replied. "It's just myself I doubt every once in a while."

"Sean, I love you to the moon and back," she murmured. "You know that, right?"

"I know that."

"Okay, good. Now I'm hanging up on you because I need some shut-eye."

The call ended.

He felt a twinge. Would her love for him and their easy relationship change in any way once she knew the other truth about him? Would it tear their family apart? Shake up everything she thought to be true about their parents, as it had for him?

Their father had been emphatic. He didn't want Sarah to know, said there was no reason for her to know.

But Sean was torn about that. He'd kept a lot of secrets in his life, but rarely from his sister, who usually wheedled them out of him.

And this wasn't a comfortable secret to keep.

A Secure Location

As usual, their call was brief.

"The game's heating up with the players," the caller reported. "It won't be long before they'll be forced to choose sides publicly."

"Then we'll see who plays it dirty and who plays it clean," the man with the deep voice said.

"So we continue to follow the trail in the meanwhile."

"Yes, see where it leads. All the way to the rabbit hole."

"You may not like where we have to go or what we have to do to get results."

"That has nothing to do with anything," the man replied. "This is about revealing what needs to be revealed. Just get it done."

"Will do."

5

WASHINGTON, D.C.

Sarah awoke the next morning to a polite but insistent rapping on her door at the Ritz Carlton.

Dazed by more than the usual lack of sleep, she glanced toward the clock on the night table—9:05 a.m. Had she really slept that long?

Yawning, she got out of bed and threw on the plush robe supplied by the hotel. Sleepily she peered out of the peephole. It looked like a breakfast delivery, only she hadn't ordered it. Still, after barely being able to eat last night after a stressful day, she was ready. Her stomach rumbled in anticipation.

She opened the door. On a white linen–covered bistro table was an assortment of bagels and cream cheese, a plateful of bacon, and a pot of coffee, accompanied by a petite, rainbow-colored bouquet. Within seconds, the efficient hotel attendants had placed the table and swiftly left her room.

Sarah brushed her curls out of her eyes and reached for the note. *A little picker-upper. Jon.*

She shook her head, amazed at his thoughtfulness. *Such a good friend. How does he always know exactly what I need?*

With Jon, there was no pushing, no questions of "How did it go?" like she got from her brothers and her father. Just a breakfast Jon knew was her favorite—cinnamon bagels, crispy, real bacon, and full-leaded coffee with no cream. The cheery flowers were a bonus to brighten her morning.

Life had been more complicated than usual lately with her flights back and forth between D.C. and her home in New York City. Jon's note was a reminder of the importance of the little things. The fact he remembered her, even with his own chaos at the *New York Times* office, warmed her.

Her thoughts rested for a minute on her friend Darcy's hints about giving Jon a chance.

"A chance for what?" Sarah had teased.

"You know what," Darcy said. "You're not stupid. And Jon's gold-plated material. Not like that other—"

Sarah had cut Darcy off. But the idea had lingered in the fringes of her mind.

Maybe someday I will. She inhaled the nutty aroma of the coffee. *Then again, maybe he's just being nice.*

After a failed romance with a jerk of a TV producer, Sarah wasn't interested in dating anyone. But if she was, Jon Gillibrand would be the kind of guy she could see in her future. He wasn't flashy, like most men who traveled in her circles. Yet she had been impressed with him from the moment Sean had introduced him. And since their work together on the Polar Bear bombing case, she'd seen even more of Jon's integrity and caring heart.

She had such good friends, she realized. And a supportive family—even if sometimes they were a bit too involved. She smiled at the impressive display of flowers that had been waiting for her from Will and Laura. Of course she knew Laura had ordered them, but the note that they believed in her meant a great deal.

It seemed like an eternity had passed since the day she stood in John Barnhill's office and he'd told her that the president had nominated her for AG. But it had only been a couple of months.

Now it would likely be several weeks until the Senate Judiciary Committee would vote on her—at their next meeting. Then the vote would need to go to the Senate floor. That could take a few weeks, even a month. Little in government circles happened swiftly.

In the meanwhile, though, Sarah wasn't going to tread water. After a quick shower, she'd devour breakfast and then pack up. If she hustled, she could be on an early afternoon flight back to New York City. Maybe even catch up on a bit of work at the DOJ. Sleep in her own bed tonight.

She looked forward to all of it.

En Route from Mozambique to John F. Kennedy International Airport

Sean was catching up on his Twitter and Instagram on the flight back to New York. Though it had been a rugged several days of meetings, sleep eluded him, and he desperately needed some. Now that he was in his thirties, he found he couldn't run as hard and fast as he had in his twenties. But he was more comfortable with who he was. That was a nice trade-off.

His life seemed to happen in chunks with his Worthington Shares work—rapid-fire long days and short nights for five to seven days, then a day or two to put up his feet on his own coffee table in New York City before he left again.

His days weren't like Will's well-ordered ones. Will's schedule was so predictable that Sean could clock exactly where his brother would be when. First, his early run through Central Park. Next, his shower. Then his usual breakfast meeting with Drew to recap and problem solve any events from the day before and strategize upcoming decisions. Weekday mornings he spent at the Worthington Shares office. He took a short lunch, usually by himself and at his desk, to regroup. That was when his brother and sister knew they could reach him most easily. In the afternoons he focused on American Frontier. Evenings and weekends were his family time, with the rare business dinner.

And *rare* was the key word. Sean grinned. Laura and Elizabeth were a lot alike that way. When it was their time, it was their time, and nobody else was allowed to mess with it.

Some days it might be nice to have a more predictable life, Sean thought. Then again, it would probably drive him crazy to have his hours boxed up like that. Will's personality was perfectly suited for the boardroom. Sean? His was meant for the seas, open skies, and flying freely from place to place. Discovering new NGOs in other countries still excited him. Meeting new people energized him. In the past, his travels had also meant an escape from the family he loved but who could be burdensome in their expectations.

Recently, however, he'd made his peace with three of the most important people in his life. Bill Worthington, the father he'd grown up with. His mother, who had thought withholding the truth about his parentage would protect him. And his brother, who had thought the same thing once he knew. Even more, Will had also withheld the truth about the Polar Bear Bomber photos. Jon was the one who had discovered them and revealed them to Sarah. Sean still remembered his shock when she'd phoned him and bluntly asked him about them. He hadn't had a clue they existed.

Only three things still hung over Sean.

One was the unfinished business with his birth father. Did Sean really want to meet him in person, get his story, or not? Should he let sleeping dogs lie? Those questions were too big, too emotionally laden to deal with in his jet-lagged state.

The second was the Polar Bear Bomber photos. He chafed when he recalled them. How could he have been so gullible, chatting away with a guy at a bar and allowing himself to be set up that way? He told himself he couldn't have known. Still, being that vulnerable to any force that wanted to take him down frustrated him. Reality was, those photos could show up again at any time. Elizabeth, Will, Drew, Sarah, and Jon all knew about them, and they were prepared.

But what havoc would those pictures wreak on his father and mother right now if they found out? Bill and Ava were still working to put their marriage back together without the secret between them. They were just beginning to rediscover what had originally drawn them together in their university days—a sweet time before Bill's job had swept him away into a whirlwind at Worthington Shares and Ava into a whirlpool of loneliness as she was left behind.

Drew and the three siblings had agreed the photos weren't something Ava should know about at this juncture. However, Drew warned, it would be wise to think about telling Bill sooner rather than later. He would need to deal with the potential ramifications of the news going public before he could deal with his wife's shock and grief.

Sean, as a middleborn, was good at keeping secrets. He'd always been secretive—slipping away from family dinners as swiftly as possible, not telling his family what he was up to outside of what he had to. But now, when he was on both the receiving and the giving ends, he realized even more how much power secrets held.

The day he'd flown out to see Elizabeth in Seattle and they had toured the Space Needle, he'd promised he'd always be transparent with her. He'd never withhold any secrets from her.

Since that day, he hadn't. She also knew about his birth father—something even their close friend Jon didn't know. Perhaps, in retrospect, it was good Sean hadn't told him. Especially if his suspicion that Jon was interested in Sarah was correct.

The time might come where Sean felt he could—and should—share that secret with his friend. Maybe even before he could tell Sarah. Perhaps Jon's calm, balanced perspective would be what Sarah needed to adjust more easily to the truth.

It wasn't that Sean didn't trust Jon. It was more that Sean still grappled with the new reality himself. Would it be easier or harder to accept if he could have a conversation with Thomas Rich? That, Sean didn't know. And it was impossible to predict.

The third thing that bothered Sean was the family decision to keep Sarah in the dark. Perhaps it wasn't as much a decision as the fear that things might change when she knew Sean was her half brother.

Bill and Ava seemed fragile right now, so Sean would let them regroup before he pushed more discussion. It had only been a short while since he and Bill had started talking about matters of importance without his father descending into a "well, you should have" diatribe—all for Sean's well-being, of course. Sean didn't want to do anything to ruin the openness of the relationship, or to cause more pain for his mother, who had suffered greatly for her one night of moral failure.

Sean frowned. He still didn't like keeping the truth from Sarah. He'd discussed his concern with Drew and Will. The three agreed the time was coming when they might have to trump Bill and Ava's wishes and tell her anyway.

For now, it was a waiting game. A very dangerous waiting game, especially with the poking and prodding happening in the vetting process.

Who else knew about Thomas and Ava's indiscretion all those years ago? Victoria, his wife? His son, Spencer, the current president of the United States? A former Secret Service operative who had been at Camp David and who might come forward with the information for the right price?

Some days Sean felt like the entire Worthington family was poised on the edge of a deep chasm, and the smallest shove could push them over it.

That was a frightening thought indeed.

6

Sarah dropped her Fendi handbag on the foyer table and kicked off her heels. It was good to be home at her penthouse in Greenwich Village and not surrounded by circling vultures. At least that's what it had felt like during the JC vetting session. Most were simply doing their jobs. Others, though, had seemed more targeted, even vindictive, in their statements and questions.

Within five minutes, she'd shed her Valentino suit and slipped into the comfort of her favorite sweats and an old T-shirt of Sean's.

She had just flipped on the Nick at Nite channel and settled on a rerun of *I Love Lucy* when her cell rang. Her first instinct was to ignore it. Then she checked the caller ID and answered.

"Jon."

"Hey, welcome home, Ms. Soon-to-Be Attorney General."

She laughed. "I'm not yet."

"No, but you will be."

Once again, his belief in her was a balm to her tired spirit.

"I have someplace I want to take you Saturday morning. Some special people I want you to meet. Please say you'll come."

She sighed. "Jon, I'm really not in the mood for anything social. I desperately need some downtime. Especially on my first Saturday home in a long time."

"You'll get exactly what you need. I promise. Casual attire—sweats or jeans, sneakers, T-shirt. You'll be on your knees a lot."

Now she was curious. She loved surprises.

The surprise factor won out over her tiredness. "Okay, you got me. I'll be ready. Just tell me it won't be before 8:00."

"Nope. Pick you up at 8:45."

"You've got a deal."

A Secure Location

"It's time to tip the balance of this game a little in our favor," the man with the deep voice declared. "Start taking down one of the high and mighty players."

He gripped the phone as he listened. He'd been waiting for this day for a long time, but he needed the kind of clearance the man had to make the events happen. "Thought you'd say that. Already have been working on it. Lining things up."

"Is the package prepared?" the man asked.

"All done. Just need your go-ahead."

"You got it. Arrange for the delivery," the man ordered, then ended the call.

He smiled. It was about time those responsible behind the scenes got their due. And this was only the beginning. He'd see to that.

7

New York City

"We're here . . . why?" Sarah asked.

Jon had picked her up precisely at 8:45 a.m. on Saturday but hadn't told her where they were going. When they pulled up to a special needs activity center, she looked at him, confused.

He smiled. "Because this is where I volunteer at least once a week, whenever I'm in town."

"Really?" She blinked. "I had no idea. How long have you been doing that?"

"About seven years. Come on, let's go inside. The kids will love meeting you."

So there were a lot more layers to Jon Gillibrand than she'd guessed.

"You're certainly full of surprises," she teased when he opened the car door for her.

"I aim to please," he joked back, giving an exaggerated gentleman's bow.

They both laughed as they walked into the center.

An hour later, Sarah was entranced by the place. There was

something so warm, so earthy and connected, about it. The kids had excitedly swarmed around her to greet her—the little ones hugging her knees, the bigger ones stretching to kiss her on the cheek. There was no "getting to know you" period here. Anyone was immediately accepted as part of the group.

Sarah sat on the tiled floor, two children and a book in her lap. More children gathered closely around her as if they were ducklings and she was Mama Duck. As she read to them, a sense of peace flowed over her. Jon was right, as always. This was exactly what she needed.

As soon as she finished the book, cries of "More, more!" abounded. She laughed. "Okay, you win. What book would you like me to read next?"

The children scrambled toward the book bin. In that moment when her arms were empty, she looked up and spotted Jon across the room. He was sitting cross-legged on the floor, engaged in a conversation with a blonde five-year-old. The little girl made a sign with her fingers, and Jon made the sign back. She threw her arms around him, then they continued the conversation in sign language.

Jon knows sign language?

In that instant, he looked toward Sarah and smiled. His eyes brimmed with happiness. She understood—she couldn't imagine being happier than she was in this very moment. The room vibrated with joy, love, and acceptance.

"Ms. Worthington," a deep voice said from nearby, and she jumped.

Turning, she saw a familiar face but grappled with placing it in this location. *Oh yes, Michael Vara. Justin Eliot's friend.*

"Michael! What are you doing here?" She got up to greet him. "It's good to see you. And please, just call me Sarah."

Michael grinned. "Jon invited me to come when I was back

in town. We've been talking ever since he interviewed me for the article about helping hurting kids through theater. Even got the director here to agree for me to do a little theater seminar today for the kids."

"You made it," Jon said, cutting in. He shook Michael's hand. "Just in time too. I'll help you set up anything you need to."

And just like that, the two men were off, talking and laughing in buddy style.

So Jon had another surprise up his sleeve too. But she didn't have long to think about it before the children piled back around her, begging for another story.

Sean was still groggy from jet lag when his cell rang.

When he saw the caller ID, his haze cleared. His heart started to pound.

"Hello?"

"Sean, it's Thomas."

Sean froze. He couldn't speak.

"I'll be in town all next week." Thomas hesitated. "I'd like to meet you, talk briefly. If possible."

Sean found his voice. "I'm not sure." Then, more strongly, "I need to think about it."

"I understand," Thomas said softly. "Call me even last minute. I'll meet you wherever or whenever."

Silence descended between the two men.

"Even if it's not on this trip," Thomas added. "Even if it's not in New York."

"Okay." Sean hung up. His hands were shaking. He had to end the call before the ache in his heart overwhelmed him.

So many years lost. Years of lies. Of not understanding who he was and why he was that way.

Pain, anger, wonder, and hope now meshed with hearing Thomas's voice.

The voice of the man who was his birth father but had had no place in his life.

* * *

"I can't thank you enough," Michael told Sarah after the theater session had ended. "For giving me the time to let Mrs. Chesterton know about Justin, to bury my friend before the news broke."

Sarah nodded. "Is she all right?"

Marie Chesterton, the former headmistress of St. Mark's, the special school Justin and Michael had attended, had a heart for all the students. But she'd grown especially close to Michael and Justin. Now the dear lady knew of Justin's sad end.

Michael's face clouded. "She's grieving. Still can't believe her boy would do such a thing." His dark eyes blazed with intensity. "Neither can I. I stand by what I said the day you told me Justin was the Polar Bear Bomber. He would never have done what he did if he'd known what was in the backpack."

Sarah reached for Michael's hand and squeezed it. "Well," she said in a determined tone, "it's not over yet." She flashed a glance toward Jon. His nod was subtle, but he clearly understood her meaning.

"Anything I can do to help," Michael added. "And I mean anything." He grinned. "Within the law, of course."

Sarah laughed. "Of course."

"Will we see you around this place again?" Jon asked. "The kids really loved you."

Michael beamed. "The next time I'm in town. I also stop in from time to time at the Nordoff-Robbins Center for Music Therapy. Theater and music are a natural combination."

"Ah, I've heard of that one. New York University. Greenwich Village," Jon said. "Right near your stomping grounds, Sarah."

She loved the way Jon naturally included her in any conversation. She watched as the two men bantered. *Such salt-of-the-earth types*, she thought. *Both quality guys, using their faith and good deeds as an extension of themselves to make the world a better place for all.*

After Michael took his leave, Sarah and Jon helped with the cleanup at the center. By late that afternoon, both exited the center more grubby than they'd entered.

Jon smiled at her. "You look happy. You know you needed this."

"All right. You win. I am happy." She'd been hugged and loved all day. She thought again of the blonde girl.

"Jon, who was that little girl you were talking to while I was reading?"

"Jessie. She's been deaf since birth. She was really shy when she first came to the center. But she'll always talk to me."

Jon—such a dichotomy, she thought. *Gentle with a little girl like that, but a die-hard news veteran who doesn't stop pressing until he has the story.* "What was she saying to you right before she hugged you?"

Jon stopped and turned toward her. "She was signing."

"Signing what?"

He extended one hand—pinkie, first finger, and thumb extended, and the two middle fingers dropped toward his palm. "I love you."

"Oh." Sarah's eyes teared. "How sweet."

They started walking again. He smiled. "Yeah, they're great kids."

"I didn't know you were fluent in sign language, or that you were keeping up with Michael. Two more things I didn't know about you."

Jon shrugged in his understated way. "There are a lot of things you don't know about me." He grinned. "But when you get to know me even more, I'm 99 percent positive you'll like them."

"Things like what?" she teased.

They reached the car, and he faced her. "Like my honesty." Eyes twinkling, he added, "So I'll tell you right now that there's a big sticky kiss mark on your left cheek. One of the kids must have had jelly before coming to the center. You've been wearing it since this morning."

Startled, she raised her hand and encountered the sticky mess. "And you've let me wear it like that all day? Without saying anything?"

He laughed. "Hey, it made the experience more authentic. I've got wet wipes in the car. I need them frequently after being here. Let's get you cleaned up and then go find some dinner."

So there *were* a lot more layers to Jon.

He was right. The more she saw, the more she liked.

8

"Sean, you know what you have to do, right?" Elizabeth's voice was warm but determined.

He cradled the phone to his ear, waiting. He knew more was coming.

"You've juggled the pros and cons in your head for almost a week, driving yourself a bit crazy. But honestly, Sean, it's simple. You have questions and he has answers. You deserve those answers. And he's in town. What better time to get them?"

And there it was—the clarity Elizabeth brought to any situation.

Sean sighed. "I know you're right. I just can't seem to make that phone call."

"Then hear me plainly, mister. It's time to get two roadblocks out of your life. Meeting Thomas is the first one. You won't be able to settle until you do."

"And the second?" he asked meekly.

"Telling Sarah the truth."

"But Dad—"

"Sean, I know your dad doesn't want that," Elizabeth said more gently. "But Sarah will feel really betrayed if you don't tell her."

"I know," he admitted. "I can still see the hurt and confusion in her eyes when I couldn't tell her why I went haywire and disappeared for a while. Weird, though. She hasn't pressed me further for answers. That's not like her."

"Maybe she senses you need time to work things out for yourself. But Sean, until you handle those two roadblocks, they'll hang over your head."

"I know."

"So meet Thomas. Today."

"Wow." He chuckled. "You're as straight-talking with me as Laura is with Will."

"I hope so," she fired back. "Now quit waffling and get moving."

"Yes, ma'am."

He shook his head with a wry grin. He really was beginning to sound like his brother.

"Looks like you need this." Darcy handed Sarah a cup of their favorite coffee from a nearby shop. "Nontoxic. Not the DOJ or DHS brand. Figured you were bogged down playing catch-up."

Sarah had been entrenched in her office at the DOJ's Criminal Division every day and evening since her return from Washington. She'd barely had time to think about the upcoming JC vote. She was focused on her work at the DOJ. Now it was Friday, and she felt the strain of the extra work hours.

"That's an understatement." Sarah laughed. "And thanks for the coffee. I needed this midmorning break more than you know."

"Hey, what are friends for?" Darcy nudged her. "I needed a time-out myself from the DHS good ol' boys. Sometimes they just get on a roll. Come on, walk with me a bit. By the time I get back, they'll have returned to normal." She rolled her eyes. "Whatever that is."

The two friends sipped coffee and walked, enjoying the city sounds and vibrant colors. Sarah filled Darcy in on her surprise visit to the special needs center the previous weekend and seeing Michael again.

"It sure seems like we're at a standstill on the bombing investigation, doesn't it?" Sarah asked.

Darcy pursed her lips. "We both know there's more to the puzzle. We'll find it."

Sarah took another sip of coffee. "I can't get Michael out of my mind. He's so sure that his friend wouldn't have done it if he knew what was in the backpack."

"I agree. From what we've been able to uncover, Justin doesn't seem like that kind of a guy. Troubled, yes, but not vengeful."

"Or suicidal," Sarah added.

The women's eyes met, and they both nodded.

"Something is going to break soon. I feel it." Darcy stopped to toss her coffee cup into a nearby trash can. "I'm going to miss this when you move to D.C."

Sarah lifted a brow. "Who says I'll get confirmed?"

"I do, because you will."

It was such a confident statement of fact—so Darcy—that Sarah laughed. "Then maybe you should tell Chairman Phelps that. He and a few others in the JC were doing their best to take things the other direction."

Darcy frowned. "Maybe I will. Phelps could stand to be taken down a notch or two. Seriously, though, you're not going to let a few old-timers stop you, are you?"

"Nope. I'm taking it all the way to the top."

Her friend winked. "I wouldn't be surprised if you do."

Sean and Thomas agreed to meet at Central Park, in the Italian part of the Conservatory Garden. The garden—actually three gardens in one—was one of eight designated quiet zones in Central Park. When Sean wanted time away from the craziness of the Big Apple but couldn't go far, he went to the garden or to the Conservatory Water, where he could watch people sail their model boats.

Interesting that his birth father had suggested the Conservatory Garden as the place to meet.

Sean had arrived half an hour early to sit on a bench by the Vanderbilt Gate. Somehow he felt more in control if he could watch Thomas arrive.

The man walking toward Sean now was an older version of himself—six feet tall, with curly, dark auburn hair tinged a bit with gray. Sean had seen him often in the news headlines in years past, when he was president of the United States. But when Thomas drew closer, Sean saw what he hadn't glimpsed before—the stature and pain of a man who had lived well in some areas but failed greatly in others.

Sean stood, suddenly feeling eclipsed.

Thomas paused a few feet away. "Sean," he said simply and extended his hand. "You must have questions. I will answer any you want to ask."

Sean reached out in slow motion to shake his hand. "Thomas." He couldn't help staring, comparing himself to the man who stood in front of him. Now that the moment was here, the questions he wanted to ask had fled.

"Shall we sit?" Thomas asked. He didn't wait for an answer but sat on one end of the bench.

Sean sat on the other end. Both men faced the garden's beauty instead of each other. For men, it was easier to talk of things of the heart that way.

"I didn't intend for the affair to happen," Thomas said quietly. "Not when she'd chosen my best friend. But I had always loved Ava. If it wasn't for my respect for Bill, I would have told her our senior year at Harvard. But Bill had already asked her to marry him after she graduated."

Sean broke in. "So you loved my mother but never told her?"

"That year, Bill plunged into his first year at Worthington Shares, while Ava and I were still seniors. We were inseparable. The closest of friends. But I could never tell her how I felt. Bill was a bright star, and I—well, I didn't know exactly what I wanted to do in life. I felt restless, directionless."

Sean frowned. How often he'd felt the same way.

"I convinced myself that Bill would be better for her." Thomas sighed. "How I missed her, and Bill, after they married. Our lives took us separate directions for a while."

A flock of birds passed overhead, shattering the quiet with their raucous calls.

Thomas straightened. "In the darkness of that time, I ached for what I couldn't have. Finally, I gave up the idea of real love with a soul mate like Ava. I did what my family expected—married a woman of status who made my mother happy but me miserable."

So, Sean thought, *the stories of the harpy Victoria are true.* He felt a flicker of compassion for Thomas.

"When Will was born, I thought I was ready to be around Ava and Bill again. Such joy in her eyes as she held that baby." He smiled as if parting the years in his memory. Turning toward Sean, he added, "You see, Ava wanted more than anything to be a mother."

Sean nodded. That he could understand. Ava wasn't truly happy unless her chicks were gathered around her and she could cluck over them. It didn't matter whether they were babies or grown-ups.

"The two families started doing things together." Thomas looked away. "Even though Victoria was missing most of the time. She never liked being around Ava. Perhaps she could sense the truth."

What? That you were in love with another woman? I can see how that could make a woman bitter, Sean thought. "So that's how you ended up at Camp David? It was supposed to be a *family* holiday?" He couldn't keep the sarcasm out of his voice.

Thomas focused on Sean again. "Yes, but to Ava, it was much more."

Suddenly Sean wasn't sure he wanted to hear the rest of the story.

9

Will sat in his office overlooking Madison Avenue and tapped his pen on his right thigh. Frank Stapleton's smug assumptions that Will would play ball in any game still rankled. Will had the upper hand—he knew things Stapleton didn't. But how could he best leverage that advantage, as he did in business opportunities? Will had been rolling that around in his thoughts ever since their dinner meeting. In the meanwhile, he'd ignored Stapleton's calls. But he couldn't put off answering them much longer.

"Stapleton not squirming enough for your satisfaction?" Drew said right by his ear.

Will jumped. He'd been so focused on the quandary that he hadn't heard Drew arrive.

Drew chuckled. "That's what has you frowning on a sunny day, right?"

Will shook his head. "You always know."

"Of course. I've worked with you too long not to guess."

"That guess is on the mark, as usual." Will scowled. "You know I have to get him off the board."

"But he's not going to go gently," Drew said. "The rest of the board will fight for him."

Will nodded. "He's been on it a long time. And they see him as the guy who stepped in when all hope was lost for AF and convinced me to come back in a bigger role."

"Agreed. So what are you thinking?"

"How to leverage our upper hand in the best way."

"Oh, you know we will," Drew said with a smirk. "But remember, timing is everything."

"You mean perhaps he should squirm on the hook a bit more first?"

Drew grinned. "Exactly."

Sean's stomach felt like lead as he waited for Thomas to explain. Did he really want to hear about the affair from Thomas's perspective? Or would the story include secrets he might have to withhold from his own mother? The irony of the tables being turned was nearly more than Sean could bear.

"It was your mother's dream that the holiday at Camp David become a time for her and Bill to reconnect, to find the love she felt they'd lost," Thomas said. "But after a few hours, Bill suddenly got a call and had to leave again."

But why? Was it a part of the plan? Or a coincidence that forever changed the paths of two families and led to my birth?

"Then Victoria left in a huff, saying she was already tired of 'camping,' and took Spencer with her. That night, I saw the pain in Ava's eyes, how lonely she was. Bill was rarely home. His travels enveloped his life. He didn't see that she was dying inside without the light from his star, just like the year he'd left her behind at Harvard."

A pang struck Sean's heart. That was the story of his entire childhood—his father rarely home, and his mother smoothing over his seeming disinterest in family for the three siblings' sake.

"After Will was tucked into bed, Ava and I opened a bottle of wine and reminisced over our Harvard years. I at last told her what I'd longed to for years—that I loved her. 'Why didn't you tell me?' she asked. 'Why didn't you give me the choice?' I told her, 'Because I respect Bill too much. Love you too much. And I knew you'd already chosen him.'"

Silence descended for a moment, as if Thomas was turning back the tides of time. "When she started to cry, I felt helpless. We shared one kiss. Then—"

Sean held up a hand. "I don't want the details."

Thomas frowned. "And I respect your mother too much to tell you," he replied in a terse tone.

Tension stretched between the two men.

At last Thomas exhaled. He continued calmly. "The instant I woke with her in my arms, I felt an inexplicable loss. I knew Ava had chosen Bill and would go back to him. It was the right thing to do—we both knew it."

"So you just let her walk away? After what happened?"

"It was Ava's choice," Thomas said firmly. "I was too much in shock to even think about the possibility of her becoming pregnant. I'm sure she was too. She and Bill had tried for several years to have another baby, with nothing to show for it. The following morning, she took Will and headed home. We both agreed it was best for her to be there when Bill returned from his business trip. I tucked away my sadness and concern when I didn't hear from her for months."

He turned now to gaze at Sean. "I didn't know about you until I read about your birth in the papers. You looked—well, too Irish. Too much like me, like Ava. Not enough like a Worthington. I started counting the months back. I realized how long

Bill had been gone on his business trip and figured it out. Saw the truth behind the preemie birth announcement in the society page. But after seeing the joy on Ava's face in the picture . . ." He sighed. "I couldn't do anything to ruin that."

"Bill didn't know?"

"I don't think so. He may have guessed, though, because after that, he and I rarely spoke. We simply drifted apart, using the busyness of our worlds as an excuse."

"So you figure out I'm your kid but choose not to acknowledge or see me—until now?" Sean asked caustically.

Thomas's eyes turned steely. "No, son."

The word reverberated in the still air of the garden and inside Sean's brain.

"I chose to love your mother, and you, and to respect your father by walking away. I thought that was best for all of you. But it wasn't what I wanted. Never."

"Then what did you want?" Sean threw the words at Thomas.

"I wanted—" The older man's voice broke. "I wanted to raise you. Be by your side. See the joy and pride in Ava's eyes firsthand. But out of love, I stepped away. I am sorry for many things. But I'll never be sorry for giving Ava what she wanted most—a child. That child of her heart and my heart is you, Sean."

Sean's anger fled. The ache in his chest pushed to his throat. He bowed his head.

"Over the years, I've kept my eye on you. Celebrated your milestones. But Bill has been the one by your side. He's shaped you into the man I wish I had been at your age. He's more of a father to you than I could have been. Somehow Ava knew, even back at Harvard, which one of us to choose. And she was right."

Dr. Kevin Leman and Jeff Nesbit

Sarah had only been back at the DOJ for a couple of hours when Darcy called.

"Aw, miss me already?" Sarah teased.

"You've got to hear this," Darcy said in her usual brusque manner. "Guess what was waiting for me when I got back to my office?"

"Okay, I'll play. What was waiting for you?"

"An anonymous package," Darcy announced.

"What? Aren't those screened by security first?"

"Yup, and it was. It was brought up to me once it was cleared because it had my name on the front."

"And?"

"Said package reveals that Frank Stapleton, the chairman of AF, *is* connected to the Polar Bear Bomber."

Sarah sat back in her chair. "How so?"

"Our source says Sandstrom and Stapleton hatched the plan together to bomb the AF building to turn the tide of public opinion about the oil fiasco. But Stapleton supplied the bomber's name and location. Jason Carson was only the point man to set up the details so Stapleton and Sandstrom didn't get their hands dirty."

"Whoa. So at least Carson's being honest about something. That might be a first. But what is Stapleton and the bomber's connection?" Sarah wondered out loud.

"Dunno. The note didn't say. But if Stapleton supplied the information, he knew the bomber somehow."

"Maybe it's time to talk to Michael again to see if there's anything else he knows without realizing it," Sarah mused.

"I already called Jon to help us contact Michael. Meanwhile, I have the lab evaluating the note for fingerprints and trying to identify its origin."

"Guess your gut instinct is working overtime for you. Earlier

67

today you said you thought something in the case would break soon." Sarah laughed. "Well, I'd call this *soon*."

"It's like a guardian angel dropped the package on my doorstep," Darcy replied. "Problem is, I don't believe in that guardian angel mumbo jumbo. This only proves our theory further—that bigger forces are at play here."

"Agreed. We just have to figure out what those forces are."

10

Sean sat in the garden, head still bowed and hands clasped together to keep them from shaking.

He heard the click of a latch as Thomas opened his briefcase.

"Here." Thomas handed him a bulky package. "I want you to have this. It contains things that might be important to you. Open it when you're ready."

"I may never be ready," Sean managed.

"Then that's all right too," Thomas said softly.

He shut the briefcase, then stood in front of Sean for a minute. Sean could feel Thomas's gaze on his lowered head.

There was a slight whisper, like a regretful sigh, and then Thomas started to move away.

Sean looked up. The world appeared to be in slow motion. He watched the back of the man who was his birth father as he receded, inch by inch, from his vision.

An inexplicable feeling of loss flooded in, and Sean battled it. *This man was never in my life. Why open my life and heart to him? And why did he want to meet me now, after all these years?*

Sean glanced back down at the package. He couldn't open it. At least not yet.

The day's revelations had been more than enough to grapple with.

Near the end of her workday, Sarah received an urgent call from Jon.

"We need to meet. Tonight at your place? Around nine? Darcy's coming too."

"We're on. Anything you can tell me now?"

"No," he said in an enigmatic tone. "This has to wait for in person."

"All right," she agreed. But she wasn't happy about it. *Wait* was one of her least favorite words.

Several hours later, the three friends gathered at Sarah's penthouse in Greenwich Village. Jon's report had stunned them all. Now their standard whiteboard was propped up on the table, ready for more notes.

Sarah stood by the board, marker in hand. "So Michael said a guy used to come around sometimes when he and Justin were young, then faded away. Does he remember what the guy looked like?"

"All his memories are shadowy. Except that the guy was tall, walked like a jock, and acted like the king of the castle," Jon replied. "When I asked him if he knew if Rebecca ever worked anywhere, he said no, she was always home. In fact, he used to go there and hang out with Rebecca and Justin when things got too tough to handle in his own house. Even slept over sometimes. That's how he knew that someone Justin called his uncle came over sometimes."

Darcy tapped her upper lip. "We've always wondered how

a 17-year-old single mom could manage to buy a house with cash and then still pay taxes even though there's no record of her working. Especially since her parents were dead and hadn't left her any money or insurance that we could find. Maybe . . ."

Sarah took over. "Someone—possibly the guy who used to come around—paid for that house. And maybe all of Rebecca's and Justin's expenses. It was an outright purchase, right? No mortgage?"

"No mortgage. Just a onetime buy in the name of Rebecca Eliot. In cash. No rent checks to track," Jon verified. "And tax records show she paid the taxes whenever they were due, but had no record of any income."

"Well, somebody paid for the expensive medicine Justin was on," Darcy added. "Rebecca didn't have any health insurance we can find, and neither did Justin. Seems they paid cash for everything."

"The person who paid for the house might have paid for the medical bills too," Sarah reasoned.

Jon frowned. "So that person knew Justin could be psychologically fragile."

"And perhaps took advantage of that," Darcy finished.

"What about your note? Did you find anything about its origin that could help us?" Sarah asked.

"Nope," Darcy said. "Whoever did it was really good. No fingerprints, so they must have worn gloves. The paper stock can be found at virtually any office supply store. Ink was general use too. No one saw the delivery boy come and go."

"Nothing on the envelope?" Jon asked.

Darcy shook her head. "Just plain brown paper. No UPS, USPS, or trackable courier service. Looks like whoever they are, they paid somebody nondescript to drop the package where DHS would quickly discover it and bring it to me."

Sarah paced. "The note said there was a connection between Stapleton and the bomber. Put that together with what Michael told us, and—"

"You thinking what I'm thinking?" Jon stared thoughtfully at the whiteboard. "That maybe Stapleton is the shadowy 'uncle' Michael remembers?"

A Secure Location

"The package has been planted," he told the man. "What happens next isn't up to me."

"No, it's up to him," the man growled.

"You knew this moment would come."

"Yes, but that doesn't mean I like it. What's in the package could expose everything."

He swallowed hard. The man on the other end of the line was additionally testy. He added in a calming tone, "You said yourself, it's time to let the chips fall where they may."

"Well, saying it and doing it are two completely different matters," the man barked. "Are you happy now?"

He paused to allow the man a minute to cool down. Then he said, "That's not the right question and you know it. The right question is, Are *you* happy?"

"That I must destroy the life of one to gain the safety of the other? There is no happiness in that."

"Nevertheless . . ."

"I understand," the man grumbled. "It must be done. So let's get it done."

11

"If I put Michael with a sketch artist on Monday, do you think he'd be able to resurrect a better image of the uncle?" Darcy asked.

It was after 11:00. A smattering of leftovers from Sarah's fridge littered her table. Jon was making a bowl of popcorn.

"I already asked him that," Jon called from the kitchen. "He didn't think he'd be able to give us anything other than the shadowy details."

Sarah chewed on the end of the marker. "What if we found pictures of Frank Stapleton from that time period instead? Showed them to Michael?"

Darcy perked up. "Sure. It's worth a try."

"Stapleton's been in the news enough. We ought to be able to find something," Jon said as he carried the popcorn into the room.

"Justin was 26 when he died. How old was Michael when he spent time at Justin's house?" Darcy asked.

"They became friends at St. Mark's." Jon peered at their notes on the whiteboard. "When they were 11."

"So we look for a 15-year-old photo of Frank Stapleton," Sarah said.

"You got it," Darcy declared.

Within minutes, the three were snacking on popcorn and simultaneously researching online photos of Frank Stapleton.

By midnight, they had eight photos—face and body shots—lined up.

"Want me to forward these to Michael?" Jon asked.

Darcy frowned. "If this were an official investigation at DHS right now, we should do it by the book. Bring him in to DHS, mix these photos in with other people's photos for a true facial recognition. Then again, it's in the archives. Nobody else is digging around."

Sarah rolled her eyes. "You know even if he did ID Stapleton, it would never stick as evidence. The kids were 11, and it was 15 years ago. No court is going to believe Michael could recognize some shadowy figure from back then."

"Problem solved then. I send them to Michael, and we see if they're even in the ballpark," Jon said. "At least it gives us something else to go on."

Sean lay sleepless on the living room couch at his One Madison building apartment. Images of Thomas walking toward him and away from him lingered. Sean recalled the haunting expressions of regret in the older man's face.

He wondered what Thomas was doing now. Was he also lying sleepless somewhere, wrestling with the what-might-have-beens?

Sorrow and relief mingled in Sean. The day he'd wondered

about had arrived. Now it was over. He had so many answers to the questions that had plagued him since that morning his mother told him the truth. He'd hated Irish oatmeal then. Now he could never face it again. The aroma and texture of it was mixed in his psyche with the worst day of his life.

He shook his head. Strange how the not important mixed with the cataclysmic on a day like this.

Turning his head, he peered at the time. It was past 3:00 a.m.—after midnight Elizabeth's time in Seattle.

Too late to call her now.

He'd needed time to reflect by himself first. But now he longed for her warmth, her clarity.

His cell rang. It was Elizabeth.

He smiled.

By early Saturday morning, Sarah, Darcy, and Jon had their answer.

"He said he can't be 100 percent sure, but he felt that involuntary shiver when he saw the photos, especially the close-up of Stapleton's eyes. He thinks it's the same guy," Jon reported to Sarah via cell. "He used to order the boys around when he was there. Michael remembers once that he told the boys to get out of the house, and when Michael refused because it was cold outside, the guy grabbed his arm and glared at him until they did. That stuck in his memory."

"That wouldn't stand up in court either. Like I said, no real evidence yet."

"No," Jon said, "but we're going to find some."

Sarah's next call was to Will. "Coffee. Now. My place."

Will sounded out of breath. "Now? I'm in the middle of my run."

"Yes, now. Get yourself over here."

"Well, when you say it so nicely."

"Will," she warned.

"I'll be there. But you better have something to go with that coffee. I haven't had breakfast."

12

Less than an hour later, Will was puzzling over Sarah's news and oversugared from the two donuts he'd eaten—something Laura would never willingly let him eat at home. Now he knew why. The sugar buzz negated his calming run through Central Park. He felt like his son Davy looked after he'd eaten a bowl of Cap'n Crunch cereal at a friend's house—all jittery.

"So let me get this straight. You think Frank Stapleton knew the Polar Bear Bomber when he was a kid? Visited his house sometimes? And later looked him up when Sandstrom needed someone to bomb the AF building? That's the connection the note is talking about?"

"Exactly," Sarah said. She offered him another donut, but he waved off the box.

"And you have irrefutable proof of this?"

She slumped. "No. Just a note from an anonymous source that Darcy received at DHS, our conjecture from earlier research, and Michael's gut that says it's the same guy as the photos we showed him. Nothing that will stand up in court."

"Then you better not go there," Will warned. "Frank Stapleton isn't somebody you mess with unless you are absolutely, 100 percent sure you can nail him to the wall."

Stapleton had a direct line to the president and just about anybody high up in the GOP. If they were in office, he'd helped put them there.

She lifted her chin. "Maybe that's exactly why we need to nail him. And find out what, if anything, the president has to do with this too. After all, he, Stapleton, and Sandstrom were pretty well tied in together. That $25M deal—"

Will leaned in. "Sarah, I'm only going to say this once. And you're not going to like it, especially coming from your big brother. But . . . be careful. I know you already took Sandstrom down, so that ended well. But it sounds to me now like maybe he was the sacrificial lamb led to slaughter. If Stapleton is involved in the way you're guessing he might be, things are going to get very messy, especially for you."

"And you too, since you're connected with AF," she fired back.

"I'm not worried about myself. Or AF," Will said. "I can handle the heat."

She bristled. "How? By walking away, like you did from the Senate race?"

He sat back and breathed deeply before he spoke. "Ouch. You know why I walked away. I had my reasons, and I don't want to discuss them anymore. If and when I'm ready and able, I'll decide if I want to tell you more. Now I need a shower and something nonsugared to combat my sugar intake."

And with those words, he slipped his running shoes back on and exited her door.

He wasn't ready to go into combat mode with his sister until he'd fully thought through every angle. Then he'd discuss it with Drew and get his perspective.

His gut, though, told him she might be right. But how to prove it?

———

"Ahh!" Sarah smacked her fist into her open palm. Her brother could be so maddening.

Still, she knew she'd done the right thing by looping him in. Stapleton had been Will's mentor for years as Will got started in the business world, even introducing him to the American Frontier board. He'd understandably be protective of Stapleton. But . . .

Sarah frowned. That was it. He *hadn't* been protective of Stapleton in their conversation, as she'd expected him to be. He was more . . . *evaluating*—yes, that was the word. As if he wasn't surprised by anything she told him, yet was puzzling to put together the pieces to a greater mystery.

She went back over their conversation.

"You know why I walked away," he'd told her. "I had my reasons, and I don't want to discuss them anymore."

And there it was. *Reasons*, he'd said. Not *reason*, singular.

So there's something in addition to the photos with Sean and the Polar Bear Bomber that caused my big brother to abort the campaign, she mused. *Something bigger. Perhaps something to do with Frank Stapleton.*

Was Stapleton the one who colluded with Sandstrom and the president to take Will out of the running? To make the odds more favorable so that James Loughlin, their favored New York senator whom they could control, would have a shot at a last run in office—an office that Will might otherwise have won because of his name and reputation?

She recalled more of Will's words. "If and when I'm ready and able, I'll decide if I want to tell you more."

It was the word *able* that caught her attention now. So something *was* holding Will back from being completely truthful with her.

Will was protective of their family. So it made sense that someone holding photos over his head of Sean with the bomber could have stopped him cold. Especially when he didn't know anything yet about Sean's side of the story.

What didn't make sense was Will's attitude afterward. He didn't strategize a plan that would again thrust him into the driver's seat and take out the opposition.

Decidedly un-Will-like behavior.

That meant the other reason or reasons were still holding Will back from making moves he wanted to make.

She straightened her shoulders. Indeed she, Jon, and Darcy were on the right track. Eventually she'd nicely wrangle out of her brother anything he knew. She'd been schooled since babyhood to do just that with her brothers. A little velvet-gloved manipulation worked every time. She simply had to find the right angle.

13

Sean hadn't connected with his sister since he was in Mozambique. Usually, they caught up quickly with straightforward information about what each had been doing, then got to the heart of why they'd called. It was a Worthington trait of communication they'd learned from their father, who said he didn't have time for blather and nonsense. So why now was his sister dancing around the reason she'd really called? Especially on a Saturday morning?

"You know, brother, you're not getting any younger. Isn't it about time you pop the question to Elizabeth? She's not going to wait around for years."

"Who says I'm ready to pop the question?" he fired back.

"Because, dear brother, you're so defensive about it. That shows you're thinking about it. Or maybe you two already have an understanding, and you just haven't told us yet." She laughed. "You can't fool me. That's got to be it. She's too great of a catch for you to let her get away. Otherwise, you'd give me the usual, 'Nah, she's not in the running.' Like you've done for years with all those what's-her-name-of-the-month who've showed up on your arm for special occasions."

"And this is your business?"

"There it is again. Defensiveness. But you know I'm right. Elizabeth is good for you. And I know you love her. It shows in your eyes when you talk about her."

"Okay, let's change the subject," he countered.

"Let's. How about you tell me what you know about why Will really walked away from the Senate race."

And there it was. The real reason for her call. She knew something. But what exactly?

He blinked, trying to clear the cobwebs from his lack of sleep. Warning lights flashed in his brain. He hedged. "Well, what do you know about it?"

"No fair. Counter tactics. Just spill the beans."

He weighed his options. But there were no options that wouldn't directly fly in the face of what Bill Worthington had directed: "Under no circumstances is Sarah to know about her mother's affair. About who your birth father is. It would destroy her."

That left Sean only one possibility, and he offered it lamely. "You already know about the photos and that they were a frame-up. So why are you asking? If you want to know anything else, ask Will."

There was a pregnant pause on the other end of the line. The truth sank in.

"You already have, haven't you? And he wouldn't tell you anything else?" Sean chuckled. "And you're playing the little sister card, trying to play your brothers against each other, huh?"

She huffed a breath. "Something like that."

"Well, we've grown up. This time it won't work. We know your moves. He'll tell you when he's ready."

"That's exactly what he said," she spouted.

"Then you have your answer. You'll have to be content with that."

"Oooh." She hung up.

Sean shook his head. Then he called Will. "Uh, Houston, we have a problem."

———

After Sean's warning call, Will's finger hovered over one of the contacts in his cell phone. Drew had given him the private number years ago and said, "You'll know when you need to use it."

Will had only used it once—right after Sean and Sarah had found out about the photos of Sean chatting with the Polar Bear Bomber at a bar near 20th and Madison. He'd placed a call to an old and powerful friend of his mother and father, trusting that friendship would encourage the man to do the right thing. He had, and all the workings behind the scenes had led to the arrest of Sandstrom for criminal negligence. His sister had no idea that Will had called on that powerful friend for the favor.

Now Will did the only thing he could. He called Thomas Spencer Rich II, former president of the United States, again.

But this time they would meet in person. Will would lay all his cards on the table. Thomas had come through before.

Will had no doubt he would do so again.

———

A Secure Location

The phone call was abrupt. "The ante just got upped. You know what to do," the man declared.

"We go after the unholy trio."

"Yes. You've got 48 hours. Make them count."

The call ended.

It only took six hours to ferret out the information. It was amazing what greasing the right palm could do—or holding a bit of information over someone's head. With unlimited funds, it was easy to find a low-level lackey who had seen something, overheard a conversation, or been asked to run an errand that might seem insignificant but revealed a big piece of a puzzle.

Through his web of contacts, he struck pay dirt.

14

NEW YORK CITY

The waiting was over. The Senate Judiciary Committee vote had been in Sarah's favor. Now it would be a few weeks before the full Senate vote.

Sarah smiled. The sunny Thursday couldn't be better. She'd crossed the first major hurdle. One more to go in the prize she sought—to become the People's Lawyer of the United States.

She reached for her cell and, almost without thinking, called her father first.

"Dad, I'm in," she said as soon as she heard his voice.

"The AG vote?"

"Yes—15 to 3 in my favor." She held her breath, waiting for his congratulations.

There was a big pause, as if he had been mid-project on something when she called. At last he said, "A big step on the way. And a big job, especially dealing with President Rich. If you're approved, it won't be long before you'll be going head-to-head with him and his policies—even if he is the one who nominated you for the position."

Not even a congratulations. Just questioning her next steps.

"Then again," he added, "people have reasons for everything."

Sarah's hackles rose. "You're saying that with the $25M quid pro quo in the balance, he's trying to buy me off?"

"That isn't what I said," her father shot back in his authoritative voice.

"No, but it's what you meant, isn't it?"

Her father sighed. "Princess, I just worry about you. You're stepping into one of the biggest jobs in the nation."

There it was again. She was in her midthirties, and he still called her by one of her many pet names.

"And I'm still the little girl playing in the sandbox, with the big wide world around her she knows nothing about—is that what you're trying to say?"

"No. I didn't say that. So get off your high horse," he commanded.

The phone was muffled for a minute. In the background, Sarah could hear her mother's warning. "Bill, change your tone. That's your daughter you're talking to."

Her father came back on the line. "All I'm trying to say is, be careful," he said more gently. "Far more events than you could ever imagine are at play here. And people aren't always what they seem."

"You got that right," she replied, still in full steam.

"And neither are positions that hold a lot of authority."

When will Dad ever believe in me? That I can do what I set out to do? Haven't I proven it in my present job?

"Dad, I have to go."

"Sarah—"

"We'll talk later." And she ended the call.

When would she learn that she could never do enough to please her father?

That was a role only Will could play. So why did she always fall into the trap of hoping she could?

———— ///————

WESTCHESTER COUNTY AIRPORT, NEW YORK

Thomas Spencer Rich II's private plane landed precisely on schedule early Friday afternoon. He had bypassed the busier Teterboro Airport in New Jersey for the convenience of the Westchester County Airport in White Plains. Will met him on board his plane, as agreed. There they could talk in complete privacy.

"Thomas." Will shook his hand. "Thank you for coming."

The older man's eyes met his squarely. "Will. At last we meet officially."

"We have much to discuss."

"Then I won't waste time." Thomas turned to the steward. "Serve the drinks and hors d'oeuvres, then take your leave onto the tarmac until I call for you again."

The steward nodded.

Soon the two men were settled into the luxurious white leather seats.

Will spoke first. "The Worthington family needs your assistance again."

"Oh?"

"Thomas, I know. I know you're Sean's birth father. I know about your affair with my mother at Camp David," Will said bluntly.

Sadness, but not surprise, flickered across Thomas's expression. "You don't know how many times I have replayed that night, crafting a different ending. Bill and Ava were my friends." His eyes begged for understanding. "But I loved Ava. Always. Still do."

Will held out his hand. "I don't think I want to, or should, hear more."

"I understand. But there's something you do need to know, Will. I respect your father. I would never have chosen to betray him."

"Yet it happened, and you didn't stop it from happening."

"Yes," Thomas said. "I can't change that path. Correct it. It's too late." He gazed out the window of the plane. "But without that path, Sean wouldn't be alive. He wouldn't have influenced the companies and people he has across the globe. I've watched—"

Will waited for his words. *Watched what?*

But Thomas didn't continue. He fumbled with his napkin and took a sip of his drink. Finally, he said, "I wish I could change the pain that has resulted for all of us. One night changed the destinies of both our families, inextricably weaving them together."

"Does Victoria know? Spencer?"

Thomas shook his head. "I don't think so. I've never told them, or anyone else."

"Then it's time to take control. Shape this in the direction we want it to go. If we don't get on the front end, what results might change a lot more destinies than merely the Worthingtons' and the Riches'."

"You're talking about the photos."

"Yes." Will leaned forward. "I have no doubt they will rise again. Mom and Dad don't know yet. We need to tell them, but as you can understand, this is a fragile time."

Thomas nodded. "I regret that I am a big part of that."

Will's next move was most difficult. It felt like a betrayal of his sister. But he had to say it. "Sarah doesn't know about Sean—that you are his birth father." Will rushed on. "Dad doesn't want her to know. Wants her protected. Especially because she's vulnerable right now with this potential move to attorney general."

"I understand. Bill always was protective of Ava. It makes sense he'd also want to protect his daughter."

"Then you understand why I'm asking for your help. No one in my family has any idea I'm meeting with you. But for Mom's sake, and Sarah's, we need to act before those photos surface. Because if they do, the digging that results may lead to more revelations about the connections between our families than either of us wants public."

"So what do you want from me, Will?"

"First, I want an honest answer. Will you help me do what it takes? Even if it means taking a stand against Spencer?"

Pain ridged the older man's brow. He looked down for a minute. But when he raised his eyes, Will saw the calm resolve there.

"Yes," Thomas said with a level gaze. "I will do what I can, and what's right."

"Okay then. We are agreed."

Together, in the privacy of the plane, the two men struck a deal that had the potential to change not only the destinies of two families but of American political history.

15

Sarah had worked extra long days at the DOJ in the two weeks since the JC vote. She was determined to finish as much of her work in the Criminal Division as possible and, where she couldn't, to leave a clear trail for her successor to follow. Though she was still waiting on the full Senate vote, chances that she'd be confirmed were fairly high, considering the JC vote.

Still, she was a Worthington through and through. That meant she went after new opportunities with gusto but didn't bank on anything until it was a done deal. As a result, she hadn't even started looking for apartments in D.C.

In the middle of the heavy workload, though, two things had weighed on her mind.

The first was that her brothers seemed to be ducking her phone calls. Sean—well, that was normal. He'd go off the grid for a while, especially if he thought she was trying to wangle information out of him.

She grinned. Which she was.

But Will? He was like clockwork. She knew exactly when she could reach him, and she always did. Except for the past couple of weeks. She'd only received a few terse text responses to her phone calls. No calls back. That alone was suspicious. Will preferred face-to-face meetings, and then calls over texts. He said it was easier to interpret what someone was really saying if he could hear the inflection of their voice.

She narrowed her eyes. If all else failed, she'd call Laura and ask her to tell Will to call her. That always worked.

The second thing that weighed on her was the missing pieces in the Polar Bear Bomber's story. She, Darcy, and Jon still hadn't been able to dig up anything else about Frank Stapleton that could link him to Justin Eliot.

She exhaled, frustrated. Why did this particular case bother her so much? She found herself thinking about it even during her other cases. Was it the fact that someone had tried to hold it over her brothers' heads? Yes, that was one reason.

But the other was stronger—that someone with enough power had taken advantage of a guy like Justin. Justin had clearly had enough odds stacked against him to make his life difficult. The person or persons who had used him had likely discarded him like a piece of trash.

Everything about that scenario caused Sarah's strong sense of justice and compassion for the underprivileged to rear its head. She couldn't stand by and let the perpetrators slide unpunished.

She sighed. There was nothing she could do about that case at the moment, so she tackled the easiest of her problems first. A glance at the clock told her it was past quitting time anyway. She'd phone Sean. He should be home from Malaysia. If he didn't answer her call, perhaps a surprise stop by was in order.

The Worthington women had a way of getting what they wanted. If not one way, then another.

Sean was lounging in sweats when his sister's number popped up on his cell. He chuckled. He'd been waiting for her to wind down from their last conversation, when she'd been digging for information. The brothers had secretly agreed that was the best strategy for now.

"So you're talking to me civilly now." He smirked.

"All right, so I was a little impulsive the last time we talked. I can get that way sometimes," she replied.

"Impulsive? Now there's an under—"

"You know you love me anyway, so let's cut to the chase. What exactly did that guy in the bar say to you? It might give us some clues as to who hired him."

He padded in sock feet toward the kitchen. "You're back on that trail again, huh? Seriously, sis, sometime you've got to let go."

"Hey, this is my family he messed with."

"People try to mess with us all the time. But this time whoever did it treated a troubled guy like a dog that could be used and kicked aside. That's really what's bothering you, isn't it?"

He'd been by her side multiple times as a kid when she stepped in to rescue cats, dogs, birds, and younger kids from the bullies of the neighborhood. Nobody messed with his sister, even the bullies. Sarah Worthington was one tough cookie, and she never crumbled.

"Yes," she breathed. "How did you know?"

Sean chuckled as he evaluated the contents of his fridge. "I know you. You never learned to back down. Even if the bully was twice your size, you still went after him."

"May I point out that I always won too," she shot back.

"Yes, you did. I would have hated to be the other guy." He laughed. "Wait—sometimes I *was* that other guy." He grabbed an iced coffee and shut the fridge door.

"Now that we're clear on that subject, what about my original question?"

He thought for a minute. "All I can remember is the guy talking about how life can be tough sometimes, but then you get a break and things seem like they're going to work out. Only general stuff like that, nothing specific. The guy seemed a little drunk, or maybe off his meds, but talkative and nice. He said his career was on the upswing. That's all I can remember."

"So did anything else happen that was unusual either before or after that?" she asked.

He rolled his eyes. Her lawyer interrogation mode had kicked in.

He thought again. "Well, I did get a strange note."

"When, and what did it say?" she fired at him.

"Whoa, let me think. It was after my little run to the Azores. When I got home, I found an odd note in a stack of mail. Basically said that if I decided to run for governor, secrets may come to light. Something weird like that."

"And you didn't think that was relevant to tell me before?" she barked.

"No, I didn't. For heaven's sake, we're Worthingtons. We get hit with crazy stuff like that all the time. Stalkers. Weirdos. Those who want to equalize the wealth in the United States and think that since we're rich, we're the spawn of Satan. It's the cost of being in the limelight. You know that."

***

Sarah was already packing her briefcase as she talked to her brother. All her senses were on alert, tingling like they did when she uncovered a critical factor in one of her cases.

"You didn't think that one was extra weird?"

"Well, on a scale of 1 to 10 . . ." he quipped.

She cut him off. "What exactly did the note say? Do you still have it?"

"I wadded it up and was going to throw it away, but then thought I should hang on to it. Just a sec." She heard rustling in the background. "Here it is. It says, 'Think twice about running for governor. Secrets have a way of becoming public.'"

"So somebody knew then about the photos of you with the bomber," she reasoned.

"That must have been it," he said quickly.

A little too quickly. What else was her brother hiding?

She frowned. "What does the handwriting look like?"

"I don't know. Handwriting. Loopy. Looks a bit uneven."

"Like somebody was trying to copy someone else's handwriting?"

"Maybe. Don't know."

"What color ink is it written in?"

"Wow, is this the day for 20 questions or what? You're on a roll."

"Just answer the question," she ordered.

"Blue. Looks like a blue ballpoint pen."

"Aha. Then you stay right there with that note until I come pick it up. I'm on my way."

16

Sean stared at the creased note and felt a shiver of premonition. Nothing about the handwriting stood out, other than the fact it seemed uneven. Even the same letters weren't formed the same way. He hadn't kept the envelope but remembered it was blank except for his name and address.

Not even a stamp. That meant someone had dropped it off. A person? A courier service?

He received so many deliveries that he doubted his house-keeper would remember a delivery so long ago. But the bell-man? Wasn't likely anything had slipped by him. He was the best place to start. Sean might as well ask while he waited for his sister to arrive.

Sarah swept into Sean's apartment door and held out her hand. "The note?"

"What? No hello first?" he teased.

She scowled, and he handed the note over. After scrutinizing it, she placed a call on her cell. "Darcy, do you still have the bomber's suicide note? And the report on the note?"

"Note's in evidence lockup. Still have the report."

"Hey, can I put you on speakerphone? I'm at Sean's. It's important he hear this too."

"No problem." There was some shuffling in the background.

"Are you still at work?" Sarah asked.

"Yep, under the piles in a major way," her friend replied.

Sarah muffled her phone and whispered to Sean, "You can take that literally. Darcy's big on piles. She's a terrible filer. But she can find anything in an instant. Kinda like somebody else I know." She grinned at her brother. "Drives her boss and colleagues crazy. Just like you used to drive Will crazy with your messes."

"You know I did that just to bug him," Sean said.

She rolled her eyes. "Of course I know that. And it worked."

"Okay, got it," Darcy announced. "What do you need to know?"

"What kind of ink did the writer use?"

"We already established that it wasn't Justin's handwriting, so this is important why?" Darcy asked.

"Remember that Michael said he and Justin always used calligraphy pens? But wasn't the note written with what looked like blue ballpoint pen?"

There was a slight pause as Darcy checked the report. "You're right. Indian-blue ballpoint pen ink."

"Anything else unusual about it?"

"Never had a chance to find out. Bomber wrote the note, jumped, end of story. People here at DHS had other things to deal with."

"Well . . ."

But Sarah didn't have to wheedle. Darcy caught on. "So you

want me to run an analysis of exactly what's in the ink, to see if we identify traces of anything unique?"

"You got it," Sarah declared.

"Okay. I'll have the lab guys analyze it. They can tag it with different rare-earth elements and see what they come up with. Back to you as soon as I have something."

Just as Sarah was ending the call with Darcy, Sean's cell rang. It was the bellman. He'd already checked his ledger when Sean phoned earlier. He'd said he was out with the flu that day, so Reginald, the new substitute bellman, had been on duty.

"Talked to Reginald," the bellman announced. "He remembered that day exactly because it was his first official one on the job. Said he was nervous." The bellman laughed. "But he told me a guy did stop by and ask whether he could deliver a letter to your door. Reginald said no, that was against the rules, and wouldn't let him go up. But Reginald agreed to deliver the letter personally to your door. Your housekeeper accepted it."

"Did the guy sign in?" Sean asked.

"Yes. I checked the records. Said he was from Jackson Couriers."

"Haven't heard of them before."

"Neither had I," the bellman announced, "so I did some checking in the last half hour. I don't think the company exists."

"Does Reginald remember what the guy looked like?"

"Already asked him that." The bellman seemed proud to have thought of it first. "He said the guy was about five ten, medium-brown hair, midthirties. Seemed too slick and professional to be a delivery boy. A little cocky too, like he was used to getting his way."

"Thanks a bunch. You've been most helpful."

When he explained to Sarah, she frowned. "That sounds a lot like—"

"Jason Carson," he finished.

"Now we just have to connect the rest of the dots and prove it." Sarah's eyes glinted. "I'll take the note to Darcy. Then we can use that minnow to catch the bigger fish we're after."

17

"We got it," Darcy announced to Sarah on Friday afternoon. "Pushed the lab guys to get it done before the weekend."

"And?" Sarah prompted.

"The ink on the two notes was an exact match. The elements of the ink are a unique mixture, found only in a very high-end pen. Specifically a Mont Blanc Ballpoint. The lab techs tell me it's one of the most expensive ballpoint pens in the world and can sell for over $700,000."

"So whoever wrote the note was definitely not your ordinary street thug. There probably aren't a lot of those pens around," Sarah said. "What about the handwriting?"

"As close of a match as possible for someone trying to fake another person's handwriting. Some of the attempted letters were almost cookie-cutter."

"So the same person wrote both notes."

"Yep. Now all we have to do is find that pen to find the person."

"I'll call Jon and see if he has any ideas," Sarah said. "He's pretty good at ferreting out that kind of stuff."

"What about Will? If Stapleton is involved somehow with

the bomber, Will's the one who knows him best. Giving Will that info might jog his memory about something he's noticed," Darcy suggested.

"You're right. He's so detail oriented. So is Jon. Though the one drives me a lot crazier than the other."

"So," Darcy teased, "the reporter is growing on you, huh?"

"Oh, hush up. I'll give them both a call."

Will was scanning a profit spreadsheet for AF with Drew when his sister called.

"A Mont Blanc Ballpoint?" Will shrugged. "There's got to be lots of those in New York City."

"No, this is a special kind. The kind that sells for over $700K. Let me send you a picture of it. I want to see if you remember anybody using anything like that."

"Okay, sis, but you're hunting for a needle in a haystack, you know."

"I know, but it doesn't mean I won't try."

"I always did love that about you. But it would help if you could give me some more information."

"That may sidetrack you from your total recall, and I wouldn't want that."

Sarah and Sean both joked about Will's ability to look at a flat image and turn it immediately into 3-D in his mind. If he hadn't ended up working with their father at Worthington Shares, he probably would have gone the route of an engineer or an architect.

He sighed. "I'll call you back."

"Yeah, I'll be waiting here patiently while you do your mind thingy."

"No you won't, but you'll have to wait anyway."

The picture came through on his cell. He showed it to Drew, then stared at it before ending the call.

Drew nodded and stepped out. He knew Will's pattern and would inform Will's secretary he was not to be disturbed.

Sitting back in his leather executive chair, Will closed his eyes and focused on the object. Had he seen anything like that? If so, where?

Half an hour later an image blurred into Will's consciousness.

Jason Carson sitting on the bench in the park. The day he showed me the photo of Sean with the Polar Bear Bomber. He'd unclipped a pen from a folder, handed the folder to me, and then tucked the pen into his breast pocket.

Will sat up straight in his chair. He could now see the pen with laser-like detail in his mind. It looked exactly like the picture Sarah had sent him.

Sarah fidgeted at her desk while she waited for Will to call back.

The instant her cell rang, she grabbed it. "So?"

"Carson. The day he showed me the photos, he was carrying that kind of pen."

"That's all I need to know. I'm on it."

A Secure Location

"I know how to get what we need," he told the man.

"Enough to make it stick?"

"That and more. I'll take care of it. He won't see it coming."

18

NEW YORK CITY

"We have to be missing something. Let's go over it all again," Sarah told Darcy that night as they sat cross-legged on the floor of her penthouse.

"The facts we already know: Justin Eliot carried a backpack bomb and blew a chunk out of the AF building. A suicide note was found in his friend Michael Vara's Brooklyn apartment, where Justin sometimes stayed. Justin jumped off a 30-story building," Darcy reported.

Sarah took over. "His single mom owned a home but never worked, had no insurance, etc. Justin had psychological issues that required private schooling and expensive medicine. He did a stint as an actor but didn't get very far. Michael was confident the handwriting on the note was not Justin's and said neither of them would use a blue ballpoint pen."

"Not to mention a $700K kind of pen," Darcy added.

"Michael doesn't believe his friend, who couldn't hurt an insect, could ever knowingly hurt another human being. But he also said Justin was desperate enough for money to do some underground shows and was happy about getting a simple acting job that would pay well. With that money, he was considering taking Michael up on his offer to leave New York and stay with him in London."

"We also know from Michael that a shadowy 'uncle' showed up and spent time with Justin's mom. And he looks an awful lot like Frank Stapleton."

"Stop. Let's follow that angle a bit." Sarah jumped up and opened the door for Jon, who'd just arrived.

"Follow what angle?" Jon asked.

"About exactly how Frank Stapleton could know Rebecca Eliot," Darcy answered.

"He wasn't a true uncle. Rebecca was an only child. Stapleton is an only child. I checked on all that," Jon said. "They didn't attend the same schools. Rebecca only attended through her junior year of high school. I can't trace anyone who remembers much about her except that she worked at a diner sometimes. Seems like she was a loner."

"Stapleton's got to be in his midfifties," Sarah figured. "That would make him about 40 when he was visiting Rebecca's house—if the 'uncle' really was him."

"And about 30 when Justin was born," Jon added. "Just when Stapleton's career in finance was flying, and he was starting to become a high roller in politics too."

Darcy stared at both of them. "What if—"

Jon nodded. "A star on the rise is nice to a waitress who doesn't get much attention. They play around. She becomes pregnant."

Sarah jumped on board. "But she refuses to get an abortion. To keep things quiet, he says he'll take care of her, buy her a house, provide for her and the baby."

"With perhaps some fringe benefits on the side," Darcy said sarcastically.

"Then why would he take care of them all these years but drop out of sight when Rebecca died?" Sarah asked.

"Maybe because Justin didn't know who Stapleton really was—his birth father—and wasn't in contact with him except through Rebecca. She was the only one who knew the truth, so after her death, there was no reason to continue the charade," Jon said.

Sarah frowned. "That's cold. Not even providing for your son, who is clearly troubled?"

"But real life," Darcy stated. "I doubt the prestigious CEO of the largest finance organization in the US would want it public that he has a son out of wedlock. He's married, right?"

"Yes, and I'm pretty sure he has a son, from what Will has said. I've seen Stapleton's wife multiple times, but I don't remember ever meeting the kid," Sarah said.

Jon did a few searches on his iPhone. "Philip. Looks like he's a few years older than Justin. But I can't find any public profile other than his birth record to Frank and Margaret Stapleton. That's odd. No driver's license either."

Darcy peered at his iPhone screen. "Plenty of media photos of Stapleton with his wife over the years, but no son in the photos."

Sarah held up a finger. "I know who'll know."

She dialed Will.

A Secure Location

"I've procured the item," he told the man.

"That fast?"

"Easy as taking candy from a baby." He chuckled.

"Fingerprints too?"

"Of course."

"Good."

"He won't have a clue where it went," he assured the man. "But when he's presented with the evidence, he'll sing any tune to save his sorry hide."

"When will the package be delivered?"

"Monday."

"Same protocol as before?"

"Yes. No one will be able to trace its origin."

19

NEW YORK CITY

Sean was glad to be home on a Friday night. The last few months he'd been traveling a lot. He loved his work assisting people around the globe with growing companies that solved real problems. He thought of the people he'd recently met in Malaysia, and their passion for purifying drinking water for the locals and providing cost-effective medical equipment. Being the money backer for such enterprises brought Sean great satisfaction. But what he loved the most was being hands-on with the locals. Helping people was in his DNA. And that innate drive allowed him to go into nearly any setting across the world and become a part of its fabric, interacting with people in every stratum.

But right now he only missed one of them—Elizabeth. Without her, his apartment felt sterile and empty. He picked up the bright yellow pillow she'd added to his black, white, and gray environment. It was just a touch, but it reflected the sunshine she brought into his life.

They'd already settled the question of love. But marriage? How exactly would that work, with her based out of Seattle for her research, and him based out of New York City? And them both traveling the world for their careers?

———————

"Hey, does Frank Stapleton have any kids other than his son?" Sarah blurted out.

Will grimaced. He'd picked up the call by instinct. Now he regretted it. His sister sounded like she was on a roll. "Hey, sis, can this wait? I'm watching a movie with the kids."

"No, just answer the question," she demanded.

He extracted Davy from his lap and got up from the couch. After he was out of earshot of the kids, he said, "No, only a son."

"What do you know about Philip? Have you ever met him?"

He sighed. She was in grilling mode. He accepted the inevitable. "Frank only mentioned him a couple of times. One was when the kid graduated from high school. Said he wasn't quite sure what the next step would be for Philip since he has some significant challenges."

"What challenges?" she asked.

"I think he was diagnosed as bipolar."

Sarah's voice raised a notch. "You're saying Frank's son is bipolar?"

"Yes. Even had tutors to help him catch up after some of his times in the hospital."

"Dad! You're missing the best part!" an energetic voice interrupted, tugging at him.

He gave Davy the one-minute sign, then asked, "Seriously, sis, what is this about?"

But she'd already hung up on him.

He shook his head and went back to the movie.

———————

Darcy's eyes were wide when Sarah got off the phone. "Bi-polar? Like Justin was?"

Sarah again held up a finger. "Wait. Jon, do you know if bi-polar disorder tends to run in families?"

"Yes, it often seems to. From all I've read about it, there's a genetic component to it."

Darcy crossed her arms in triumph. "So we've found another connection."

"You still have a DNA sample of Justin at DHS, right?" Jon asked her.

"Yup. You guys thinking what I'm thinking?"

Sarah nodded. "There's got to be a blood test or DNA sample somewhere of Frank Stapleton, right? Enough to see if it's a match for paternity?"

"I'm sure there is," Darcy declared. "I'll get going on it first thing Monday."

20

Saturday morning, Will woke up grumpy and disconcerted. When he'd barked at the kids for the third time in an hour, Laura lifted an eyebrow and jammed a thumb in the direction of his office.

He knew what that look meant. He'd better hightail it into that office, shut the door, and deal with his attitude before he came out.

So he did what he didn't usually do—he phoned Drew on the weekend.

After explaining Sarah's line of questioning, Will concluded with, "What do you think she's up to?"

"She's on the trail of something. You know Sarah. She won't give up until she's ferreted out every clue."

"I just don't want her to get in over her head."

Drew laughed. "Sarah's always up to her eyeballs in something. But let me assure you, she's never been in over her head. Unlike you now, for instance."

Will scowled. "What do you mean?"

"You're calling me because Laura quarantined you in your office for your bad mood, right?"

Will sighed. "You got it," he said meekly.

"Well then, you better deal with the alligators in your own swamp for now."

———————

Sarah hated waiting. She wanted to be able to snap her fingers and have that DNA test pronto. But since that wasn't possible, she focused on the upcoming week. By the end of it, she should know what was next in her destiny. The full Senate vote was slated for Thursday.

Her mind had been so full of her DOJ work and the Polar Bear bombing that she hadn't started looking for a place in D.C. yet. She'd thought about asking her mom to help out, but Ava had seemed more introspective than usual lately. Maybe it was because her father had been home a lot recently, and she was adjusting to a new schedule. Sarah hadn't wanted to push.

Maybe she should start scanning possibilities in the D.C. area this weekend. After all, if she was confirmed, she'd be swept into a whirlwind of responsibilities.

Just then her cell rang. It was Jon.

"Have any more thoughts about our theories from last night?" he asked.

She chuckled. "I'm trying hard not to, since there's nothing else we can do about it until Monday."

"Ah," he said. "To change the subject then, how are you doing with finding a place in D.C.?"

"That's assuming I get confirmed," she replied.

"You will. So, have you started looking?"

"No time." She sighed. "I was just thinking about that."

"I'd be happy to help, but I'm not exactly a connoisseur of fine apartments. You've seen mine." He laughed. "But I bet Drew could help out with that. I already told him I'd be more than happy to help you move whatever you want to take there. I deserve a few days off."

"Actually, I'm keeping the place here so I can come back on weekends, so I won't be taking much. Just some clothes and a few basics to get me started. I can get the rest there when I get a place. But I'd welcome the help in hauling a carload." She paused. "You two have been talking about me, huh?"

Somehow that didn't bother her, like it did when Will and her father talked about her.

"Yes, we have," Jon replied. "Drew's a really good guy, Sarah. What he does isn't merely a job."

"I know," Sarah said. "Dad has always surrounded himself with people of integrity. He says if you can't look somebody straight in the eye and they can't look straight back at you, no waffling, he doesn't want them around his family. He's built a lot of his business on handshakes. But he did a great thing when he hired Drew all those years ago when we kids were little."

"Where did he find Drew anyway?"

She thought for a second. "I think an old friend of Dad and Mom's recommended him right after he got out of university."

"Anybody I know?"

"Yeah. Thomas Rich."

"The former president of the United States? That Thomas Rich?"

"Indeed."

He whistled. "That's some friend. But then again, why should I be surprised?"

"We're not as high and mighty as you might think," she teased. "Hang around us even more and you'll find that out." She sobered. "Mom and Dad don't see him anymore, though. Life just got too busy and all that, I think."

"I can imagine. The president of the United States and the

president of Worthington Shares probably didn't find much time to inhabit the same space."

"I don't remember doing anything with Thomas and his family when I was young. But Drew? He's been around since my earliest memories."

"He says you Worthingtons are family. I don't think he'd ever let anything bad happen to you on his watch."

"No, he wouldn't."

"Nor would I," he said softly. Quickly he added, "I've got to go. My editor's flagging me down with that 'potential big story' look in his eye. Talk soon."

With Jon, there was no guessing. She knew he'd do just what he said.

Her next call was to Drew to take him up on his help. He said he and Jean would contact a couple high-end realtors they trusted and let them start the hunt.

Drew chuckled. "You know Jean. After the realtors do their job, she'll take a look and narrow the field herself before we pass any choices to you."

"I know, and I'm grateful."

After the call ended, she refocused on the attorney general next steps. If she was confirmed on Thursday, she'd likely be sworn in sometime the following week. Then she'd need to move to D.C., a short distance from her finagling and sometimes over-protective family. That might be a bit of a relief. Then again, the Worthingtons stayed in close contact no matter where they traveled.

A thought leaped into the forefront of her mind, startling her. *Jon travels to D.C. a lot to report on events there.*

She recalled his comment, "Nor would I."

Had he really said that, or had she imagined it?

21

Jon's call on Monday morning was short. "I just received a surprise you have to see. Can you get to the *Times*—my desk—within the next hour?"

"Any hints?" Sarah asked.

"Nope. This one you have to see to believe."

She was there within 45 minutes.

Jon held a baggie out to her. It was tagged with a note: *Check this against Justin Eliot's suicide note. Run the fingerprints.*

"Wow," she said, "can't get any clearer than that. I can get it to Darcy on my way back."

"No need." He pointed.

An out-of-breath Darcy hustled toward his office. "Hey, I was working on the DNA match. What's so important that—" She stopped in her tracks when Jon dangled the baggie in front of her.

By Tuesday noon, they had their answer. The fingerprints on the pen were undeniable. It was Jason Carson. A direct match to Will's crystal-clear recall.

Now Darcy was moving heaven and earth to get a warrant as swiftly as possible for his arrest.

Will was on a call with the CEO of a potential acquisition when Drew walked into his office.

"Sarah," Drew mouthed, holding out his cell.

Will knew Drew wouldn't interrupt him on a call unless it was critical. He put the CEO on hold and took Sarah's call.

"Carson will be arrested as soon as we can get the warrant," she declared. "He won't have a chance to see it coming."

"Well, you certainly have been busy. But arrested for what exactly?"

"A surprise package dropped into our laps. A $700K pen with Carson's fingerprints on it, and the ink matches that on the suicide note," she reported.

"Wow. You think you have enough to make it stick against Carson?"

"Yup. But if the little minnow can help us catch the bigger fish, then, depending on how deep the waters the minnow got himself in, he may swim free to cause havoc elsewhere."

"That stinks, but I got it. And now I have to go back to my other call."

Drew nodded, looking satisfied. Evidently Sarah had filled him in as well.

Will didn't know the details, but he knew Drew had been tracking Carson ever since the aborted Senate race, looking for a weak moment. All they needed was one in order to get Carson talking. Drew had said they were close. What Sarah had just learned tipped the balance of the scale in their favor.

On Thursday, the full Senate vote was in—58 to 41. Sarah would be sworn in on Wednesday, the following week, at the Warner Theatre in D.C.

The media flew into a frenzy, swarming the outside of the DOJ office for an official statement from her. She gave a simple one: "I am honored by the American people's faith in me in leading this department and committed to preserving and pursuing equal justice for all."

Her supporters ramped up their news comments.

"She's tough, well-respected, and a veteran in the area of law."

"Her proven record and significant experience in handling difficult cases says it all."

"I have no doubt she'll use the law to protect equality for Americans, since she's a devoted champion of all the law protects."

"Even in law school, she worked pro bono and defended the disadvantaged. She can't be swayed from doing what is right."

Her detractors didn't dispute her qualifications or background but took issue with her potential politics and her connection to President Rich.

"She's part of a wealthy, pro-Democrat family. How can she not be biased in her rulings?"

"She was nominated by Rich. She'll protect him at all costs."

"With Rich's ratings dropping after the AF scandal, she'll do what she can to support issues that could get him reelected."

She rolled her eyes. If they only knew what she thought of President Spencer Rich . . .

22

NEW YORK CITY

"Found the perfect place for your sister in D.C.," Drew announced as he walked into Will's office Friday morning. "Or, shall I clarify, my wife found it. She's spent more time with it than I have, so the realtors started calling her."

"They know where the real power lies." Will grinned. "But I already knew," he admitted.

"Jean called Laura?"

"Yesterday, as soon as the vote was announced. Laura filled me in."

"So you know they've settled on a place in the Longwood neighborhood of Bethesda?"

Will nodded. "Laura said Sarah loved the idea, especially since it's close to the McCrillis Gardens."

"Sarah's going to take a look as soon as she gets there this weekend, just to confirm. If she likes it, Jean will handle the details with the realtor and push things along. Sarah will stay at the Ritz in the meanwhile. Jon offered to drive her to D.C. and haul anything she wants to take."

Will lifted a brow. "Really? You know Sarah. She'll likely just pick up whatever she needs in D.C."

"You're saying Jon really doesn't need to drive with her." Drew said it straightforwardly, but Will caught the amusement in his eyes.

"At least not for practical reasons."

"Oh, but I think he does." Now the enigmatic Drew was smiling.

Will crossed his arms. "If you have something to say, come right on out and say it."

"Okay, I will. I think Jon is far more interested in your baby sister than a simple colleague would be. And I think, even if Sarah doesn't realize it yet, the attraction is mutual." Drew cocked his head. "That wouldn't be a bad thing, would it?"

"No," Will said shortly. "Maybe that's why it bothers me."

"You didn't think Sarah would ever find a guy? Get married?"

"After that jerk of a TV producer, she signed off on dating in general. Said she had more important things to accomplish in life than to be used by some fatheaded, pompous—"

Drew held up his hand. "I get it. You hated that guy. You want to protect your sister." His tone gentled. "But with Jon, there's nothing to protect her from. You asked me to check him out long ago, when you first had an inkling that Jon could be interested in her, or vice versa. I did. The guy's clean. Sterling reputation. Impeccable career. Doesn't back down in the face of anything. Always does what's right. As close a match to Worthington character as I've ever seen. Even volunteers with special needs kids."

Will sighed. "You're right. I just want my sister to be safe . . . and happy."

Drew nodded. "Understood."

A Secure Location

He'd received multiple calls from the man over the past couple of days. The warrant for Jason Carson hadn't moved as swiftly as they'd hoped. Finally, the man ordered him to intervene by pulling a few strings.

It was a done deal by 10:00 a.m. He phoned the man to report the news.

"Carson was looking rather squeamish as he was led away."

"Now they—and we—will get some more answers. If he can fill in the missing pieces," the man said.

"Then we both know what's going to happen."

"But it's got to happen quietly. No one can know we're involved—that I'm involved," the man said. "You know what's at stake."

"Leave that to me."

New York City

Sarah had bid her co-workers good-bye at the DOJ's Criminal Division that afternoon. No one was surprised by her swift exit. They'd all known the vote was pending. Even John Barnhill, her now ex-boss, had shaken her hand, looked her in the eye, and said, "Nicely done." It was the closest thing to a compliment the gruff, no-nonsense veteran had ever given her.

It had only taken her 20 minutes to pack up the few personal belongings from her office. It was a strange feeling walking away from the building where she'd spent so many years.

Now, finally, she had the opportunity to return Darcy's earlier call.

"Carson's in custody," Darcy declared with satisfaction.

"Was there a holdup on the warrant?" Sarah asked. "I wondered when I hadn't heard, but I've been too busy to check in."

"Don't even want to go there with what I've been through to get it." Darcy's tone was caustic. "But then suddenly, as if Oz was pulling the strings behind the magic curtain, it came through this morning."

"So now everybody gets their crack at him—NYPD, FBI, DHS, you name it."

"Yeah. He's not going to be sitting comfortably anywhere."

"At least we might get some answers, even if I can't technically be involved anymore," Sarah said.

"Well, unofficially involved person, we'll still keep you up-to-date on what's happening."

She grinned. "I'm counting on it."

23

Sean was grappling with the financials of a new NGO when his sister called to announce Carson was in custody.

"What took you so long?" he teased.

"What's taking *you* so long?" she fired back. "You still don't have a ring on Elizabeth's finger. What are you waiting for?"

"Give it a rest, sis."

She laughed. "You know I won't give up until I get what I want. What I know you want."

He knew she was right. What *was* he waiting for?

But he also didn't want his sister to know how close she was to hitting the mark. So he employed an age-old technique—he changed the subject.

"Jon is going with you to D.C., huh? How exactly did that happen?"

Sarah was silent for a moment. "Are you implying . . ."

He grinned. "You can dish it out, but you can't take it, can you?"

"Oooh," was all she said before she hung up.

Now he knew the interest was mutual. He couldn't wait to tell Elizabeth.

Will was happy for his sister. He had no doubt she'd be an excellent attorney general. Not that it would be easy, but Sarah never backed down from any challenge.

He was also uneasy. She'd never explained why she was digging more into Frank Stapleton and his son, Philip. Will hadn't pushed her. Only he and Drew knew that Stapleton was behind trying to take the Worthingtons down, but neither could prove it.

Will hated it when his hands were tied, and when his sister was potentially pursuing an angle that could get her in big trouble.

Maybe this career move was exactly what they all needed—to distract her from the Polar Bear bombing case and get her out of harm's way.

Late evening, Darcy called Sarah again to report on Carson's interrogation.

"Started with the song and dance of 'Sandstrom made me do it or I'd lose my job.' Basically the same info he'd given when he blew the whistle on the $25M quid pro quo."

Sarah cut in. "Which doesn't get us anywhere, with Sandstrom already behind bars."

"Carson said Sandstrom didn't like Will pushing for more research before AF moved into the Arctic. When the fiasco happened, he was convinced Will would use it to take over AF, rallying the board and shareholders around him. Sandstrom was shocked when Will just walked away. But that didn't solve the problem, with Sean and Jon being eyewitnesses in the Arctic.

When news leaked of what was really happening, the president went ballistic on Sandstrom for making him look bad. Loughlin threw a fit when Will decided to run for Senate and cashed in his favors with Sandstrom. Sandstrom told Carson it was time to take care of the Worthington problem."

"So that's when they set up Sean," Sarah reasoned.

"Yep," Darcy said. "Sandstrom handed Carson a name and address and ordered Carson to hire some guy—who we now know was Justin—at an underground show. All Justin had to do was show up at a local bar, have a few drinks, and chat with the guy they described to him. Carson gave Justin a disposable cell for contact. He also hired a photographer to hang out at the bar and paid a woman a couple hundred bucks to act like she was an executive assistant for one of Sean's clients and set up a meet via phone. As soon as Sean left the bar, Carson met the photographer and picked up the photos."

"What about the backpack?"

"Sandstrom asked Carson to pick up a package and contact Justin again. Carson claims he only saw Justin one more time—to deliver the backpack and instructions in a sealed envelope. Says he showed up at the apartment to pay Justin, but he wasn't there. So Carson left the envelope inside the apartment."

"Let me guess," Sarah said. "Carson claims he didn't know the contents of either the backpack or the envelope."

"You got it. Says he never opened them, just delivered them. After the bomb went off, Carson says he confronted Sandstrom, but Sandstrom threatened him, saying he was in too deep to get out now. That he had to finish what he started. Carson admitted to the photo setup. Shrugged and said that kind of stuff happens all the time in big corporations. But he insisted he had nothing else to do with the bomber. He didn't have a clue about the suicide note until the press announced it."

"So if Carson didn't kill Justin, who did?"

"A good question," Darcy said. "Now we have to dig up the answer."

A Secure Location

He placed the call the man was waiting for. "Once confronted with the evidence, Carson was singing like a songbird."

"What exactly did he say?"

"Everything we already know, except he insisted he didn't write the suicide note."

"And you believe him?" the man growled.

"He offered to take a lie detector test."

"Did he say anything about the C-4 and the bomb elements stashed in the apartment?"

"Claims he didn't see anything like that when he was inside the apartment. He just left the envelope on a desk."

"Mr. Eliot's death?"

"He insists he had nothing to do with that."

"So the other players are more involved than we originally thought."

"Certainly looks that way."

24

NEW YORK CITY

Saturday morning Sarah was wildly throwing a few personal essentials and some clothing into a couple of suitcases. Jon would arrive at 10 to drive her to D.C. She'd decided to leave her car in New York City for the time being, until she was settled in a more permanent location in D.C. Jean Simons had set up an appointment with the D.C. realtor for Sarah to look at her potential new place on Sunday. If she confirmed interest, she'd close on her new home within a month. In the meanwhile, she'd be at the Ritz.

Though she wouldn't be sworn in as attorney general until Wednesday, Sarah had wanted to be there early before the media hoopla kicked in. That way she could scope out the area more effectively than she had in her visits there and also shop for furniture once she'd seen her new place. Unlike Sean, who simply let an interior decorator have her way with his abode since he was rarely there, Sarah liked to do her own decorating. She'd already decided on Asian minimalistic—other than her walk-in closets. She planned on stocking those thoroughly with apparel appropriate for an attorney general.

But for today, she was just Sarah—in jeans, a sweatshirt, and tennis shoes.

As she was dragging one of her suitcases toward the door, a knock sounded.

She smiled. It was Jon—right on time, as always.

WASHINGTON, D.C.

Will waited in the audience on Wednesday, the day Sarah would be sworn in as attorney general. The Worthingtons had arrived the previous evening and had enjoyed a late family dinner. All knew with Sarah's schedule it might be awhile before they'd have the opportunity to do so again.

Now, minutes before the ceremony, Spencer Rich entered the room.

Will studied the president's expression. Smug. As if he'd played a tennis match and won.

That meant the president thought somehow he'd gotten the upper hand.

So he thinks he can control Sarah—or us as a family—by getting her into this position, Will reflected. He grinned. *He doesn't know my sister.*

Sarah was officially sworn in by Chief Justice Larsen, with President Rich looking on. With her left hand on a Bible, Sarah raised her right hand and vowed to use the law to protect equality.

Then, with cameras flashing, she addressed the American people. "My sacred charge is your protection, your liberties, and your rights. I will be a devoted champion of all the law protects. Thank you for your faith and trust in me," she concluded.

When she looked out into the audience, she saw her family. Will and her father sat stoically, as usual. Sean was clapping. Her mother was teary-eyed. Everything she had expected.

Her gaze moved toward the press wing. Jon was smiling at her. When he caught her eyes, he mouthed, "Well done."

She basked in his approval.

25

Sarah tightened her scarf against the January chill of D.C. as she stepped out of the taxi and hurried toward her office building. Her new job was even more intense than she'd been forewarned.

Her father was indeed right. Protecting the rights of an entire nation *was* a big job. But after her time in the DOJ's Criminal Division and the long vetting process, Sarah had gone into it with eyes wide open. She recalled the ancient saying, "Be as wise as a serpent and as innocent as a dove." With the current presidential administration, she definitely had her hands full.

With her role now, Sarah had had to recuse herself officially from the Polar Bear bombing case and anything having to do with American Frontier. But Jon and Darcy had promised to keep her quietly in the loop, and she could still give them her input on any theories.

Carson was the small fish, if he'd only made the connections and handoffs that he admitted to. She frowned. Not that the man hadn't done multiple dirty deals before, per all the rumors. But until now, he'd never been caught. It would be nice to see him tucked behind bars, like Sandstrom. But the big fish were the ones they most needed to catch.

Jon was doing additional digging behind the scenes, so she knew the facts that had sounded so sensationalist—as news about events occurring in Washington often was—were the truth. President Rich had received $25 million from the Big Oil companies for his reelection campaign, with American Frontier providing the largest share of the funds but Sandstrom himself cajoling other oil companies to buy in. Frank Stapleton, the GOP kingmaker, had been at the hub of Rich's campaign. Shortly after Rich was elected, American Frontier had easily secured exclusive drilling rights in the Arctic without going through any of the usual red tape that could take months. That meant Stapleton also had a lot to lose publicly when all the connections were made.

And privately, if her, Jon, and Darcy's guesses were right.

Besides that, Jon had been strangely quiet. She knew what that meant. In his brilliant mind, the pieces related to the $25M still weren't completely adding up.

Also, Darcy hadn't been able to obtain a sample of Stapleton's DNA. There was no way to force him to contribute one without revealing the cards in their hand. Then he'd lawyer up and would be far harder to touch.

In her gut, though, Sarah was convinced Stapleton was exactly who they thought—Justin Eliot's birth father. But how exactly would she approach her skeptical older brother with the possibility? Without more to go on?

NEW YORK CITY

Stapleton called on Will in his Worthington Shares office.

They'd barely exchanged the usual morning pleasantries before Stapleton got to the point. "Will, you and I have been friends for a long time. I've recently heard a rumor that your sister and a couple of her old colleagues are continuing to pursue the Polar Bear Bomber case—off the books, you might say."

Will watched as Stapleton clicked his pen, an irritating habit and sure sign that Stapleton was nervous.

"There's no need to do so," Stapleton said. "The case is closed. The guy's dead, and all evidence is in. Any continued digging for rabbit trails will eventually come to the press's notice. For AF's sake, I want to ask you—as a friend—to advise your sister and the others to back off. There's nothing to be gained other than unwanted attention for AF as we're trying to get ourselves back in the good graces of the world."

"So you're concerned about the stock prices. The media attention. Is that all?" Will studied Stapleton. "Or is something else at stake too?"

The typically even-keeled Stapleton lost his cool. "Of course there are other things at stake here, Will," he exclaimed.

At the outburst, Will's office door opened. Drew poked his head in. Will waved him off but knew Drew would hover close by outside his office.

"You know President Rich isn't happy," Stapleton said in a lowered voice, "and that means I get phone calls. None of us can afford any more media attention right now." He clicked his pen again.

"First of all, I've never been able to tell my sister what to do, and I won't this time either." Will paused. "But I will talk with her."

Stapleton held up his hand. "That's all I'm asking."

Will nodded. "Done."

Stapleton got up from the chair opposite Will's desk. "Oh, and let me know what she says, will you?" he asked casually. He clicked his pen, reached for the notepad on Will's desk, scribbled something, and laid the slip of paper on the desktop. "I'll be in Marina di Portofino for a few days." He grimaced. "A forced vacation with the wife, you know. Her birthday. This is the number. My cell doesn't always work well there."

Will didn't promise anything but stood to shake Stapleton's hand.

Drew entered as Stapleton exited.

Will sat back in his chair.

"Why the frown?" Drew asked.

"Because something's not right." Will pondered, his analytical mind tracing back over every detail of the conversation.

He saw Stapleton's pen.

A Mont Blanc Ballpoint pen.

He stared at the slip of paper Stapleton had tossed on his desk.

Blue ink.

The exact same combination as Jason Carson's pen.

Will gestured toward the paper. "Take a look," he told Drew. "But don't touch it."

Drew raised a brow.

Grabbing his cell, Will called Sarah.

WASHINGTON, D.C.

Sarah's cell buzzed. It was Will.

"You're not going to believe this," he began.

"Then don't make me wait."

"I remember two pens."

She frowned. "Pens."

"Mont Blanc pens," he said curtly.

"Two? Jason Carson and—"

"Frank Stapleton."

"Stapleton?" Her brain scrambled to connect the dots. "You sure?"

"Absolutely. He just paid me a little visit, trying to get me to tell you and your friends to back off the bombing investigation. He used the pen right in front of me."

"Used it? As in, on paper?"

"A note he gave me with a phone number. I still have it, untouched."

"Don't touch it. I'll call Darcy. I'm sure she'll be right over."

NEW YORK CITY

Will stared at the phone, then raised troubled eyes to Drew.

"So," Drew said, "Sarah thinks there's more going on than she's saying."

Will frowned. "Exactly. And I intend to get to the bottom of it, sooner rather than later."

26

WASHINGTON, D.C.

It was late afternoon when Darcy phoned Sarah.

"It's a match," Darcy declared. "Same ink, from the same type of pen as Carson's."

"You're absolutely sure?" Sarah asked.

"Of course I'm sure," Darcy scoffed. "To quote the guys in the lab: 'We tagged it with rare-earth thenoyltrifluoroacetonates by inductively coupling plasma mass spectrometry and instrumental neutron activation analysis.'"

"Wow, that's a mouthful."

"And that mouthful says there's no shadow of a doubt. Exact match. The warning note Sean received. The suicide note. Stapleton's note to Will."

"And the handwriting?"

"Similarities in style, though we couldn't match with a high probability since the note Stapleton wrote for Will only had numbers on it."

Sarah sighed. "So we don't have enough to go after Stapleton."

"Not yet," Darcy said, "but we will. I have our handwriting experts going through any public documents we can find with Stapleton's signature, matching it against the notes."

A Secure Location

"Checked some of my sources," he told the man late that evening. "Applied a little pressure. Looks like Stapleton's got a bigger role in this than we thought."

"And?"

"One of my contacts said a guy delivered some C-4 on a cash deal to a man matching Stapleton's description."

"When?"

"A couple days before the bombing."

"Anything else?"

"Yes, curiously. He also paid for the assembly and delivery of a bomb and a bag full of the parts left over."

"Extra parts?" the man asked.

"Yes. My contact identified some of them. What he could remember matches what DHS and the FBI found in the Brooklyn apartment."

"So part of Stapleton's plan—and whoever all is involved in this—was to frame that troubled young man from the start."

"Sure. Probably seemed foolproof. Justin Eliot had enough history of mental illness that anybody could believe he went over the edge."

"He went over the edge, that's for sure," the man agreed, "but you can bet it was with some help."

"This is getting messier by the minute," he said. "I may have come across another connection as well. You're certain you want to proceed?"

There was a slight hesitation. Then a curt, "Yes. I'll do what I need to do."

Late that night Sarah stared at the wall of her bedroom. She'd been adding up the pieces for hours. Stapleton was likely in much deeper than they'd originally thought. Had he written the suicide note? Stashed C-4 and AF building fragments in Michael Vara's apartment to frame Justin and set up the suicide? How had he known about Justin's continued friendship with Michael? Had he been tracking Justin even after his mother's death?

She checked the time. Darcy was a night owl. She wasn't likely to be asleep yet.

"Hey, did Carson say who delivered the backpack, instructions, and disposable cell phone to him?" Sarah blurted out as soon as Darcy answered.

Darcy laughed. "Hello to you too. And nope, he and his lawyers are dancing around answering that question. They're working hard to assign the blame in this to Sandstrom, who's already wrapped up."

"You think it could be Stapleton?" Sarah asked. "They're protecting him since he's linked closely to the president? The reelection money?"

"So you're saying Sandstrom, Stapleton, and the president have been working together as a sort of unholy trio? And Carson thinks that if he stays mum about Stapleton, Stapleton and the president will protect him?"

"That's what I'm thinking."

"Mmm." Darcy pondered a minute. "If it was Stapleton,

then he not only set up the bombing but picked his own son to bomb the building." She exhaled in disgust. "That's just sick, almost beyond belief."

Sarah plunged on. "And he would have had a cell phone number to contact Justin, if he set up that disposable phone Carson delivered. Carson said he showed up to deliver the money, but Justin wasn't there, right? So what if—"

"Stapleton called Justin and changed the location to the top of that 30-story building?"

"Maybe because he didn't trust Carson?"

"Well, would you?" Darcy asked.

"So Stapleton had Justin followed, or called the cell number to change the location."

"But then that means whatever happened on the top of that building either caused Justin to jump—"

"So maybe Stapleton told Justin he was his father, and the kid couldn't handle it? Went ballistic and decided to end it all?" Sarah suggested.

"Or he was pushed or herded that way, more like it. That's pretty sick too. Meet your own kid, tell him you're his father, then herd him off the roof to his death?" Darcy exhaled. "I've processed some cold people in my line of work, but that . . . wow."

"Either way, if Stapleton had anything to do with the suicide note, he had to know Justin was going to die," Sarah reasoned. "Maybe Stapleton wasn't on the rooftop. Perhaps he just arranged for another party to meet Justin there."

"Seems more likely, but still sick," Darcy threw in.

"You and I both know that guys like Stapleton rarely do their own dirty work. But they're also smart enough to use different people for various aspects of the job, so no one person can connect all the dots."

"Since Carson talked about the cell phone, we've had a team searching for it. It wasn't in Justin's pocket or anywhere near his body."

"But you'll find it."

"Yes, we will. And we're searching for more video footage of the building."

A Secure Location

"You thinking what I'm thinking?" the man asked.

"Yes. We've got to get eyes on any surveillance of people going in and out of that building. See if any cameras in that building or surrounding ones recorded images of Stapleton entering or leaving."

"Starting the day the goods were delivered to Stapleton through the time of Eliot's death," the man clarified.

"Agreed."

"And one more thing." The phone went silent for a minute. "I need you to check on something else. See if during that time, or even a day or two before, Stapleton made any visits to the White House and, if so, exactly who he talked to."

"You got it."

27

New York City

Will was used to getting late-night calls from his sister, but this one moved him from a sluggish state to full awake within a minute.

"The ink on Sean's note and Stapleton's note was an exact match," Sarah reported. "The elements of the ink are a unique mixture, found only in a very high-end pen. Specifically a Mont Blanc Ballpoint. The lab techs said it's one of the most expensive ballpoint pens in the world."

"Sounds like Stapleton," Will whispered as he made his way out of his bedroom and to the kitchen, leaving Laura sleeping. "But Carson? He doesn't have that kind of money."

"Not unless it was a gift. Maybe from Stapleton?"

"So you're saying—"

"Will, there's something else you need to know." There was a slight pause. "It's also a match for the ink on the suicide note."

"Wait." He grappled to process what his sister wasn't saying. "You're saying Stapleton—"

"Just shut up and listen," she said.

So he did. He knew better than to argue with his sister when she was in that mode.

Finally, when she'd finished filling him in, he sat back in shock. Rebuttals raced through his mind. "So you have a DNA test that backs this up?"

"Not yet. That's been tricky. We haven't been able to find a DNA or blood test sample on file. It was required for some of his positions, but mysteriously, all records have gone missing, Darcy says."

"So let me get this straight," he said. "You think Frank Stapleton might have gotten some teenage waitress pregnant, bought her a house, and taken care of her and the kid for years to keep her quiet? Then, after she dies suddenly of some congenital heart defect, the kid becomes a recluse and loses the place, because he no longer has income from the anonymous source. When Stapleton and Sandstrom need someone to bomb the AF building to take the heat off the oil fiasco, he hires his own kid, who has mental and emotional problems. Is that all?" Will whistled. "Look, I know Stapleton can be a wily ol' fox, but that's . . . just crazy."

"But what if it's true?" she insisted. "Think it through, Will. What other conclusion could we come to?"

The wheels turned in his head as he considered the options.

"See?" she said triumphantly after silence reigned for several seconds. "Told you."

"But what about the girl's parents? Did he buy them off too?" he argued.

"He didn't have to. They were killed right before she had her baby."

Silence again.

"A little convenient, huh?" she asked him.

He gave an exasperated exhale. "So now you're saying Frank

Stapleton killed the girl's parents, or had them killed, so they wouldn't reveal who he was, if they even knew? No. Now you're way over in Candy Land, sis."

But what if she's right? Will's gut constricted. At last he said aloud, "I don't think it's Stapleton's style to get a teenager pregnant. And he's not a killer."

"But he did potentially make one mistake we know about," she argued. "Writing that note and leaving it with you."

"I still can't believe he could get away with a kid out of wedlock all these years. No one knowing about it, as much as he's in the press. Or that he wouldn't say something if he had a connection to the bomber in any way. Especially since he's the AF board chair."

"Will, you're still an innocent, aren't you?" she exclaimed. "You think Stapleton would risk his reputation to say, 'Oh, by the way, the Polar Bear Bomber is my son. I funded him and his mom for a lot of years'?" She took a breath, then gained steam again. "Why does it bother you so much about Stapleton—that he's likely not on the up-and-up—other than the fact he was your mentor?"

He sighed. "Maybe because I'm loyal. And one of my faults is seeing the best in people."

"Except yourself," she corrected. "Yes, sure it's a fault to look blindly for the best in people." Her voice softened. "But it's a good thing too, Will. Remember when I was at university, and there wasn't much direction in my life? You kept telling me you believed in me and that I'd find my way eventually. Well, now I have."

Will laughed. "You're giving me some credit now, after years of putting up with you, for you turning out all right?" he teased.

"I wouldn't go that far," she teased back. Then she sobered. "But you know it's true. This is my way to give back a little and to take down the people who not only tried to take down my family, but have likely done a lot of things to hurt others behind the scenes too. People who don't have the clout to fight back or stand up for themselves."

"Like Justin Eliot, you mean."

"Yes."

"Okay, I'll think through everything you said," he replied.

"That's all I'm asking, Will."

A Secure Location

His call to the man was swift. "I pulled a few strings. Secured a bit of footage already."

"And?" the man demanded.

"Should get the parties that need it moving in the right direction."

New York City

Will sat silently in the dim light of his kitchen. He needed to let Drew know the potential latest developments as fast as possible.

Drew had once told Will, "Desperate people do desperate things."

Once on the downward spiral, people would do anything to protect themselves. *But hiring your own kid to do a hit? A hit that leads to his death?*

Will shivered. Frank Stapleton was many things, and he'd betrayed Will. But he couldn't believe Stapleton would or ever could stoop to those depths. Such actions would make his betrayal of Will—and the possibility that he, Sandstrom, and the president had all colluded to try to take the Worthington family down—a mere blip on the screen of depravity. Carson was amoral, an anything-goes-to-get-to-the-top person. Likely, all three powerful people had used Carson as a pawn to get exactly what they wanted—a clear road ahead, without any interference from the Worthingtons.

Will's determination hardened. He'd given in once to protect his family. He wouldn't do so again. There was no protection against people like that, other than revealing their evil acts in the light of day.

With Drew's help, he would do exactly that.

28

WASHINGTON, D.C.

The next day Darcy phoned Sarah at her office. "The hand-writing on all three notes looks like an 85 percent match—as close as we can probably get—with Stapleton's signature on documents. And that's not the only clincher," she reported. "We took another look at the footage we had from the building. Came across some I don't remember seeing before, at least not in the same light."

"How so?" Sarah asked.

"Two cops entered the building a couple of hours before Justin was found at the bottom of it. The footage also reveals a man with a dark hood that matches Justin's clothing, but no face was revealed. He entered the building about half an hour before the jump. The two cops exited the first floor of the building before NYPD arrived to set up a perimeter around the body."

"So they weren't NYPD. Just dressed in cop clothing," Sarah reasoned.

"No one at NYPD could identify them. The partial views we have don't match anything in our databases—US or otherwise."

Sarah swiveled in her chair toward the window. "So somebody hired them to make sure Justin went over the edge of that building."

"Yup. Found something else too."

"So out with it."

"Carson. He tried a good disguise with a hat and trench coat, but it was him. He entered after Justin and waited by the first-floor elevators."

"He didn't go up?"

"No, just hung around. Seemed nervous and kept checking his cell phone. Then the reflection of lights from NYPD flashed into the video. Carson fled out the back door an instant later."

"So Carson didn't kill the kid. But he may have been directing the two guys up top."

"Or maybe he was supposed to pay off the kid, but Stapleton changed the game plan without telling him," Darcy suggested.

"You know what that means."

"We play the two little foxes against each other to see who's all in the den."

A SECURE LOCATION

"Surveillance is now all in on the building where Eliot died," he reported to the man.

"And?"

"No Stapleton. Two cops in before Eliot, two cops out after the kid supposedly jumps and before NYPD arrives."

"So they were dirty cops," the man said.

"Not likely cops at all. My friends at NYPD say nobody recognizes them."

"Then we dig a little deeper."

"I'm on it."

"The White House?"

"Still working on it."

Washington, D.C.

That afternoon Darcy patched in Sarah confidentially via video loop on her just-concluded interrogation of Jason Carson.

Sarah watched the video with fascination as Darcy strode into the conference room and deposited a pen in front of Carson. "Do you recognize this pen?"

"Yes. I have one like it. Usually carry it around with me."

"Do you have it with you now?"

He made a show of searching his pockets. "No. Must have left it at home or at my office."

Darcy crossed her arms. "So, if we accompanied you to your home or office, you could lay hands on it immediately?"

Carson blanched. "Uh, no, I think I lost it."

"When?"

He shrugged. "Maybe a week ago, or a few days. Don't know."

"Now we're getting somewhere. It might interest you to know that this is your pen. It has your fingerprints all over it. Where did you get the pen, Mr. Carson?"

"How am I supposed to remember that?" he asked. "It's a pen, not a Ferrari. And owning a pen isn't a criminal action."

"But a most unusual pen, Mr. Carson. That's why we're interested in it. Did you buy it? Or did someone give it to you?"

"I don't remember."

"Let me tell you what I think. This is a pretty expensive pen, even for a guy on your salary, unless, of course, you've got some accounts stashed on the Cayman Islands or elsewhere."

Sarah laughed to herself. Darcy was at her intimidating best in interrogation mode. She hadn't seen any perpetrator yet who hadn't backed down. Carson, though, was a tough case. Only his knuckles tightened. But that was enough to tell Sarah that the rumors and her gut instinct were true. The guy did have his ill-gotten gains stashed somewhere out of federal tax reach.

There was no response from Carson, so Darcy went on. "I think someone gave it to you."

"Could be. Maybe someone my old boss did business with. I get gifts all the time."

"I bet you do. But which guy in particular gave you the pen?"

"I don't remember."

"Someone gave you a pen that's worth $700,000, and you don't remember who gave it to you? I find that hard to believe."

He shrugged. "I deal with high rollers all the time."

"But you remember it was some guy your old boss did business with? Just not any specifics."

"That's right."

"And why would he give you a pen? Especially one this expensive?"

Carson's cockiness returned. "Maybe he liked me. A lot of people do."

Darcy zeroed in for the kill. "More like because you did a job for him under the table. Mr. Carson, we have a signed affidavit from a bartender that specifically states you paid him a thousand bucks to allow you to set up a video cam inside the bar. The only thing he had to do was move two men you had described to him within viewing distance, click the remote to start the cam, and then meet you outside in the alley late that night so you could pick up the cam. Those two men, Mr. Carson, match the description of Sean Worthington and Justin Eliot, aka the Polar Bear Bomber."

Jason Carson blanched again.

"That was a mistake—setting up those photos," Darcy said. "But you made an even bigger mistake by accepting that pen. It's the one that wrote the suicide note for the bomber. And, Mr. Carson, it has your fingerprints all over it, which can easily lead to a murder charge that sticks. Now, I'm sure we'll discover many more connections between you and the man who gave you this pen as we continue digging. Including the fact that you tried to bribe Will Worthington to leave the Senate race by showing him those falsified photos that you yourself had set up. What did you have to gain, Mr. Carson, other than money? Is that money really worth a prison sentence for murder? Or do you want to make our job easier and maybe your jail sentence a little shorter, and tell us about your employer?"

At that point, Darcy stopped the tape for Sarah.

"Wow, that was quite the song and dance, wasn't it?" Sarah said.

"Very typical," Darcy retorted. "Only this one carried his snobbery a bit further than usual. At that point he demanded to talk to his lawyer privately. But from the look on the lawyer's face, he's going to encourage Carson to tell the truth and nothing but the truth. I'll let you know what floats up to the surface."

A Secure Location

"Stapleton was there, at the White House," he told the man.

"Private meeting with the president?"

"Indeed."

29

It didn't take long before Sarah found out what had floated
to the surface. Within minutes of entering her office the next
day, she was summoned to the White House for a confidential
meeting with one of President Rich's closest advisors.

"Ms. Worthington." He rose to shake her hand. "I hear good
things about your work."

"Thank you, sir."

He cleared his throat. "I'll get right to business. It has come
to the president's attention that you and some colleagues are
continuing to dig into the Polar Bear bombing instead of con-
centrating solely on your attorney general responsibilities. As
you know, President Rich has backed you fully in your nomination and the proceedings. But pursuing a line of questioning that
could bring this matter back into the light could be, shall we
say, not good for you, your colleagues, or this administration.
We respectfully ask you to step away and consider the matter
closed. Especially since you have publicly recused yourself from
anything to do with the bombing."

Sarah straightened. "And if I decide that this 'line of questioning' is in the best interests of the American people, then what?"

His eyes narrowed. Then he relaxed. "Ms. Worthington, we're not threatening you. We're simply asking you to consider the ramifications of what you are pursuing."

"I am," she replied with a determined lift of her chin. "You can be absolutely certain of that."

NEW YORK CITY

"So you're now directly in the president's gun sights?" Will asked his sister. "Wow, you certainly know how to pick a fight."

"Indeed. But it only proves that we're on the right track," she insisted.

"Watch out for any stray bullets," he warned, "or targeted ones."

"Nothing I haven't faced before."

"But this is on a whole new level."

"And they are grossly underestimating me," she fired back.

He knew his sister. Still, he worried about her.

A SECURE LOCATION

He knew what the man had promised long ago when he'd started working for him. But when that promise conflicted directly with something else he was deeply invested in, what then? Would the man still hold to his end of the deal?

The connections were coming together from all sides now. When they could be proved, the public would have something else to point fingers at in their claim that the US government had run amok and that crooks were at the helm. There would be a plain-as-day connection between Washington powers and American Frontier, the most powerful oil company in the world. Not only that, but . . .

No. He halted his thoughts. The full plan couldn't be launched until it was more than conjecture and disparate pieces. They would need absolute proof that would stand up in court, because the vitriolic White House would go into attack mode, fearing the potential of impeachment proceedings.

There was no doubt what Sarah Worthington as the new AG would do. Her track record at the DOJ's Criminal Division spoke for itself. She was like a freight train, never stopping. This time, though, her path would collide with the most powerful boss of all—the president of the United States. It was more power than she'd ever had to deal with. And clearly, President Spencer Rich would fight dirty to keep his own hands clean.

Will Worthington still had a big fight on his hands with the White House media, who continued their attempt to separate the president's actions and AF's regarding the oil fiasco. Yet each time, among combative questioners and the throngs of reporters, Will came out on top—the good guy who had walked away when he couldn't sway the old CEO into doing what was right for the planet, but then had walked back in when the company needed saving.

Nobody seemed to care anymore that Will had aborted his Senate race. The rumors as to why had faded in the light of more pressing national issues. To the rest of the world, Will truly was the knight in shining armor who would literally save the planet from ecological disaster. The media highlighted his research into new methods of cleaning up the oil along the shore and in the waters, and also in pioneering safer ways of extracting oil. Will had halted all of AF's oil efforts in the Arctic.

Yet the biggest fight for the Worthingtons was still to come. He was convinced of that.

What the end result would be, though, was anyone's guess.

The players all had to play to win. With the high stakes, there was no other option.

30

WASHINGTON, D.C.

"Jon!" Sarah happily flung open her door at the Ritz Carlton upon seeing her unexpected visitor. "Didn't know you were going to be in D.C."

"I didn't either," he said. "It was kind of a spur-of-the-moment decision."

She tilted her head. "Oh? Come on in. I just ordered some coffee. Want some?"

Once they'd settled across from each other at the small table with coffee mugs in hand, he eyed her. "Actually, I'm here because there's something I need to tell you. I'm about to break a story. One that concerns you. I wanted you to know about it first."

She lifted a brow.

"The $25 million supplied by AF and its affiliates for the quid pro quo came from foreign funds, Sarah."

She set her coffee cup down. "Using foreign funds to contribute to a presidential campaign and to be spent in America is treason."

"See why President Rich is desperate not to have that known?" Jon asked.

"So you're saying the president of the United States knowingly used foreign funds for his campaign? Jon, that's—"

"That's what I'm saying. I have reputable sources that told me he knows exactly where it came from."

"Most of the money came solely from American Frontier," she argued. "So you're saying AF knowingly donated foreign funds to influence an American election?"

He nodded.

She stared at him. "If you break this story, you know how tough the media is going to be on my brother? And on me, just becoming attorney general? You know what the press is going to say—that the Worthington family has been manipulating things behind the scenes for a presidential election."

Jon looked her straight in the eyes. "Yes, I know. But it gets worse."

She threw her hands up in the air. "How could it get worse?"

"I've now identified the origin of the majority of the funds coming from AF."

"And?" she pressed.

"They're from ISIS."

Dread swept over Sarah, sickening her.

"That's why I wanted you to know first. And why I wanted to give you the heads-up so you could also warn Will."

"But you still feel you have to break the story, knowing how it will affect me. How it will affect Will."

Jon sighed. "Sarah, I'm an investigative journalist. It's my job. Beyond that, it's about integrity. I have to do what's right for the *Times*. For America. People deserve to know the truth, especially since this is an election year and Spencer Rich will be on the campaign trail."

She raised her chin. "Then do what you need to do." There was an uncomfortable pause. Then she added, "I've got other plans."

"Like what?" Jon asked.

"I'm not certain it would be wise to tell a journalist."

"Sarah—"

"I think it would be best if we didn't communicate for a while."

"Sarah—" he tried again.

"I need you to leave."

He nodded slowly. "Okay," he finally said. "But this isn't what I want. It isn't the way it has to be."

"Maybe. Maybe not. But it's the way it has to be for now."

There was a brittle silence between them, and then he turned toward the door.

Without another word, he stepped out and shut the door behind him.

NANNING, CHINA

Sean was standing in a rice paddy in southeastern China when the back of his neck started to prickle. He rubbed his neck and surveyed the locals standing around him.

Suddenly his sister and brother came to mind. He frowned. Was something up with Sarah or Will? The only times his neck prickled were when one of his family members was in trouble. It was an uncanny, disturbing feeling, but he'd learned to trust it.

He scanned the area for a cell tower. No such luck. As soon as he had cell coverage back at the hotel in Nanning, he'd have to call Sarah. In the meanwhile, he needed to focus on the potential

NGO he'd come to visit. He looked around at the group. Eyes were on him. The expressions of trust and hope—and yes, worry too—seemed to ask him, "Can you help us? Will you help us?"

An ox bellowed from where it pulled a wooden cart on a nearby dirt road. Bamboo shot up tall and vivid green on the left of him. It was a good year for the villagers, after two years of too much rain had nearly destroyed their rice and bamboo crops.

Sean realized again the huge responsibility he had in choosing the right NGOs for Worthington to back. Some he knew would make money—both for the locals and for Worthington Shares. Not a lot, but some. Others he knew would simply sustain the area and be flatlined on a financial graph. A select few would fly and pay for all of the other efforts, making the Worthington shareholders happy.

But he knew now how important all three types of NGOs were, because on every trip he met the real people behind the dreams and labor. He ate simple meals with the families who would be affected, knowing that the gift of food they gave him meant they all went a little hungry that day and the next. He played with the children who would have food in their bellies, clothes to wear, and the potential of education if Worthington Shares backed them.

Every time Sean boarded the plane to go back to New York City, he did so a bit older and wiser. Excess that he used to consider his right as a Worthington now bothered him. Both the people behind the NGOs and Elizabeth had changed him.

His dad's mantra surfaced again: "To those who are given much, much is required." Sean thought back to the many ways his wealthy father had made sure his kids brushed elbows with and served those in need.

Sean was grateful every day for his and Elizabeth's ongoing work. No, they could never do enough to save every child, every family. But as long as they were on this earth, they would do all they could.

———※ / / / ※———

NEW YORK CITY

Will knew the instant he heard his sister's voice that something big had just happened.

Big didn't even describe the shock he felt at the news. "So you're telling me that AF used money from ISIS to pull off the $25 million quid pro quo? Jon's sure?"

"Absolutely certain. He wouldn't have come to D.C. to tell me in person if he wasn't."

Will blinked. So Drew was right. There was more between his sister and Jon than Will had known. Now, though, wasn't the time to bring it up.

"Okay. I'm going to do some research of my own," he said.

"Thought you would." Sarah hung up.

Five minutes later, Will was out the door and headed for the AF office. He phoned Drew on the way.

———※ / / / ※———

A SECURE LOCATION

"As expected, the story will break soon," he told the man.

"The *Times*?" the man asked.

"Yes. No turning back now."

The silence on the other end of the line hung heavy before the man sighed.

"You knew the time would come where you'd have to choose. You can't protect both. It has to go one way or the other," he told the man.

"I know," the man growled. "Let's just get this done."

31

Sarah didn't waste any time after the story broke in the *Times*. She immediately appointed a special prosecutor to go after the president of the United States. Now, less than six hours after that appointment, she was in the Oval Office of the White House, staring down an angry president.

President Spencer Rich was on his feet, index finger pointed directly at her. They were the only two in the private meeting.

"I need you to back off immediately," he demanded.

"Back off what? The truth?" She shook her head. "No, I won't do that."

"I put you in this position. You owe me," he insisted. "You need to do your job."

"That's exactly what I'm doing," she replied in a steely tone.

His eyes narrowed further. "That doesn't mean you'll win."

She matched his glare. "No, but I'm going to give it my best shot."

"We'll see about that. For now, this meeting is over." The president turned his back toward her.

Sarah strode out of the White House with determined steps.

Her next moves would make her life extremely difficult. High-powered influencers around the president would swiftly realize that the impeachment proceedings could end their own political careers. She would receive mounting pressure from all sides to shut the prosecution down.

But Sarah would not cave like the attorney general had done during Watergate, when he'd been pressured to cover up Richard Nixon's actions instead of prosecuting him. Rather than allowing the prosecution to go forward, the attorney general had buckled under the pressure and had resigned.

As long as I'm AG, I won't back down. Ever, Sarah resolved. Even if that meant taking on her boss, the sitting president of the United States.

New York City

Will wasn't surprised by the phone call from his sister. "So you've done it."

"Yes." Her tone was calm, calculated.

"You sure about this?" he asked.

"Never more sure."

"Okay then." He had no further questions except one. "Did you tell Dad?"

"He's my next call. And Will? Thanks for believing in me. For trusting me. This is going to get messy."

Messier than you might ever guess, he thought. "I know," he said simply. "I'll let Sean know."

"Just remember, I love you to the moon and back."

He smiled as she ended the call.

He had a couple calls himself to make—the first to Sean and the second to his father, after Sarah had talked with him.

The time was coming swiftly where they could no longer hide their secret from Sarah.

Washington, D.C.

Will had taken the news better than Sarah had expected. Perhaps because he'd known her actions were inevitable.

After working for the Criminal Division of the DOJ, she'd seen a lot of unscrupulous big players. She wasn't so naïve to think she could halt the dirty plays from happening. But as AG, she was determined to at least make a big enough dent so the dirty players had to think twice and work harder to accomplish their purposes.

The little things—even the $25M quid pro quo where AF had received special privileges—wouldn't be enough in themselves to impeach the president. What would seal the deal was President Rich's behind-the-scenes dealing in foreign funds for his reelection campaign. Worse, the foreign funds had been from ISIS. That cover-up would pave the way for President Rich to be impeached.

Sarah knew what was at stake in going after her boss. She'd need to do her job thoroughly and without bias during the impeachment process. She'd have to expect public and private jabs at her, at her family. It wouldn't be pretty, or easy. Her family deserved to know, to be forewarned.

But what she wouldn't tell anyone yet was the next step in her dreams.

A Secure Location

The phone call he received was curt. "So Ms. Worthington is exploring what it would take to impeach the president."

"Indeed," he replied. "Let's just say Spencer isn't happy. He's making enough noise that no one at the White House is happy either. Lots of ranting about the Worthington family in general."

"Their meddling in affairs of state, I'd guess," the man said. "Probably thought he'd put an end to that."

"Clearly, that didn't work with Sarah. Will already stepped out of the Senate race. So that means—"

"There's only one remaining Worthington sibling to target again," the man finished.

"With another round—but public this time. The photo with the Polar Bear Bomber."

"It's the one and only card Spencer has left to play," the man said.

"Unless he figures out . . ."

"Yes, there's that."

32

WASHINGTON, D.C.

Sarah had been hard at work with the lead prosecutor to provide everything the House Judiciary Committee needed to sway the decision to proceed with the impeachment of the president. The chairman had just proposed a resolution calling for the Judiciary Committee to begin a formal inquiry into the issue.

So, it has officially begun, Sarah thought. No matter the cost, even to her personally, she would do all in her power to edge Spencer Rich out of office.

NEW YORK CITY

Will stared out his large office window overlooking Madison Avenue, pondering his sister's gutsy move. Some of the power brokers in D.C. were calling it idiotic—a real career ender for Sarah. But to Will, it made sense. Each time they had talked over the past several years, he had sensed in her a targeted drive to do battle with people in positions of power who didn't use that power honestly or wisely.

The entire Worthington family had a growing dissatisfaction for the way President Spencer Rich was running the country—far different from the way his father had, years earlier. Thomas Rich had always been an honest man. But Thomas's integrity and best character traits had not passed to his son. His quid pro quo deal with Eric Sandstrom during reelection infuriated Will, once he'd understood why the Arctic research had been bypassed. That one decision, made because of two men's greed and drive for power, would have incalculable effects on the ocean systems and the shores bordering oceans around the world, not to mention the economic impact on hundreds of thousands of fishermen.

Add to that the collusion between Spencer Rich, Eric Sandstrom, and Frank Stapleton to control or bring down the Worthingtons . . . It didn't sit well with Will. He knew Jason Carson was only a pawn. But he would also be glad to see that smug expression wiped off the lawyer's face. And Stapleton? If Sarah's gut was on target, and it usually was, then Will's disgust for the man was unparalleled.

Will had already held an emergency AF board meeting to have Stapleton removed as board chairman, due to the investigation of foreign funds and the connection with Spencer Rich. Stapleton was apoplectic but had agreed to step aside.

"For now," he'd warned Will with a steely glint in his eyes.

Now Sarah was up to her eyeballs in alligators. So was Will, following up on all of American Frontier's records to see where exactly the ISIS funds had entered the picture. He'd given the DOJ and DHS complete and unfettered access to the AF archives.

Yes, Sarah had made the right move. He'd told her so. But he still worried.

"You know I'll do whatever I can to help. And you know I'll back you," he'd said.

161

"Of course I know that. You don't have a choice. If you didn't, I'd put you in a headlock or send Mom after you," she teased.

"You always were good at that," he joked back.

"Then again, you always let me win, because if you didn't, I'd run and tell Mom."

"You did hold all the cards, you little manipulator."

"And I still do. Only the president doesn't know it yet. But that's all about to change."

He'd smiled at the authority and determination in her voice. His beautiful, bubbly sister who could befriend anyone was far from the belle-of-the-ball pushover that people expected her to be from an initial look. Before they knew it, she would gain control of the situation. But she never did it just to get the upper hand. She did it because she could orchestrate events and edge them toward balance and justice.

She'd make a great president of the United States.

He sat back in his chair, stunned. Where had that thought come from? But the more he pondered it, the more sense it made.

Dad always said it would take a Worthington to turn the ship of this country around and get it headed in the right direction. He had his sights set on me. I let him down.

And Will had still never told him why.

Next, Sean had dabbled in the political realm, letting the idea dangle around to keep the press busy for a while, then he'd taken his fishing pole and left the water.

What if Sarah is the one? Deep in thought, he absentmindedly rubbed his clean-shaven chin. *The one Worthington who is destined to be the next president of the United States? Not only that, but the first woman president?*

WASHINGTON, D.C.

President Rich had tried his best to derail Sarah in her pursuit. So had his advisors and a plethora of other Washington, D.C. veterans.

When that didn't work, he played his highest card.

The president's official order to stand down came on a Wednesday. She knew what her refusal would mean—that he would ask for her resignation.

She was prepared to resign rather than back down in her convictions.

Darcy phoned the next day. "So how are you holding up under all the pressure?"

"I'm going to resign," Sarah told her friend.

There was silence on the other end of the line. "I understand. After all, you don't have much choice, do you?"

"Not on that end," Sarah agreed. "But I do about what happens next."

"What exactly is that?" Darcy asked.

"I have a few thoughts brewing."

"Any you want to share?"

"Not yet. But suffice it to say, I'm not going to let him win."

The following day, Sarah resigned as attorney general. As she walked away, she prepared mentally for her next move—one that would stun even those who knew her well.

33

CHAUTAUQUA INSTITUTION, WESTERN NEW YORK

Sarah sat beside the rock-lined koi pond in her mother's green room, listening to the rush of the waterfall. It was her favorite place in their family's vacation house—filled with tall, leafy palms and ferns—and a great place to think. The coming weekend was Sean's birthday, and the family always gathered from wherever they were around the globe to celebrate birthdays together. Craving quiet to help her strategize her next big move, Sarah had decided to go a day early, to spend some time with her mom before her dad was back in town and her siblings descended.

Ava had seemed quiet and withdrawn since Will's aborted Senate race and Sean's disappearance and return. Sarah knew her mother had to be worried about both of her boys. She was such a mama bear with her cubs. Still, that didn't explain her evasiveness toward Sarah.

"Ah, there you are," her mother said, entering the room. "Our shared favorite place."

Sarah smiled. Ava had spent hours there adding colorful fish and various flowers until it was a garden extraordinaire.

Ava gestured toward the beloved sea chest that had belonged to her grandmother. "I have something for you." She moved toward the weathered chest, opened the lid, and extracted a small package wrapped in gold tissue. "I've been saving it, but somehow I think now is the time to give it to you." She extended the package to Sarah. "Here, open it."

Sarah took the package. "But it's not my birthday."

"I know," her mother said gently. "But I want you to have it."

Sarah unfolded the tissue. A princess-cut flawless tourmaline diamond ring emerged. Two carats. Platinum. "It's beautiful!"

"It was my mother's," Ava explained. "Her father gave it to her right before she married. He said it was because she was his princess and always would be."

"And you want me to have it? Now?" Sarah asked, puzzled.

Her mom gazed at her. "Sarah, no matter what, I want you to know how much I love you. How much your father loves you. You always have been, and will be, our princess. I hope the ring will be a reminder of that when you need it most."

Sarah stared at the luminescence of the ring. Of course she knew her parents loved her. But this time the way her mom said it seemed different—tinged with something else.

Sadness? Regret?

Not being able to identify what it was made her uneasy.

"Thanks, Mom. I'll remember that."

En Route from Jakarta, Indonesia

Sean settled in for the long flight from Jakarta to New York City. From there he'd hop on a flight to Jamestown, the closest airport to his family's home in Chautauqua.

He smiled, thinking of the upcoming festivities. One of Bill's few quirks was an old-fashioned jukebox that Ava had bought him on his thirtieth birthday. The kids had grown up listening to it. On birthdays, they'd turn on the jukebox, gather pots and pans from the kitchen, beat on them, sing at the top of their lungs, and parade around the house. Sure, it was crazy, but it was one of those things that made the Worthingtons a family.

Sean sighed. He loved that birthday tradition. It had been Sarah who had started the tradition when she was about five years old. Now, even though they were all too old, they still did it. Will and Laura's kids—the next generation of Worthingtons—heartily joined in.

Suddenly, inexplicably, he missed Elizabeth. He texted her and got an answer an instant later.

Elizabeth
So, you ready for the birthday parade?

He shook his head. She always knew what he was thinking.

Sean
You bet. Maybe next year you can be a part of the craziness. See it for yourself. Your dad too.

I'd love that.

I can just see the look on his face now.

He laughed to himself. Dr. Leo Shapiro had seen many things, but the birthday parade might give even the eccentric scientist a jolt.

Me too. But I bet he'd love it.

Sean sensed her wistfulness. She'd said many times that it would really be something to have a larger family, like Sean did. After Elizabeth's mom left, life for Elizabeth and Leo had been mainly on board research vessels—just the two of them. "I wouldn't exchange time with my father for anything," she had told Sean once. "But sometimes I miss . . ."

She hadn't finished the statement, but Sean knew what she meant. She missed having a mom. Having siblings. Doing crazy things together, like birthday parades.

Then she had looked him in the eye. "Sean, never stop being grateful for your family. I hope you know what you have."

"Believe me, I know," he told her.

But he'd meant more than just his family. He'd meant Elizabeth.

Right now, though, she was half a world away, and that was much, much too far.

Chautauqua Institution

Sarah woke to warm light flooding through her large bedroom window at Chautauqua. Squinting around the room, she smiled. It still had all the touches reminiscent of her teenage days, when she'd gone through a retro stage—an infatuation with the icons of the sixties, flower power, and the Beatles. She'd outgrown it long ago, but somehow, in the swirl of life, the bedroom had stayed the same.

Today she'd awakened earlier than usual.

She grinned. This time she'd be the one waking Sean on his birthday. He should be sleeping on the tail end of his flight from Indonesia.

Sarah grabbed her cell but found it was dead. She'd forgotten to charge it overnight.

No worries. She'd just use the landline in the kitchen.

She padded down the hall and entered the kitchen. Picking up the landline, she was startled to hear a deep male voice.

"Ava, it's Thomas."

Her mother's voice replied, "Thomas?"

"I had to call. Had to talk to you."

Sarah frowned. Thomas? Thomas who? But it was the catch in her mother's voice that made her keep listening when normally she'd hang up.

"Why now? After all these years?"

There was a long sigh. "Because, Ava, I've tried. I thought I could set it aside, but I can't."

Set what aside? Sarah wondered. Her protective instincts kicked in, keeping her grip clenched on the phone. Was her mother in trouble?

"Thomas." Her mother's voice shook. "You can't do this. I can't do this—"

"I was coming to see you." Another sigh. "Then I saw you, Sean, and Bill standing on the back porch. A family. And I couldn't."

"You saw us . . . when?" Her mother's voice broke off. "Oh, I see." There was a pause. "But then you would have been . . . You were in a boat, watching me? Watching us?" Anger tinged her mother's tone. "Have you done this before? When? For how long?" Her words came out rapid-fire.

"Ava, I love you. I've stayed away all these years. But now I want you—no, I need you to know . . . I've never stopped loving you."

"No," Ava said firmly. "It's too late. I made my choice. You made yours. This conversation is over."

There was a definite click, and the call ended.

Stunned, Sarah stood in the kitchen and slowly hung up the phone. *Thomas? Thomas who?*

Then a shaft of reality hit. *Thomas Rich? Her old friend? The former president of the United States? That Thomas?*

Sarah's heart raced as she tried to sort out what she'd heard. Was her mother having an affair? *Did* she have an affair? Was her parents' marriage, which she had always thought was so solid, in trouble?

Hearing a sob from her mother's green room, Sarah tiptoed toward it and peered in.

Ava was bent over, her shoulders shaking.

Paralyzed by her mother's grief, Sarah couldn't intervene. Slipping back to her room, she softly closed the door with trembling hands.

Once inside her bedroom, she started to pace. Recalling everything she'd heard, she attempted to puzzle it out. A picture of her strong, business-minded father flicked into her mind. Did he know? Or would the secret she now guessed destroy him? What about her brothers?

She sank onto the floor, her back to the door.

Time passed, and she remained in that position until she heard the cheerful arrival of Laura, Will, and their kids.

There was no opportunity to discuss what Sarah had heard with her mother, even if she'd had the courage to do so.

34

After dinner and the usual noisy birthday parade, Sean and his mother went for a quiet walk around the lake.

"I'm okay, Mom. Really I am," he answered in response to her questions. "Knowing what I know now, well, so many things make sense. *I* make sense."

He didn't tell her that he'd already met Thomas in person. He wasn't ready yet to share that meeting with anyone other than Elizabeth.

"And you and Elizabeth make sense," his mom said, a sly peek in his direction.

He grinned. "Yes, we do."

Her eyes sparkled. "There's no time like the present. I even have something you might want to use, until you both can pick out exactly what you want." She grabbed his hand and tugged him back toward the house, then drew him into the green room.

She opened her sea chest and took out a tiny package wrapped in white tissue. "This belonged to my grandmother. Part of her Irish heritage. Now it's yours."

He unwrapped the gift and held it delicately between his right thumb and forefinger. "I just might find a purpose for this."

"I thought you might." She smiled. "And the sooner, the better."

He laughed. Now she was sounding like the mother he'd grown up with. In charge and a bit pushy where the welfare of her children was concerned.

But this time he didn't mind. It was what he wanted too.

"Hey, sis, you okay?" a voice asked near Sarah's ear.

She jumped, startled.

Will extended a cup of hot decaf in her direction. "You seem a bit distracted. Not in the usual birthday weekend mode."

"Oh." She waved away his concern but took the cup. "Just have a lot of things on my mind."

That was certainly an understatement.

"Yeah, I bet you do." He sat next to her. "I'm sure you're still thinking about the impeachment."

Yes, she was. The JC had already sent another resolution to the full House of Congress, stating that the impeachment was warranted, with articles explaining why. The House was in the middle of debating and voting on each Article of Impeachment. If any article was approved by a simple majority vote, the president could then be formally impeached. Then the next step, which could take months or more, would be a trial, with the president represented by his lawyers before the Senate to determine if he'd be removed from office.

Will swiveled toward her. "You wish you were still involved?"

"Yes. No. I guess. But it's a moot point, since I can't be."

"But you're still conflicted," he pressed.

"Not about what I did," she said quickly.

"Then about what you're going to do next," he clarified.

"Yes."

"Well, sis"—his arm encircled her—"I have no doubt you'll find that path."

They were only a few reassuring words, but exactly what she needed.

Sean stared at the platinum and gold circle in his hand. It was so small but heavy with meaning. Would Elizabeth too be ready for it?

He had to try.

Sean booked a flight to San Diego for the next morning. The Shapiros' research vessel would be docking there in the afternoon, and he was determined to be there.

But he had one thing to do first. He checked the time on his cell phone. If he hurried, he could get to the little store in Chautauqua before it closed.

35

///

Darcy surprised Sarah with a call late that evening. "Hey, I know you're technically on vacation, but thought you'd want to know. We've now made direct connections between Sandstrom, Stapleton, and the president. All three had knowledge of the funds being foreign. Sandstrom is the only one who has acknowledged they came originally from ISIS. He claims Stapleton and the president also knew it."

"But those two are denying those claims," Sarah reasoned.

"Of course. But us asking the question has Stapleton and the president plenty nervous. Both have been steering a wide berth around each other since Jon's story hit," Darcy said. "Speaking of Jon, what's going on with you two anyway?"

"We're steering a wide berth around each other for now too," Sarah said quickly.

"Mmm." Darcy's tone was sarcastic. "Seems to me that berth is a little one-sided. You sure you—"

"No more on that subject. Let's turn to a different one." Her friend's inference stung because she was right on, and Sarah knew it. She hadn't been entirely fair to Jon.

"Like what?"

"Like the fact I'm thinking of throwing my hat into the ring," Sarah declared.

"You're thinking of running the country? Seriously?" Darcy was uncharacteristically quiet for a minute. Then she said, "I should be surprised, but I'm not. Had a gut feeling this would come someday."

"Really? Why?"

"Because you understand justice and hate injustice. You're uniquely equipped to restore faith in the political system to Americans. You handle tough situations and never back down . . ." Darcy was off and running with a list of Sarah's best qualities.

"Wow," Sarah teased once Darcy took a breath. "I had no idea you entertained all those thoughts about me."

"You know I, of all people, don't blow smoke. America needs new, fresh leadership. A person who has everyone's best at heart. Those are pretty big shoes to fill. But I believe your feet might be just the right size." Darcy laughed. "And it doesn't hurt being a Worthington either."

"No, it sure doesn't hurt." Sarah laughed too. "So you don't think I'm crazy?" she asked.

"Crazy? You're always a bit crazy. But you're also right on target."

As soon as she hung up with Darcy, Sarah mentally began preparations to throw her hat into the ring in the February primaries. She'd have to be on the fast track to jump in. Worthington money would help, but that could only give her a kick start. She'd need to raise funds just like every other candidate.

First things first, though. She had to tell her family about her plans. As her father had said long ago, "It's about time a Worthington steps into the presidential race." He just didn't know yet that the first Worthington to make a run in six generations would be his daughter.

Perhaps it would be best to test the news out on Will first.

Will knew something was bothering his sister as soon as he returned from taking Sean to the Jamestown airport the following morning. So did Laura. She'd given him the head jab in Sarah's direction right after breakfast. He knew what that meant: "Go find out what's wrong with her, and do it now, buster."

What was wrong with Sarah far exceeded any guesses he might have had. Simply stated, he was stunned.

"You're going to *what*?" He stopped in his tracks at the edge of Lake Chautauqua.

"I'm going to run for president," she announced.

He blinked. After the initial shock cleared, it was strange how his own earlier thought drifted back to him. *She'd make a great president of the United States.*

"As a Republican," she added.

Will flinched. His family, like most New York money, was publicly Democrat in its leanings. So were their friends and contacts. Will understood personally, though. He had been torn himself when running for Senate. Though his values aligned more with the Republican Party, his thinking on most issues tended to be more in the Democrat camp. He wasn't quite one but wasn't quite the other either.

"Well," he said drily, "that will certainly raise some eyebrows."

A vision of a furious Kiki Estrada flitted into his mind. After backing and then being shafted by both Worthington brothers, she'd certainly have something vitriolic to say if a Worthington ran on the opposing ticket.

"Are you saying I'm wrong?" Sarah demanded with fire in her eyes.

"No. I get it. But you've got an uphill battle going against the conservative, antigovernment voice that's in the minority but too loud to ignore. Like some of the people I have to deal with every day, all backed by the big guns behind Big Oil and Tobacco."

"But that's just it," she argued. "It's time for a balanced voice in the party. Someone who can unite both Democrat and Republican parties through common causes that can benefit all of America."

"And you think you're that person," he shot back. It was a statement, not a question.

She opened her mouth, then shut it just as she was clearly about to lambaste him. "Yes, I think I'm the one for the job."

"And you're willing to stake your career on it? Our family's reputation on it?" he asked.

"Yes."

He started to pace. "You talked to Dad?"

She shrugged. "Not yet."

"Ah, I see. You're putting the fleece out in front of me first, because I'm most like Dad. But I'm not as likely to blow a gasket."

"Something like that," she admitted.

"So I'll just run you through what Dad would say then. You sure you want to do this? Put yourself through the kind of public scrutiny that running the presidential race means? Far worse scrutiny than you had to go through in the attorney general process?"

"Yes, I'm sure."

"And you know what this means for every single one of us? The entire Worthington family?" he fired at her.

"Yes, I do." She gazed directly at him. "But Will, I'm not only going to run against Rich. I'm going to take his job."

"I can't change your mind?" Bill asked Sarah a few hours later.

Their conversation had gone exactly as she'd expected, including the grilling that far outranked Will's in intensity.

Strangely, he hadn't argued as much with her running for president as he had with her running as a Republican.

"That's simply crazy." He shook his head. "That'll make it a lot harder to get backing from our family's contacts. You know they're all pro-Democrat. That's where all the money is. And you've got to start by nailing the votes in your home state."

"I *will* run as a Republican," she insisted more than once.

Finally, her father had backed down. "All right. Do what you feel you have to." Then he sighed. "Sarah, you know this family will back you."

She knew that, but she wished he'd said, "I know you can do this and will do this. I believe in you."

Will placed a call to Drew while Sarah was talking with their father.

"So your sister's thrown the family one of her biggest curveballs yet," Drew said. He chuckled.

"She always was good at that. From babyhood on," Will agreed.

"Just don't ever mistake whimsical in your sister for being soft."

Will laughed. "No, I never could and never would."

36

SAN DIEGO, CALIFORNIA

Sean was waiting on the dock in the late afternoon for the Shapiros' research vessel to land. The warmth of the California sun was a welcome change from New York's wintry scene.

Dr. Leo Shapiro, Elizabeth's father, appeared first, both hands full of heavy equipment. He spotted Sean and gave him an approving nod.

A few minutes later Elizabeth emerged from below deck. Gusts of wind from off the coast tossed her long blonde hair around her face as she walked down the gangplank. Her cheeks were tinged with sunburn from long days on board ship. To Sean, she'd never looked more beautiful.

The instant she spotted him, she set down her duffle and the equipment she was carrying and ran to hug him. After retrieving her luggage and stowing it with her father's in his rental vehicle, Sean grabbed her hand.

"It's such a beautiful day. Let's take a walk," he suggested. "Maybe find a place where we can dangle our feet in the water. Since I can't do that in New York right now."

She grinned. "I know the perfect spot."

They headed there hand in hand. By the time they'd settled by the water and removed their shoes, the sun had turned to a dark golden glow.

"I thought you might be hungry, so I brought a snack to hold us over until dinner." He took a mini picnic out of his backpack—crackers, cheese, strawberries, bottled fruit waters, red-checked napkins.

"Impressive." She nudged him. "You did this all yourself? Even cloth napkins?"

He grinned. His quick visit to a gourmet food store had been worth it. "Yeah. You bring out the romantic in me."

She laughed. "I'm starving. Let's eat."

As they munched, they caught up on what couldn't be said as easily via text or phone. By now, with their world travels, they were experts at it.

"One more thing," he said when they'd polished off the snacks. "I brought us some dessert." He whipped out a box of Cracker Jacks and presented it to her.

Her warm brown eyes lit up. "Cracker Jacks? I haven't seen these since I was a kid. My dad would get them for me sometimes when I'd have to go with him to a really boring meeting. I love these!"

"My mom used to take us to an old-fashioned candy store in Chautauqua when we were young. It's still there. We always loved the little surprises inside. Bet they still have them." He opened the top of the box. "Should we see what's—"

"Oooh, I love surprises." She grabbed the box from him and peeked inside. Extracting a couple kernels, she tossed them into her mouth. "But I hate waiting to see what's inside." She upended the box into the napkin on her lap. "There it is!" Grinning, she pounced on the yellow plastic capsule amid the caramel kernels.

"So, what's the prize inside?" he asked.

Elizabeth unscrewed the capsule. "It's—" She squinted at it. "It's the most beautiful ring I've ever seen. This can't be a toy—" She raised startled eyes to Sean.

He smiled. "It's real. Actually, from my Irish grandmother." He reached over and picked the claddagh ring out of her trembling fingers. "I thought it might do for a very special occasion."

He moved in front of her and knelt in the sand, the sunset behind him. Holding the ring, he said, "Elizabeth Anne Shapiro, you make my heart smile. Will you do that every day for the rest of my life? Will you marry me?"

"It's about time you ask, Sean Worthington," she shot at him. Then tears of joy brimmed. "Of course I will," she whispered.

He slid the beautiful 1.5-carat heart-shaped diamond on her finger. The platinum and gold ring had a Celtic engraved band encircled with emeralds. He smiled at her. "This is for now. We can go together to pick out anything you like, or have one specially designed."

She gazed at him. "No need. I can't imagine anything more perfect. And Sean? My heart has always felt at home with you too. Since the beginning." She laughed. "Sheesh, that sounds like a Hallmark card, doesn't it? But I mean every word. I love you, Sean."

"I know you do. And I love you, Elizabeth."

Their tender kiss was framed in the light of the sun setting over the ocean.

Chautauqua Institution

In between spending time with Will and Laura's kids during their last day at Chautauqua, Sarah had made some preliminary calls to rally the parties she'd need to swiftly launch into the February primaries. She'd have the immediate financial backing of the Worthington family, but she'd need to raise additional funds. Her father and Will had promised their help and connections. They'd already started making some phone calls on her behalf.

Once Sarah had announced she was running, Ava had been strangely quiet. She'd kept herself busier than usual in the kitchen and with the activities of her grandkids. Twice Sarah had tried to broach the subject of the conversation that she'd overheard, but both times she and her mother had been interrupted.

Sarah hadn't been able to reach Sean in the last 24 hours. But his unavailability made her smile. It meant her brother was busy with Elizabeth, and that was a good thing. Still, she wanted him to know her plans before anything hit the press. And it would very soon, she knew.

Nothing about the Worthingtons stayed private for long.

Her thoughts flickered back to the conversation between her mother and Thomas. Clearly, her mother wasn't ready to talk. Sarah knew she couldn't force the conversation, and she wasn't sure she really wanted to know the answers to the questions that brewed.

A Secure Location

He phoned the man. "The ante has just been upped. Sarah Worthington is about to announce she's throwing her hat into the presidential ring in the February primaries."

"Ah, so she's going to give the other Democratic candidates a run for their money," the man reasoned.

"No. She'll run as a Republican."

"A what?" The man's tone was incredulous.

"A Republican," he repeated.

"That means—"

"Yes, directly against the current sitting president."

There was a long silence on the other end of the phone, and then a click as the man hung up.

37

Sarah exited her bedroom the next morning, bag in hand, and was surprised to find her father waiting for her.

"I always knew it would be one of you kids," he said simply.

She didn't have to ask what he meant. "But you didn't expect it to be me, did you?" she fired back.

"No, I didn't. But before you get any more heated, hear me out," he commanded in his best lecturing voice. "Princess, I want you to listen to me." His tone gentled. "You know I'm proud of you, right?"

She nodded. Yes, she knew in theory, but he'd never really stated that.

"All you've accomplished—" His voice broke. "Well, those things are just added on top of who you are. Not only as a Worthington but as a person. Achievements don't make you who you are. I don't ever want you to fall into the trap of thinking that. I went down that road once and—"

What exactly was her father trying to say?

He cleared his throat. "I've been watching as your expertise develops in so many areas. And you're right. It *is* time for a Worthington—a Worthington *woman*—to run the country." He chuckled. "Your mother has been running things in this family for years. It's time to broaden the scope." Tilting his head, he added, "And you're the one to do it. It makes sense."

Sarah's bag dropped to the floor. Stunned at the turn in the conversation, she stared at her father.

He had softened somehow. As he gazed at her, she saw he'd suddenly seemed to age. His hands were shaking.

The changes in her strong father unnerved her. First after Sean had disappeared. Now even more so.

"I've always loved you." Thomas's words to her mother flickered back into her consciousness.

Did the conversation she'd overheard have anything to do with her father's weakness now? Compassion flooded over her. She reached toward her father and hugged him hard. "I love you, Dad."

"I love you too, princess."

Their embrace was the warmest she could remember. When she at last drew away, she was surprised by the dampness on her father's cheeks before he turned his head.

"I'll carry your bag to the car," was all he said.

But she knew he meant much more than that.

<hr />

Two hours after Sarah left Chautauqua, Will was packing the Land Rover to return to New York City. Laura handed him another overstuffed bag.

He shook his head. "How exactly is it that we always have way more going home than we came with?"

Laura shrugged. "You know, Grandma and Grandpa."

At that minute, Will's cell rang.

"Hey, big brother," Sean said in a mysterious tone. "I have some news."

"Ah." Will quirked a brow at Laura. "And this news—does it have anything to do with Elizabeth? And a certain ring Mom said she gave you? Not to rush things, but when's the big day?"

Sean laughed. "My brother. So practical and to the point. You probably already have your Google calendar pulled up."

"Not yet, but I will soon." Will's words ended there, because Laura snatched the phone from him.

"Well, Sean, it's about time. Now give me Elizabeth."

Will rolled his eyes and tried to grab the phone back.

Laura frowned and slapped at his hand. "Don't even think about it." Her face brightened. "Elizabeth!" she squealed into the phone.

Will sighed. So it was a done deal at last. All he needed to know was the date and he was good. But the girls? They'd be running for a couple of hours with the "what did he say, what did you say, where did it happen exactly?" replays. Shaking his head, he headed for the kitchen. He'd use the landline to tell Drew they'd be a little belated heading back to the city.

San Diego, California

Sean waited patiently through a record two-hour phone call with his family. Between Laura, Ava, and Elizabeth, he'd barely gotten a word in edgewise. But he didn't need to. The women in his life were all happy. Things between Elizabeth and himself were settled. That's what mattered the most.

Elizabeth's face was radiant when she got off the phone. "Wow, they were pretty excited," she told him.

He chuckled. "They've been waiting, or more like pushing, a long time for this day. They finally got their way."

She elbowed him. "*Their* way? You saying it wasn't your idea?"

"No, it was always my idea. I just strung them along for a while so they'd think I was going with their idea." He laughed. "We haven't even had time to set a date—"

"As soon as possible," Elizabeth said.

Sean lifted a brow.

"What? Now you've got cold feet? Too late for that," she teased him. "Seriously, I don't need or want a big event. I just want you. No big crowds. No grand high-society wedding. Just simple."

"Then how about a week from Saturday? You've got the ring. I've got the girl." He grinned. "What's to stop us?"

Elizabeth smacked him in the chest. "Nice try, but that's a little too fast."

"So when are you thinking?"

She mused aloud. "I have a four-month research project with Dad that starts in a week. The grant we have won't allow us to change the time frame. It'll be done around the first week of June. But then I'd be able to take a few months completely off."

"How about the end of June then?" He waggled an eyebrow. "I'm sure Mom and Jean would be happy to help pull things together. Just tell them what you want and don't want. You could hang out in Chautauqua with Mom when you're done with your research project until time for the wedding."

"You've got a deal."

Sean smiled. "How about on the water? Our favorite place to be?"

She nodded. "I always wanted a ride on the *Summer Wind*."

"Perfect. Lake Chautauqua it is. The season will be open

by then. All we have to do is say the word and Mom will get it booked. Privately too. The owners will do anything for her."

"Like keeping quiet about it?" She frowned. "I don't want our wedding to be a media field day."

"There's a solution for that too. I just remain an eligible bachelor in the eyes of the tabloids for now. So long as you don't mind them concocting stories about my single status and the rumors of who I'm currently seeing or not seeing, we're good. They won't know anything about you until after we've returned from our honeymoon and someone catches us holding hands in public." He shrugged. "The shock waves will skitter around for a while as they try to figure out who you are. We'll give them some straightforward answers to cut off the gossip at the knees, and eventually it'll all settle down."

"And our honeymoon?"

"Oh, you can leave that up to me."

EN ROUTE TO NEW YORK CITY

Sarah was getting ready to merge onto the I-80 express, crossing into Pennsylvania, when she got a call from Sean. After fumbling for her Bluetooth, she said, "About time you called me back."

He laughed. "Pushy. Got something on your mind?"

"Yes. I'm going to run for president."

There was a pause, then, "You're serious."

"Darn right I am."

"Good for you. You're just the kind of candidate Americans can rally around. Ronald Reagan was a baby of the family too. Smart, charismatic, and people loved him. Just like you."

"Wow, I had no idea you thought so highly of your sister,"

---

she teased. "Then will you be my campaign manager?" She paused. "Even if I run as a Republican?"

There was only a slight hesitation in the conversation. "Would I let you choose any other? But Republican? You sure?"

"Positive."

"I don't mind playing the other side of the field. Always was in the middle myself too—just not publicly. The switch in what the public thinks about Worthington politics may give us an added media kick too. If nothing else, it'll confuse the other candidates for a while." He chuckled.

"See, you're already talking like a campaign manager," she said.

"But I have one stipulation."

"And what's that?"

"I get two weeks completely off, starting the last weekend in June. In fact, you can't be busy that weekend either."

"Okay, I'll check my calendar to see if I'm open."

"No, you won't," he insisted. "You'll be there."

"There, where?"

"Chautauqua. The *Summer Wind*."

"Oh, a little family cruise?"

"Yes. But something more too. A wedding. Mine."

38

////

SEOUL, KOREA

Sean peered out his hotel window at the night sky. Since his engagement a few days ago and Sarah asking him to be her campaign manager, he had been at lightning speed. His mother and Jean were working their magic on the details of the upcoming wedding. Jean had booked the *Summer Wind* under her own name, as well as some other arrangements, so the tabloids wouldn't get a whiff of the news.

As Sean and Elizabeth had agreed, they didn't want a reporter-infested wedding—except for Jon, that is.

Only a few people were on the guest list—the Worthington family, Leo Shapiro, Jon, Drew and Jean and their kids, Darcy, and . . . Thomas.

He paused, reflecting on that last decision. Elizabeth had suggested it. They'd gone rounds on it. But he knew in his gut it was the right thing to do.

Still, at a quiet time like this, he wrestled with that decision and the implications of it—for himself, for his family. Yes, he now understood why the affair had happened and why Thomas had chosen to stay away all these years. But where did Sean want to go from here? Did he want an ongoing relationship with his birth father?

That, he didn't know.

He sighed. Best to focus on completing this last trip for Worthington Shares before hitting the campaign trail with Sarah.

Speaking of that, he checked the time on his cell phone. He had calls to make.

NEW YORK CITY

"We found it," Darcy announced to Sarah a few days after her return to New York City. "The cell phone."

"Hold it. You're saying—"

"Yes. The cell phone Justin was given as a contact."

"Where on earth—"

"On a homeless man recently found deceased in an alleyway. He was known to hang out near the building where Justin died. The phone likely fell out of Justin's pocket or he dropped it when he plunged off the building. The homeless man found it and stashed it in his pocket with other trinkets he'd scavenged. NYPD wouldn't have thought anything about it except for the bulletin DHS had sent, saying they were looking for a phone in that area. The phone was smashed and still had traces of blood on it. Justin's blood."

"His contact list? Any texts? Phone calls?" Sarah asked.

"That's where this gets good. Tech support was able to trace the few calls—all from a single number except for one. The single number was Carson's cell. They back up his story. But the last call is from a different number. Another burner cell. Its ID number shows that it was shipped to the same store."

"So the two burner cells—Justin's and the unknown caller's—were likely purchased at the same time, from the same store," Sarah reasoned.

"You got it. A little visit to the store and a check of their records confirmed it. And there's more."

"More?"

"The clerk remembered the person who bought it. A big guy. Athletic. In a hurry. Pushy. We showed the clerk a few pictures."

"Let me guess."

"Yes, Stapleton. As soon as we can bring the clerk in and get his statement, we'll have enough on Stapleton to get a warrant to search his apartment and to get that DNA test."

To make a mistake like that, Stapleton must have been desperate, Sarah thought. Power brokers like him didn't make mistakes. They had others do their dirty work. But maybe this time the work had been too personal. He had too much invested to leave the odds in someone else's hands. He'd had to take control himself.

That action would be his undoing.

A Secure Location

"So the mudslinging has already begun," the man with the deep voice said.

"Did you expect anything else?" he asked. With no response to the rhetorical question, he went on. "Spencer's camp is in defense mode. They'll do their best to smear Sarah's reputation. They're already saying she betrayed his trust after he nominated her for AG. That she's been working behind the scenes to dismantle his administration. Raising rumors about his involvement in the AF scandal."

"Which we now know are true," the man replied.

"Yes. Stapleton did visit the White House for a private meeting with President Rich before the bombing. The timing is right to have allowed him time to arrange for the purchase of the C-4, etc. And Stapleton had several interactions with Carson right after that. Carson has confirmed the nature of those conversations. Stapleton's temporarily removed from the AF board. Will saw to that."

"So the noose is tightening on both of them."

"Uncomfortably so," he told the man. "Sarah won't back down. She's got the power, influence, and brains to take this all the way to the top."

"That means Spencer's campaign will get more vicious. He's got too much to lose."

"Agreed. But remember—"

"We hold the last card in the deck."

NEW YORK CITY

"I've got the best present you can imagine," Darcy announced to Sarah several days later. "The DNA is a match."

"So Justin Eliot was Stapleton's biological kid."

"Indeed. Stapleton has his team of lawyers working overtime trying to explain that one. He finally admitted he had a little fling with a waitress he'd thought was 18 at the time. When she got pregnant, he took care of her and the kid financially. Said he felt bad that she didn't have parents to look after them. Even took care of Justin's schooling and medical bills when he found out the kid was bipolar. After Rebecca died, he says the kid disappeared. Couldn't trace him."

"And that he had no idea the kid had become the Polar Bear Bomber, am I right?"

"You win the lottery," Darcy said sarcastically. "Finally admitted that he knew about the bombing—Sandstrom's idea—but claims Carson did the dirty work, yada yada."

"What about the pens and handwriting?"

"His lawyers are arguing that they're circumstantial. That Carson is covering his own behind."

"What about the cell phones?"

"Stapleton says he bought a couple cell phones. Who doesn't buy burner phones, he says, from time to time? But he has no idea how one of them got into Justin's hands or ended up with his blood on it."

"And you couldn't track the whereabouts of the other cell phone—the number of the person who talked to Justin last?" Sarah asked.

"Nada. If we could find that cell phone—"

"Then you could close the loop on a murder charge."

39

Will sat back in his office chair at Worthington Shares with a satisfied smile. His brother and sister had been hard at work. While the Rich primary campaign had focused on raising questions about Sarah's background and integrity, Sarah had wisely sidestepped all that, choosing to zero in on the issues Americans in general were concerned about.

Instead of bringing up the Rich administration's failed election promises from his first term, which were many, Sarah offered practical solutions on taxes, America's education system, increasing jobs for America, and immigration concerns. She reached into the hearts and minds of young people with her enthusiasm, honesty, and fresh approach. The public, tired of the usual Washington politicians, was responding positively to Sarah, while Spencer Rich's ratings slipped day by day. People in their twenties who said they'd declined to vote in the last election because there were no candidates they felt good about were now showing up in droves at the Republican state primaries.

In February, Sarah had won the New Hampshire primary with an astounding 11 percent margin over Spencer Rich, and the Iowa Republican caucus with a 7 percent lead. In March, she'd nailed an 8 percent lead in Colorado and a 14 percent lead in Virginia, and won Illinois with an 18 percent lead. She'd also received startling support at the Republican Party convention in D.C. In April, she'd led by 17 percent in Pennsylvania and 22 percent in her home state of New York.

Will scanned the most recent May news headlines about Sarah.

A Voice of Reason in the Political Realm

Now Neck and Neck with President Rich in the Race

Focused on Real People, Real Issues

A Trusted Advocate for Minorities and the Disadvantaged

Young Voters Turn Out in Groundbreaking Numbers to Support Sarah Worthington

Photos appeared on a daily basis of Sarah visiting everyday people—an African American church in Georgia, a steel workers' plant in Philadelphia, a politics forum at Stanford University, a farmers union in Iowa, an orphanage in New Jersey. Sean was doing his job well. Sarah was the candidate people of all backgrounds could talk to—one who would care about them and their needs.

She wasn't a politician who kissed babies just to get votes. Sarah was real. Though she'd been raised in privilege, not only had she rubbed shoulders with people in nearly every stratum of life in America and across the globe, but she had worked to understand them, find common ground with them.

Will smiled. She'd always been like that. Sarah shone even more brightly when under fire.

Just like now.

———————

INDIANAPOLIS, INDIANA

Sean scanned Sarah's upcoming schedule. For the last part of April and early May, they were focusing on Indiana, West Virginia, Oregon, and Washington. For the rest of May, they'd focus on California and New Jersey, then circle back to New York, Colorado, Virginia, and Washington, D.C.

Their goal was to knock President Rich out of the race by July, in time for a single-minded Republican focus at the conventions.

Sean and Sarah were both highly aware that no one became president by winning the national popularity contest. She had to nail 270 or more electoral college votes to accomplish that.

The truth was that presidential elections were now fought and won in just seven states—Florida, Ohio, Virginia, Colorado, Nevada, Iowa, and New Hampshire. So those swing states would be the ones they concentrated on the rest of the campaign. The votes of the other 43 states had been largely preordained since John F. Kennedy's era as either Democrat or Republican.

Not unexpectedly, the media at first had a field day with a Worthington emerging as a Republican. Bill, Will, and Sean all experienced vitriolic phone conversations with colleagues who couldn't understand Sarah's choice.

Sean winced. Kiki Estrada in particular had some choice things to say, and rightfully so. But she was also enough of a professional and long-range strategist that he'd managed to complete the conversation with her in a professional manner.

As a staunch Democrat himself, Bill still struggled with Sarah's choice to run as a Republican. But Will and Sean had gradually worn him down to understand that Sarah's core values and leanings were much more Republican. Also, within that camp she had the opportunity to make a tremendous impact—even change the very nature of the political race.

With Worthington money and power, the influence of their vast network of colleagues, and Rich's alarming decline in the polls and the impeachment proceedings, Sarah Worthington was a shoo-in for the top Republican candidate.

Unless anything is revealed that could sway her to step out of the race, Sean thought.

He narrowed his eyes. That had already happened to their family. It would never happen again, at least not on Sean's watch.

With the stakes upped, they needed to carve out the time for a family meeting. His mother and father needed to know about the photos. Sarah needed to know what had happened between Ava and Thomas.

He sighed. Neither were secrets that could be revealed by phone. They required a face-to-face meeting. But that was harder than it sounded with the Worthingtons. Will was still in the throes of a massive investigation by DHS and the FBI over the foreign funds. He personally had been cleared, but that didn't mean the stress was much less. With Sean and Sarah on the campaign trail, they'd only been able to carve out the couple of weeks for Sean's wedding and honeymoon in late June and early July. It meant an even faster-paced schedule, though, in the meanwhile, since they'd be missing a critical window in the campaign.

Still, the Worthingtons needed to find the time—soon.

Sarah stood looking out the large plate-glass window at the crowd below that had gathered to meet her. So much had happened in less than a year that it was sometimes difficult to believe it.

She'd taken on the attorney general position, all the while harboring her secret dream—to become not only the youngest president of the United States but the first female. Now, if the primary state polls were any indication, she was on her way to doing exactly that.

Even in the tumult of her campaign, she'd managed to keep tabs on the impeachment process. It was still proceeding. If the president was removed from office before the end of his term, the vice president would become president automatically in the interim, before the newly elected president took office. In this case, it would be disaster for America, as the current vice president didn't have what it took to be a sitting president. Spencer Rich was many things, Sarah thought woefully, and she didn't like most of them. But the man at least made decisions, unlike his waffling vice president.

The chief justice of the court was now presiding over the president's trial, with all 100 senators in a private session as the jury. Two-thirds of the Senate had to vote for a conviction.

Sarah knew the odds. No president in American history had ever been removed from office.

Bill Clinton had been impeached by the House on charges of perjury and obstruction of justice but was acquitted by the Senate.

Nixon, though impeached over the Watergate break-in, had resigned before he could be removed.

Andrew Johnson had been impeached due to some post–Civil War issues but was acquitted by one vote and remained in office.

Congress's resolution to impeach John Tyler had failed.

But Sarah also knew what Article II, Section 4 of the Constitution said:

The President, Vice President, and all civil Officers of the United States, shall be removed from Office on Impeachment for, and Conviction of, Treason, Bribery, or other high Crimes and Misdemeanors.

A simple majority could vote to prohibit Spencer Rich from holding any public office in the future. He could be convicted of bribery, violation of public trust, and real criminality—breaking laws, abusing his power, and employing the power of the office for personal gain. Using foreign money to influence a US campaign was treason itself. That it came from ISIS should be the final nail in the coffin by law and also in the eyes of the public.

She sighed. The results of the impeachment were not in her control. She had done all she could in that regard when she was attorney general.

"Ready, sis?" Sean asked from behind her.

She swiveled to face him. "Always."

With determination, she swept out of the room and down the stairs toward the waiting crowd.

40

NEW YORK CITY

"Mom, you sure you want to do that?"

Once again, Will found himself treading lightly on relational matters. He hated it. Business was easy. Personal was just that—personal. It wasn't his forte.

"Thomas is our oldest friend and Sean's father. I didn't invite him to the wedding. Sean did," she said defensively.

So Thomas and Sean made their peace—at least for now, Will reflected. Sean hadn't said much about that, except for a slight reference to father and son meeting in person for a short discussion.

"Does Dad know?" Will asked.

"Yes, he understands. But he doesn't like it."

Will could imagine. It would be the first time the two old best friends had seen each other in years, with the woman they both loved sandwiched between them.

"What about Sarah?"

"She only knows that Thomas is on the guest list as your father's and my closest friend from university."

"Mom," he warned, "that's pretty risky. Especially if any news of that leaks to the media."

"Don't use that tone with me. I am fully aware of the risks," she announced with a voice he couldn't argue with, so he didn't try. "But I must do this for Sean . . . and for Thomas. It would be unconscionable not to."

He knew his mother would defend Sean to her dying day—because of her love for him and because of her guilt. This was one way to deal with a portion of the guilt that she would feel for a lifetime. He backed down. "Okay."

But her actions further reinforced his resolve. His mother could never know about the threat that loomed over their family—that Sean's name could potentially be linked to the Polar Bear Bomber. She'd already been through enough and was more fragile than she looked.

Will had to protect her at all costs.

CHAUTAUQUA INSTITUTION

The evening before the wedding, the Worthington and Simons families, plus Elizabeth and Leo Shapiro, gathered at the Athenaeum Hotel in Chautauqua Institution for a celebratory meal. Jon, Thomas, and Darcy couldn't make dinner, but they would arrive the next day to board the *Summer Wind* in the single-stop-sign town of Celoron.

As Sean held his soon-to-be bride's hand, he glanced around the room and sighed gratefully.

Elizabeth's eyes met his. "Your family," she whispered, "and mine too. We're both really fortunate, you know that?"

Indeed, he knew that. Even more, he knew he belonged.

The day of the wedding, Sarah propped her hands on the railing of the *Summer Wind*. The sleek, 130-passenger, state-of-the-art, all-white yacht was perfect for viewing the beauty of Lake Chautauqua. The wedding itself would be on the semi-open upper admiral's deck of the two-story boat. The small reception would be catered in the luxurious dining salon. The deck was decorated simply with white ribbon, baby's breath, and white roses. Elizabeth had said they didn't need any more than that, with the natural beauty surrounding them.

Sean always said he felt most at home on the water. It was also the place Elizabeth felt most comfortable. So the location made perfect sense.

It was the first wedding Sarah had been to in several years. In the beautiful and quiet surroundings, she suddenly missed Jon. Since the day he had told her he was breaking the story, they hadn't been in contact. He was giving her the wide berth she'd asked for, she knew. He would be respectful like that.

As time passed and she grew busier with the campaign, it had been easier to use her fast track as an excuse not to contact him. But it didn't mean she didn't miss their friendship.

Now, as he boarded the *Summer Wind*, she felt a twinge of regret. That day she had acted in haste, out of emotion. If she could go back and do anything differently . . .

In that instant, he spotted her and moved toward her. "Sarah," he said simply. "You've certainly had a lot to deal with. It's good to see you."

Any awkwardness was wiped away. His eyes rested on her warmly. *It's all right*, they said. *I understand*. She nearly sagged in relief.

Throughout the short but meaningful ceremony, Jon stayed by her side, his gentle presence a comfort.

When Sean and Elizabeth exchanged their rings, Sarah grew

misty-eyed. Not only had her brother, the noted most eligible bachelor in New York City, found the love of his life, but he'd found his center. He and Elizabeth seemed so happy, so content with each other.

Will that ever happen for me? she wondered. *Or is my destiny in another direction?*

She felt someone's eyes on her. Turning her head, she saw Jon smiling.

So he'd been watching her. Yes, he'd stepped away for a while, because she'd asked him to. But he was still Jon, and again he was by her side. She was content.

———————

Because Thomas had arrived only minutes before the *Summer Wind* cast off, Will barely had the opportunity to shake the ex-president's hand before the ceremony began.

Thomas now stood to the side, chatting with Dr. Leo Shapiro, Elizabeth, and Sean.

Will grinned. The quirky doctor was a perfect foil in difficult situations such as this, and Elizabeth had clearly prepped him to help out. Leo was doing his best with entertaining stories about research missions gone awry. The group was laughing.

Will's gaze swept to his father. Bill had greeted Thomas with a rather stiff handshake, Ava by his side. Ava was playing the part of the mother of the groom to a tee, fussing over food already perfectly arranged and interacting with her grandkids.

Jon, Darcy, and Sarah stood in another group, clinking champagne glasses. Will was relieved. The tension that had existed between Jon and Sarah clearly had dissipated.

A hand clapped Will's shoulder. "All is good, right, Will?"

Will swiveled toward Drew, who always meant more than he said. "Yes. Sean and Elizabeth."

Drew chuckled. "Jon and Sarah."

Will wrinkled his nose. "Yes, that too."

"Thomas," Drew added. "Being here. Helping to close a loop for Sean."

Will nodded. "It is as it should be."

He meant exactly what he said.

———

Darcy had just gone to get a slice of wedding cake when Sarah saw her mother start to pass by Thomas. When Thomas touched her mother's arm and drew her toward the bow of the boat, Sarah inexplicably flinched.

Jon followed her gaze. "You think your mom feels bad for Thomas, since they're old friends?"

She scowled at Jon. "Why would she feel bad for him?"

Jon lifted a brow. "You didn't notice that Thomas came solo to the wedding—no Victoria? Rumors abound that their marriage is on the rocks. Sure looks like it, or she'd be here for this type of occasion. I feel bad for him. Victoria was no catch, but breaking up a marriage, that's rough."

Does Victoria know about the affair? Is that why she didn't come? Does my dad know? Why is Thomas here?

The conflicting questions hit her in a wave. Suddenly she felt dizzy. A headache mounted. She reeled.

"Hey, you okay?" Jon's voice was concerned.

"I must be feeling a little seasick," she said. "Too much champagne."

He tilted his head. "Too much of something, that's for certain. But I'm not sure it's the champagne."

He turned back toward Thomas with an evaluating gaze.

41

The morning after Sarah arrived home from Chautauqua, Jon arrived with a bag of her favorite bagels.

"Thought you might be a little short on breakfast food," he said. "And I wanted to make sure you were all right. You seemed a little distracted at the wedding. You're good with your brother's choice of Elizabeth, right?"

"That's not it at all. I love Elizabeth. Guess I just have a lot going on right now."

He studied her. "More than the election, you mean."

"Yes. I mean, no." She shook her head. "I don't know."

She thought of her father's warning. *"Far more events than you could ever imagine are at play here."* His gentle nudge for her to stand down from her quest for the AG position. His concern about her pursuing the presidency.

"There are things going on that are"—she hesitated—"or might be, bigger than all of us."

He shrugged. "There always are."

205

"No." She frowned. "I mean, really big. Things that could change all of our lives."

"Like what things?"

She avoided his eyes. "I can't say any more. At least not right now."

"Sarah, you can trust me," he said gently. "You should know that by now." After a moment, he added, "And I might know more than you think."

She flinched. "What's that supposed to mean?"

He met her glare with a steady look. "I know about the affair. That your mom had one. And with whom."

She stiffened.

"I've always shot straight with you. I'm doing so now," he said in a calm tone. "I know it isn't what you want to hear—"

Her fear spewed forth in anger. "You're telling me this now—when Sean's off to wherever land for his honeymoon? When Will's neck-deep in the foreign funds mess? When Mom and Dad are headed to Australia? I can't deal with this right now, Jon. Not in the middle of the presidential race. And you know it."

His face was stoic. "I thought you deserved to know, before you found out from someone else. In case you didn't already know. But I'm guessing you did."

"You need to leave," she said in a horrible replay of their earlier conversation. She pointed a shaky finger toward the door.

"Okay." He lifted his chin. "For now. But I'll be back when you're ready."

As soon as he left, Sarah started to shake. The weight of two secrets was too much. Sean's photo with the Polar Bear Bomber—something her parents still didn't know about—could show up anytime.

But worse, how did Jon know about the affair? Was it real? And if Jon knew, who else did?

THE MALDIVES ISLANDS

The day was perfect—blue sky, azure water, and the scent of tropical flowers. Best of all, Elizabeth was next to him, in the quietest spot he could imagine. He plucked a single bloom from the bush nearby and tucked it behind her ear.

"Hey, just like in the Azores," she said, smiling. "When I was half sleeping and half admiring you."

He laughed. "And when I was half working and half admiring you. But now it's way, way better." He tugged her closer. "I have a lot more benefits for fully admiring you." He cocked his head invitingly toward their hut.

She took his offered hand. "I like the sound of that. So what are you waiting for? Lead away, Romeo."

NEW YORK CITY

Sarah sat on the couch in her penthouse in Greenwich Village. Her head ached with the disparate pieces that barraged her mind.

A flash of Will's aborted Senate race surfaced. Jason Carson lurking in the shadows for a brief interaction with him. Will's determined expression as he strode off the stage and out through the crowd.

She inhaled sharply. Surely Will couldn't have believed, even in the shock of the moment, that their brother would be connected with a bombing.

Or was it also because Carson knew somehow about her mother's affair and threatened to reveal it to the world? Had Will known that, hidden it all these years from his brother and sister, but then stepped away to protect his family—especially their mother?

Sarah's grip tightened on the throw pillow she held on her lap. She couldn't talk to Darcy or Jon, even as much as she trusted them. This was too deeply personal. She had to know as much as possible first.

There was only one place to go. Her oldest brother.

42

Will had been expecting this call for some time. It finally came.

"Why didn't you tell me?" his sister said bluntly.

"Hi to you too," he said.

"Don't mess with me, Will."

"Okay, so evidently you have something to tell me."

"The phone isn't a good place. Meet me. Now. My place." She hung up.

He sighed. When his sister got that authoritative tone, he knew he couldn't do anything but hop into a cab and hightail it over. But what exactly did she know? That their mother had an affair? About the fact Sean had a different birth father? Or was she guessing? Still trying to put together the pieces?

First, he did what he always did when he was feeling squeezed by the women in his family. He talked to Laura. "She knows something," he said as soon as he walked into the kitchen.

"She. You mean Sarah, right?"

His wife always knew how to read him. "Yes."

"Well, what exactly does she know?"

He scratched his chin. "I have no idea."

"So you're walking into a she-bear cave with no idea how many cubs she has, huh? Then you just take them on one at a time." She paused. "And as gently as possible. Your sister may be a force to be reckoned with, especially when she's determined or upset. But Will, she's still your baby sister. Right now my guess is she's as vulnerable as she's ever been. Whether she knows one part, both parts, or more."

He nodded slowly. "You're right."

"Just get over there, let her vent, and keep your mouth shut until she's done. Then walk her calmly through what you know about the situation, piece by piece. Sure, she'll be firing questions at you, but do what you do best—sort them out one at a time." Laura's advice, per usual, was straightforward. "And Will?" she added. "Don't worry. You'll know what to do when you get there. You always do."

Her support and belief in him astounded him, even after two decades.

THE MALDIVES ISLANDS

Sean inhaled the scent of the ocean as he stood on the veranda enjoying the soft breeze. Besides the waves, the only sound was the gentle call of birds in the trees nearby.

So much had changed since he had fled New York City after discovering he was the product of an affair. Learning who he was had explained so much about his restlessness and their family's dynamics. Secrets, once revealed, were freeing.

The revelation had not destroyed his parents' marriage, as he had feared. Instead it had seemed to remind them of what was truly important. Sean had never seen his driven father so affectionate with his mother. Now Bill lingered over coffee at the table with his family. He and Ava would soon be on their way to Australia, affectionately calling it a second honeymoon while Sean and Elizabeth were on their first.

Sean himself had realized, through the wrenching pain of the past months, what—and who—truly mattered. Elizabeth. His family. Trusted friends he could count on one hand, such as Drew, Jon, and Kirk Baldwin, who was rough around the edges but solid gold at his core. As he glanced back at Elizabeth, asleep on the couch just inside the door, he made a vow—to always treat her as his beloved bride.

Settling into the rattan chair on the veranda, he picked up the wedding present Elizabeth had given him. He flipped open the pages of the book to the inscription and read it again in the subtle glow of the lamplight.

For the man you are, and the man you will be.

My love always,
Elizabeth

She had known how much he missed the Bible Sarah had given him, as much as he had tried to ignore its wise words for years. Then, in his darkest of times on Corvo, he had at last leafed through its pages. The truths revealed indeed had been light for his path. Then, when Sean had realized suddenly that he loved Elizabeth and needed to return to civilization, he'd unwittingly left the book behind in the little white house. So the gift he held now was a precious one indeed.

He sighed, his thoughts weighed by the two secrets that still hung over the Worthington family. The Polar Bear Bomber photos would come out eventually. The question was simply when.

The media would play it up, of course, and wear any angle thin. People would think what they decided to think.

Elizabeth had said it best: "Those who matter won't mind. Those who mind don't matter."

He chuckled. Leave it to Elizabeth to streamline anything to a cryptic punch.

Together they would weather any chaos. He was convinced of that.

But it was time for his parents to know about the Polar Bear Bomber photos. Earlier they had seemed too fragile. But Bill and Ava would both want to know. As soon as he and Elizabeth were home from their honeymoon, Sean would tell them. Or perhaps he and Will would, since those photos were the other part of the reason Will had walked away from the Senate bid, never explaining his reasons.

As the book now spread in front of him said, there truly was a time and a season for everything. It was time to bring the pieces of the puzzle together for his parents.

The only secret that would remain was the one they were all holding from Sarah—about Sean's parentage. Sean was intensely uncomfortable withholding it from her. But Sarah had so much going on in her career, Bill continually argued. "It's not the time to give her something else to think or worry about," he'd insisted.

But perhaps Sarah was much stronger than they all gave her credit for.

***

A Secure Location

"Perimeter closing in, as we discussed?" the caller asked.

"Right on target," the man said. "They won't have anywhere to run or hide."

"Good. Let's get it done."

43

///

NEW YORK CITY

The time for family secrets was over. Will didn't hesitate. He phoned his father.

"There's something you need to know. I'd rather tell you in person, but since you're leaving early tomorrow, that isn't possible. I'm on my way to Sarah's right now."

"Is something wrong with your sister?"

"No," Will said. "Not physically."

"What exactly does that mean?"

"She's hot under the collar about something, but I'm not sure what. She just demanded that I meet her at her place, pronto."

Bill sighed. "That sounds like your sister. So what do you think she knows?"

"I'm not sure. But if she has put the pieces together about Sean, I'm going to have to tell her."

There was a long pause. Then, at last, a quiet, "I understand."

"As for what I wanted to tell you in person—actually, what Sean and I wanted to tell you together—I need to tell you now."

His father was strangely silent, not interrupting at all, as Will explained about the photos of Sean with the Polar Bear Bomber.

"So that's why you stepped out of the Senate race? Not only because you knew about your mother's affair but also because you thought Sean might be involved with a bombing?"

"Dad, I didn't have time to think. I simply had to act—to protect all of us as a family. So I did what I had to. I got out of the race so I could sort it out."

"And sorting it out meant not telling me about it?"

"Do you honestly think you were ready to hear about anything else at that time?"

Bill blew out a breath. "You're right. I wasn't. But I'm listening now. Does your mother know?"

"No, and it will be up to you to tell her in the timing you choose."

"Then I will tell her tonight. We promised each other no more secrets. I will not fail in that promise."

When Will disconnected the call, he was relieved.

One secret down, one left to go. He doubted dealing with his feisty sister would be as easy.

———

As soon as Sarah heard Will's familiar step on her landing, she flung open her door. "You've been holding out on me," she accused.

"Whoa." He raised his hands in a defensive gesture. "How about at least offering me some coffee before you start in on me?"

"Coffee is already brewing."

He grinned. "Now we're getting somewhere."

She held in her words until she and Will sat facing each other at the small table nestled in the nook of her kitchen.

"So, what do you want to talk about?" he asked as he cradled his cup of steaming brew.

"Why didn't you tell me that Mom had an affair?" The words burst out with no filter. It was her brother, after all. They always shot straight with each other. At least she'd thought so, until now. "And with the president of the United States?"

He lifted a brow. "So the double barrel all at once," he shot back at her. "Got any other ammunition you want to fire at me? You might as well get it all over with."

She slumped. "Why do you always make me feel juvenile?"

"Because I'm your older brother, and that's what older brothers do."

"True." She sighed. The heat of the moment dissipated. "Okay, let's start over. I'll tell you what I know . . . or what I think I know."

She filled Will in on the startling phone conversation she'd overheard between Ava and Thomas as she'd stood in their Chautauqua kitchen. As she did so, she studied Will. There was no hint of surprise, no shock. So her brother knew. Who else knew?

When she'd concluded her story, he said simply, "You believe from what you heard that Ava and Thomas had an affair."

"What else could I conclude? I do have some pretty good instincts, being an attorney and all."

He brushed the comment off. "Did you ask Mom about it?"

"No. I couldn't bring myself to. Mom has finally seemed normal again, after recovering from Sean going missing. I couldn't stir the pot, especially with Sean getting married. Mom deserves some happiness after all she's been through." She zeroed in on him. "Will, did you know?"

He looked down briefly at his coffee cup, then up again. "Yes. I was very young when it happened, but I knew something was wrong. Mom was sad. I tried to comfort her, but nothing seemed to help. I remember feeling very lost during that time. I didn't know exactly what had happened until recently, when Mom told me. After that, the memories I had from childhood seemed to make more sense."

Her eyes teared. "So Mom told you? But not me?"

He reached over to clasp her hand on the table. "She wanted to protect you. She didn't think you had to know. You've had so much going on with your job at the DOJ, the attorney general vetting, the Polar Bear bombing, that she didn't want to worry you or throw you off your trajectory. Then, with you resigning from the AG position and launching into the presidential race, well, she didn't want to trouble you."

"Does Dad know? Does Sean?"

He nodded. "They do now."

She swallowed. How difficult that must have been for her father, thinking of his wife in the arms of another man. "Anybody else besides Laura?"

Laura was a given. Will would never withhold any knowledge from his wife.

"Drew," Will said softly.

"That doesn't surprise me. That man knows everything."

"And he's been with our family a long time. You know he's loyal. He would never let it leak to the press."

"But would Thomas?"

Will frowned. "From what I know of the man, never. He was a good friend of Mom and Dad's for a long time. He's never said anything in all these years. He wouldn't now."

"Then how could Jon know about it?"

Will's eyes widened. "Jon? What does he have to do with this?"

"He told me Mom had an affair and that I deserved to know from him before I found out from somewhere else."

Now Will turned into the interrogator. "Did Sean tell him? And if so, when?"

She chewed on her lip. "I don't know how Jon knew. He just knew."

"And you didn't ask him?" Will scowled.

"No." She sighed. "I kind of flew off the handle and ordered him out the door."

Will sat back. "Ah."

A wave of remorse washed over Sarah. Jon had only been trying to protect her by telling her the truth before someone else did. "Guess I owe him an apology. Take two."

"There's an understatement." Will chuckled. "I've seen you when you're in full firing mode. The only thing we guys can do is batten down the hatches and wait until the storm blows over."

She smacked his arm.

Will left Sarah's late that night with a mix of feelings. His sister knew about the affair but still didn't know that Sean was the product of that affair. So Will had done as Laura had suggested earlier—answered the questions Sarah asked one at a time, giving out no more information than she requested.

Drew was right. Secrets would indeed be revealed, but some had so many interweaving threads that they could only be pulled one at a time without making a mess of the complete tapestry.

It wasn't Will's place to pull the last thread. That should come to Sarah from their mother and Sean. Some secrets were not Will's to tell, as much as he hated leaving things unfinished. The idea grated against everything he was at his core. But since the two revelations of the photos and Sean's parentage, his axis had wobbled. His world didn't seem as black and white anymore. The grays in between resulted from his protectiveness toward those he loved.

At least his dad now knew about the photos. His mom would know soon, if she didn't already. Will had updated Sarah on that, and she'd seemed relieved. He would alert Drew of that fact tomorrow morning and fill him in on his discussion with Sarah.

Before Will had reached his home, Bill phoned.

"Your sister?"

"She's okay, Dad. But she knows."

"About Sean?"

"No, about the affair."

"You didn't—"

"I didn't. But you and Mom and Sean need to figure this out. Someone needs to tell her everything."

"I talked to Drew a few minutes ago, after I told your mother about the bomber photos. He said the same thing. Your mother agrees, as much as she hates to do it. But she doesn't feel comfortable saying anything unless Sean can be there too."

"So as soon as possible after Sean and Elizabeth get back, and you and Mom return from Australia?"

"Yes." His father's tone had switched to his business one, distancing all emotion. "You should probably alert Sean to what Sarah knows."

"Sarah will leave it alone until he's back from his honeymoon. Even she wouldn't dare intrude on that. But just in case, I'll text him a heads-up sometime tomorrow so it's waiting for him. Elizabeth said she was going to hide his phone and not give it back to him until they hit JFK on the way home."

44

Sarah had tried texting and calling Jon. She still hadn't heard from him. Often when he was on assignment, he couldn't get back to her immediately. But he always got back to her within six to eight hours, if not sooner. It was now midmorning the next day. He would never betray the Worthingtons and break the story about the affair, would he?

Now she was worried. Where had Jon's information come from? Sean? But why would Sean reveal that to Jon and not her?

Or had it come from another source—someone who was trying to stir up trouble for the Worthingtons? Especially now, with one of them in the presidential race? It wouldn't be the first time, or the last.

She needed to talk to her mother, her father. But no, they were on the flight to Australia.

How was it that her parents could survive one of the worst events in a marriage—infidelity—and emerge stronger? Sarah thought back to their interactions at the wedding. No, their affection hadn't been a show. But it had likely taken everything they had to refocus as a couple and figure out how to go on after the betrayal. Somehow they had been able to forgive and love again.

And I can't even let a fight with a friend go. She hadn't been able to sleep all night.

"A friend, huh? Jon's just a friend?" Sean had teased at the wedding. "Somehow I think there's a lot more going on."

Ever since her failed romance with the TV producer, Sarah had taken a pass even on casual dating. She wasn't about to admit to anyone, especially her brothers, that she had more than a passing interest in a *New York Times* reporter, even if he was someone they all knew and trusted.

So she'd faked disinterest in response to Sean's gibe. But she knew he hadn't been fooled.

"He's a good man," Sean had told her quietly. "You won't find a better one."

The look in her brother's eyes had been unsettling then. Recalling it now unsettled her even more. Had she blown something she could have had with Jon Gillibrand just because . . .

Because you're too hotheaded sometimes, she chastised herself. *You couldn't just listen to his side first. You had to go all crazy on him. You really need to apologize.*

Then, in the midst of the tumult, the still, small voice spoke. *Be patient. Wait.*

She exhaled. Patience wasn't something she was naturally good at.

Maybe Jon was giving her time to regroup. After all, she'd basically thrown him out of her place. The memory of the time she'd done that at the hotel in D.C. smarted too.

She winced, remembering both scenes. Jon didn't deserve any of it. At the very least, she needed to text him two words: *I'm sorry.*

Sarah poised her fingers over the keypad of her phone.

The voice spoke again. *Wait.*

As hard as it was, she did. She knew from past experience that the still, small voice was always right.

Turning her thoughts from personal matters, Sarah refocused on the area where she could make a difference—the next steps of her political campaign. With her campaign manager gone during his honeymoon, the rest of her team had stepped up to help fill in the gap. She'd only missed the few days she'd been in Chautauqua for the wedding and the day of her return. But even that small lapse in her schedule meant the remaining time until the national conventions would be intensified.

She only had a couple of days coming up that weren't scheduled in the next several months. She looked forward to them.

A Secure Location

"We now have some specifics about Stapleton's visit to the White House in regard to the bombing," the caller reported to the man. "Our inside source says Stapleton went into the Oval Office and the president kicked even his closest aides out. Stapleton was only in there for five minutes or less, but the two were alone."

"What did Stapleton do afterward?"

"Made a call. We tracked it to a contact who told us—after we put a bit of pressure on him about his unscrupulous dealings coming to light—that he owed Stapleton a favor. The contact made another call and connected Stapleton with the bomb dealer."

"So we were right. Spencer is involved," the man said.

"Yes. What we don't know is whether he ordered it or simply knew about it."

"How the mighty have fallen."

"Only the world doesn't know it yet."

"But they will," the man stated. "It's only a matter of time, and the right strings being pulled."

45

JFK International Airport

Sean and Elizabeth exited their flight holding hands. A tropical flower was still tucked in Elizabeth's hair. Their honeymoon had been all too short, they'd agreed. But they had a lifetime to take vacations in paradises far from the crowd, just the two of them. For the time being, Sarah needed Sean for her campaign, especially now that it was the critical month of July.

Instead of the usual limo that greeted him after a flight, Sean had arranged a different mode of transportation. Elizabeth disliked the traditional fanfare that accompanied Sean's arrivals and departures, often spotlighted in the media. Sean hoped to sidestep the paparazzi for now. So Drew had arranged for Sean's Jeep to be parked in a quiet spot at the airport.

The two honeymooners had gone with streamlined baggage, so it wasn't long before they had their single lightweight bags plucked off the revolving belt and slung over their shoulders.

They were discovered by paparazzi when they were about 40 yards from the Jeep. Tightening his grip on Elizabeth's hand, Sean tugged her along faster to avoid the oncoming wave. It hit right after he had deposited her and their bags safely in the Jeep. He jumped into the driver's side and revved up the engine.

Just before he drove toward the exit, he paused to smile widely for the reporters. Then he held up his left hand, wedding ring finger visible for the cameras to capture.

An instant later, the tires of his Jeep squealed down the curves of the exit ramp.

Elizabeth lifted a brow. "Seriously? How old are you?"

Sean laughed. "Have to give them something to talk about. Might as well be the truth." He winked at her. "This longtime bachelor is off the market."

NEW YORK CITY

Will had been spending most of his time with American Frontier lately, exploring the new vision of pursuing clean energy that would benefit the planet. He also had worked hard with Drew and AF's chief operations officer to put into place a system of checks that would make it nearly impossible for investors to come to American Frontier without first going through an intense grid. All current investments and investors were also being thoroughly analyzed.

Will had worked long hours juggling his increased responsibilities at AF with his continuing Worthington Shares leadership. He would have to continue to do so in the next couple of months to pave the path for AF's success after being hit so hard by scandal. This was a critical time, when he would need to be involved with each of the AF department heads to ensure they were all on the same page about how AF would be run under Will's leadership. He'd already made some difficult decisions with Drew about which department heads would need to change. More such decisions would likely be made over the next month.

As a result, he and Laura had agreed that she alone would take their three kids to Malawi for the month of July to work with the local villagers. His family had left shortly after Sean and Elizabeth's wedding, and he'd missed them as soon as they were on the plane. It was the first year he hadn't been able to accompany them, even for a couple of weeks.

However, his month while they were away would be more than full. Will was already connected with Kirk Baldwin of Green Justice and other grassroots leaders he'd met at the environmental summit. The environmental community, who had been gun-shy around Will at first—even though his brother had previously backed several of the ecological NGOs with Worthington money—now welcomed him with open arms. Sean had helped to pave the way so the leaders could see Will's heart and the road he was passionately pursuing toward clean energy.

The two most important steps were establishing common ground and a relationship of trust. Both were not easy between grassroots organizations and large corporations such as Will's. An innate distrust of the other party existed. Will, though, had been able to make significant progress toward a working plan that both sides could agree on.

At the moment, his thoughts flicked to Sean, who would be returning to New York today and soon have access to his phone. Hopefully Sean would read Will's text before Sarah reached him.

"Okay, now you can have it," Elizabeth said 24 hours after their return to the renowned One Madison building that housed Sean's penthouse, now their New York City home. She tossed

Sean's cell phone in his direction, and he made a grab for it. She laughed. "Talk about addicted."

Their first day back in the city had been busy with more important activities than reading text messages. They'd wanted a day all to themselves.

But with the return of Sean's cell, real life intruded into their bliss.

Before he attacked his emails and texts, he trolled through the usual tabloid stories that were mostly trumped-up but often had a kernel of truth to them. Several carried front-page stories that featured various photos of Sean and Elizabeth in the Jeep from the previous day.

He grinned at the headlines.

Sean Worthington's Mystery Woman Revealed

Sean Worthington—Off the Market?

Sean Worthington's Secret Marriage

Sean Worthington Ends Rumors

All carried basically the same text: Sean Worthington was clearly taken. Rumors about why he hadn't married yet were laid to rest. Speculation swirled about when he had gotten hitched and who the mystery bride was. He knew the furor would continue until they'd ferreted out who Dr. Elizabeth Shapiro Worthington was. For an instant he debated making a simple public relations call to a couple of the key tabloids. Then he decided it would be more fun to watch them scramble to find it.

He'd announce his marriage first to his Facebook and Twitter circles. Not long after that, it would leak to the paparazzi. Elizabeth would be stalked for a while when she was in New

York. Thankfully, with the type of work she did, tracking her in remote locales would prove to be difficult.

That was fine with Sean. He was ready to take breaks from the media spotlight. Once Sarah's campaign was completed, he planned on accompanying Elizabeth on many of her research trips. What he did for Worthington Shares would easily work hand in hand with locales that Elizabeth would visit for her work with her father.

He grinned. Elizabeth truly was a perfect match for him in every way.

46

Drew entered Will's office and quietly laid his tablet on Will's desk. A tabloid news story adorned the screen. Sean's cocky smile beamed back in a grainy picture. One inset photo showed the taillights of his disappearing Jeep. Another featured a blowup of Sean's hand, with his wedding ring circled in red and an arrow pointing to it.

Will rolled his eyes. "At least we know they're home."

"With fanfare. Sean's usual style." Drew chuckled. "I told him coming home in the Jeep wouldn't throw the paparazzi off for long. Have you heard from him yet?"

"No, but you know Sean. He'll contact me when he's ready, and not before. At least he's been forewarned."

"There's something else you need to see." Drew scrolled to another page of the tabloid.

Will squinted at the page. Victoria Rich, Thomas's wife, was pictured strolling hand in hand with her lover in front of a series of quaint boutiques. The article stated that divorce proceedings with Thomas Rich were under way.

Sadness swept over Will. So Sean's birth father was now experiencing the other side of his marital infidelity. Will thought of the paths the three friends chose out of university and how each step they took had impacted their lives.

"Do the right thing," Will said softly. "Dad's mantra. And he did, even when it was hard. Even when it seemed impossible."

"Yes. Bill is a good, honorable man." Drew leaned over Will's desk. "So is Thomas Rich. But even good, honorable men aren't perfect. We all fail. But it's what happens after each failure—who we listen to and how we choose to go on—that makes the difference."

And there it was again—Drew's clarifying wisdom that helped Will stay on the right path. All those years ago, when Bill was constantly on the road for business, he had known how much Will would someday need a good, honorable man like Drew by his side. Bill had chosen his right-hand man carefully—someone whose life philosophy matched his own. For over three decades, Drew Simons not only had served the Worthingtons in various capacities but had become family, as loyal and protective as if he had been born into the Worthington family himself.

Will looked up at Drew. "Thank you."

Two small words that would never be enough.

But the smile in Drew's eyes said he understood the volumes of expression behind the scarce words.

While Elizabeth soaked in the tub—a rarity for her when she spent so much time on board ship—Sean attacked his electronic in-box. It was cluttered with well-wishers who had already spotted the tabloid stories. His mom and dad weren't texters and had left him alone. Sarah had sent him multiple texts, as usual.

There was only one from Will. He checked that one first, since

Will would never interrupt his honeymoon with any contact unless doing so was critical.

> Sarah knows about Thomas. But not about you.

Sean sat back on the sofa. Life had just gone from tropical paradise to extremely complicated.

Sarah exhaled in frustration. Leave it to Sean to be enigmatic about when exactly he was getting home from his honeymoon. But she had been sure she'd know as soon as he was, because he'd check his texts first. And of course he'd respond to his sister right away.

She had held back, starting with sending only nice little messages:

> Welcome back to reality.

> Call me when you get a chance. There's something I'd like to ask you.

They had progressed to just:

> Call me. We need to talk.

However, after seeing the tabloid stories, she knew he was home and likely ignoring her.

Now she'd resorted to toe tapping. Will had said all he was going to, so she had determined to pry any other information out of Sean, who could usually be wheedled for details more easily. Jon was still silent, and her parents were in Australia. Sarah felt out of the loop, and she didn't like it.

Once again, she was the baby of the family, the one no one took seriously. The one they wanted to protect from any emotional upheaval. Will had always had their father's respect and backing. But she couldn't pinpoint the reason for the change in Sean and Bill's relationship, and that bothered her tremendously.

Or perhaps what bothered her most was that, in spite of everything she'd done in her career, she couldn't achieve what she longed for most—her father's respect. Yes, he'd given his nod at last to her entering the presidential race and had extended his full support to her in regard to finances and his personal and corporate network. But did he really believe at his core that she could handle such a big job?

Asking the question, she knew, was in many ways ludicrous. She was in her midthirties, for heaven's sake. Why did she still crave her father's approval?

Nevertheless, the ache was there.

47

Sean looked up as Elizabeth padded barefoot into the living room. She was wearing one of his shirts. They had yet to move any of her possessions, other than the light honeymoon bag she'd traveled with and the few clothes they'd purchased in the Maldives. But neither of them was in any hurry to do so. They'd keep Sean's place in New York and also find a flat in Seattle, close to the university and Elizabeth's work. Until then, when they were in Washington, they'd stay with Elizabeth's father.

She gestured around the stark living room. "This has got to change. Not homey at all. Who decorated it anyway?"

He winced. "A high-end decorator who came with good recommendations."

Elizabeth lifted a brow. "Uh-huh. And you fell for that, did you? There's absolutely nothing feminine about this place."

"That's where you're wrong." He reached for her. "Now you're in it. And you're the best décor of all."

Finally, the penthouse wasn't just a place for him to land. It was home.

A SECURE LOCATION

The real forces trying to take the Worthingtons down had been known to the contact for a long time. With the backing of the powerful man and his own growing, trusted network, he acted as the hub of information. In a game that had become more high stakes and dangerous every day, only he knew exactly where each chess piece was likely to move. He and the man had agreed on that stipulation from the beginning, as a protection for everyone involved.

Most of the time, he succeeded in removing the threat toward the Worthingtons before it surfaced. But sometimes even he was surprised by the height and depth of the depravity that was revealed.

He'd known about Spencer Rich's tirade in the White House after hearing that Will was running for Senate. Will was too dangerous as a player in the Senate. Irritating New York senator James Loughlin in running against him was only a small thing compared to the shoo-in Will would be as the top Democrat candidate in the presidential race. With Spencer Rich's ratings down and Will Worthington shining like a star after the AF fiasco, there would have been no contest.

Stapleton had been around the block a long time as the GOP kingmaker. He had a big stake in Spencer Rich's reelection, far more than the American public would likely know. On top of that, his goal as chairman of American Frontier's board was to see that the company continued to rake in money for the shareholders, even if that meant short-circuiting critical research parameters. When Will pushed the AF board to stay out of the Arctic, Stapleton began greasing a few palms on the AF board to back Sandstrom and counter Will.

Spencer Rich and Stapleton had agreed between them that

Will Worthington had to go down. The only question was when.

Sean was known for his public statements against Spencer Rich's tirades and his inept administration. For Frank Stapleton, that meant walking a constant tightrope between remaining friendly with Will to stay in the Worthingtons' good graces and make the AF board run smoothly, and dealing behind the scenes to sidetrack the Worthingtons in order to keep the American president happy. Stapleton had been playing both sides for years. As Will's early mentor in business, Stapleton had thought he could swing another bright star his way. Instead, the bright star had gone his own way.

Then Sarah had popped up as an additional irritant. She was, in President Rich's and Stapleton's eyes, a crusader who still believed in good and evil. She couldn't be bought. After the Arctic fiasco, she determined not only to take down Sandstrom and set things right, but to take things all the way in finding out what had really happened with the Polar Bear Bomber.

It was no wonder that all three Worthington siblings had come into the gun sights of the White House and Frank Stapleton.

Senator James Loughlin meant nothing. He was a pompous old windbag who would soon be voted out of office or have a heart attack during one of his petty tirades.

Jason Carson was simply a pawn who moved any direction the highest bidder ordered him to. First it was Sandstrom, until Carson saw the writing on the wall and made a play for presidential protection. That move had worked temporarily. Sandstrom went to prison and Carson got his stay-out-of-jail card. It would have been better for Carson if he had disappeared after that. But his ego and greed had overwhelmed his common sense. He'd gone to Stapleton, demanding a large monthly addition to his salary from American Frontier for his "additional services."

American Frontier had that day increased Carson's stipend for "exemplary service, going beyond the call of duty in trying times."

But that day Stapleton had also set up Carson for a hard fall. When they'd signed the agreement Stapleton had drafted, Stapleton had waved off Carson returning the pen.

"Keep it. My gift to you," Stapleton had said magnanimously.

So Carson had walked away, congratulating himself and carrying the pen that was now the reason he was secreted away by the FBI and DHS.

The contact smiled. It was indeed satisfying when a plan came together. And soon Darcy Wiggins at DHS would receive a surprise package—video footage of Sean Worthington and Justin Eliot's meeting at the bar, with Jason Carson's fingerprints all over it.

The copy Carson had made to protect himself would lead to his downfall.

Sometimes you had to catch the small fish to use them as bait to catch the much bigger ones.

NEW YORK CITY

Sean still hadn't called his brother or his sister. He knew he was delaying the inevitable as he flipped through the stack of mail. Then he spotted the package that Thomas had given him the day they'd met in person. He held it for five minutes, turning it over and over. He lacked the courage to open it.

Elizabeth stepped back into the living room after scouting out the ingredients in their fridge. "I was thinking mac and cheese—" She eyed his expression. "Is that the package from Thomas?"

He nodded.

"Then it's time to open it." She perched on the edge of his large chair.

"But—" His protests were pointless. He knew she would get her way.

She rubbed his shoulder. "It's okay, Sean. Whatever it is, or says. You need to know."

He sighed, then eased open the package. The first object he drew out was wrapped in tissue paper.

Elizabeth nudged him gently. "Go ahead."

The object he unwrapped gingerly was a white baby shoe, scuffed on the toes from a child's learning to walk. Turning the shoe over, he traced the delicate lettering that said "Thomas" and, beneath it, "of Love."

"Oh, Sean," Elizabeth whispered.

They both looked toward the bookshelf, where another white baby shoe rested. Elizabeth got up and retrieved it. "Look." She placed the two shoes next to each other. "A perfect match."

Sean reached for them and turned them over. He held them together and read the message across the back of the shoes. "To Sean Thomas. A Gift of Love."

"The missing shoe," Elizabeth breathed. "Thomas must have had it all this time."

Sean nodded. "But how did he get it?" He stared at it.

His mother never said she had been in contact with Thomas through the years. But she never said she hadn't either. When she'd given Sean one of the baby shoes, all she'd said about the other was, "I no longer have the other shoe. I wish I did." He would have to give that angle some more thought.

"What else is in the package?" Elizabeth asked, propelling him out of his reverie.

The next item was a tiny white shirt, embroidered with distinctive purple and pink flowers. He passed the shirt to Elizabeth.

She studied the soft fabric. "Those are fuchsias."

He nodded. "They grow wild along the roadsides in Ireland, near my mother's family's castle. I don't remember wearing this shirt, but I have seen a picture of me as a baby in it somewhere."

A third item was a photo of a happy red-haired baby, revealing one tooth and clapping his hands.

"A chubby little guy. I never would have guessed," Elizabeth teased.

There was one more item in the package. He breathed deeply before he opened it. It was an expensive, handmade leather journal that appeared to have weathered decades. Sean opened the first page, and his hand started to shake.

Elizabeth read the title of the page aloud. "The Story of My Son, Sean Thomas." She flipped to the next page and read, "Today I discovered that I have a son—you, Sean Thomas. It has to be true because you look like me, and your mother gave you not only an Irish name, for our shared heritage, but my first name for your middle name."

Sean held up his hand. In a broken voice, he managed, "What else is in the journal?"

She took it from his hands and flipped through it for a few minutes. "His thoughts about your mother, pictures of you growing up and from all around the globe on your travels, articles about you starting NGOs . . ."

He took a shaky breath. "No more for now. I need to make a phone call."

She hugged him. "I understand."

48

Sarah walked away from the set of *The View*, satisfied with her talk show performance. The hosts had been friendly and clearly were in her court politically. Her campaign team was already giving her a thumbs-up in the greenroom. Within minutes of the show concluding, her public rating had already increased by several percent. It would likely jump 3 to 5 percent more, just as it had done when she was on *The Tonight Show*. Sarah was the fresh voice in politics and the confident change agent that the American public, tired of bureaucratic and unapproachable men in their fifties and sixties, craved.

Though the media was clearly following her with nearly all positive feedback, she'd be glad when Sean was back. She counted on him to filter key information and strategize the next moves of her campaign.

Thinking of Sean, she frowned. He still hadn't called or shot a text back. Good thing they had strategized early to keep a couple of days clear for her in her schedule and to allow him time to settle back in after his honeymoon.

However, they needed to talk, and soon.

Sean called Thomas. "I opened the package," he said. "I had no idea. All these years . . ."

"Yes," Thomas answered in a gravelly voice. "I was following you."

"So you knew, somehow." Sean paused. "I haven't read the journal, but . . . when are you coming to town next?"

"Whenever you say, and as fast as you say."

"Then today."

"All right. I'll be there."

"This time I want you to come to my place . . . our place. Elizabeth's and mine."

"I'll give you an ETA as soon as I land."

Sean's hand was shaking slightly when he ended the call. Thomas hadn't even asked where Sean lived. Clearly, he already knew. As crazy as it seemed, though, that didn't disturb Sean.

Elizabeth covered his hand with both of hers. "So he's coming?"

Sean nodded. "Today."

"Good." Then she chuckled. "What exactly do you feed a former president of the United States?"

He smiled at her. "The same thing we were going to eat. Homemade macaroni and cheese."

It was one of the best dishes Elizabeth made. Her father's favorite, it had become one of Sean's favorites too. Sean's housekeeper had stocked the fridge and pantry with the simple ingredients, upon his request.

A SECURE LOCATION

The call from the man was short. "I'll be in New York City for a day or so," he said in his gravelly voice.

"Understood." A pause, then he asked, "Sean?"

"Yes."

The ball had been in Sean's court. So, he had finally called.

What the outcome would be, he didn't know. But he had learned long ago to trust both in the man's patience for accomplishing results and in Sean Worthington's integrity.

Both were used to being in the line of fire.

Father and son were much more alike than even they guessed.

49

Sarah was back in her penthouse by early afternoon. Finally, she had the opportunity to call Sean again. This time he picked up.

His greeting didn't sound like his usual nonchalant self, but she didn't linger long on that thought. She didn't even ask about his and Elizabeth's trip.

"Sean, why didn't you tell me?" she demanded.

"Tell you what? And what's with the full frontal assault before you even say hi?"

"That Mom had an affair?" She heard what sounded like the phone dropping on his side. "Hey, are you still there?"

"Still here," he answered in a tone that sounded like Will's steely one. "Could we have this conversation another time, maybe in person?"

"You knew and you didn't tell me," she accused. "Even more, Thomas was at your wedding. If you knew, how could you let Mom invite him to a *family* event?"

"No, sis, Mom didn't invite him. I did."

"I don't understand. Why would you—"

"Because he's my birth father."

The air around her suddenly turned arctic. Her world stilled as if it were on pause.

Sean's "Hello? Hello?" dimmed into the background. Suddenly the clues shifted into a complete picture. All made sense.

Sean's disappearance, never explained. He must have fled after he found out the truth.

Her mother's distress and remoteness.

The change in her father—both with Sean and with Ava. His aged appearance.

Thomas suddenly showing up at a family event after all these years.

Her parents' second honeymoon trip.

So her mother's secret had been revealed to Will, Sean, and Bill, but she hadn't trusted her own daughter. The baby of the family never would grow up in their eyes, would she?

As tears clouded her eyes, she grabbed her purse and slipped out the door.

There was only one place she could go.

To Chautauqua.

Sean should have known better than to answer his sister's call before he talked to Will to get any details of what she knew. Will would be patient and await his call. His sister, on the other hand, always demanded an immediate response. He'd picked up her call from simple habit.

Now he did what he should have done first. He phoned Will. "Talked to Sarah, and it didn't go so well. Maybe you or Laura could call her after a while."

"How much did you tell her?"

"That Thomas is my birth father."

"So she knows the whole enchilada," Will said flatly.

"I didn't have the opportunity to say more than that. The line went silent on her end. But she knew about Mom's affair, so I'm certain she's now put together the rest of the pieces." Sean sighed. "Wish I could head over to her place right now, but that's not possible. I have a visitor arriving any moment."

"Visitor?" Will asked. "More important than what's going on with Sarah right now?"

"It's Thomas. He's on his way. I asked him to come."

Will cleared his throat. "I see. Looks like things are heating up for our family. Okay, I'll handle Sarah. You've got your hands full."

At this moment, he missed Laura even more.

CHAUTAUQUA INSTITUTION

Sarah's anger overshadowed her exhaustion by the time she reached Chautauqua. With her parents both in Australia, their home was empty. That was a good thing. She needed time to process, to get her emotions under control. Once in her bedroom, she donned an old T-shirt, hoodie, and sweats—comfort wear.

Her phone beeped again. She scrolled through the long list of calls from Sean, Will, and Laura. She'd ignored them the entire drive. Thankfully, she was on her agreed-upon break from campaign responsibilities to allow Sean a window upon his return, so she didn't have to respond to any texts immediately.

At that moment she saw a single text from Jon. She frowned. He had to know about Thomas. Jon was Sean's best friend. Was this what Jon had been trying to tell her when she cut him off and ordered him out of her penthouse? Had he stayed silent up until then because Sean had asked him to?

She called Jon. "You know, don't you?" she fired at him as soon as he picked up.

"Know what?" he said in his maddeningly calm manner.

"About Sean. Where he came from?"

Jon chuckled. "You mean from the moon?"

"That's not funny. No, that he came from—my mom's affair."

"Your mom and Thomas." Jon clicked into reporter mode. "Is that what you mean?"

"So you knew and you didn't tell me?"

"No, I didn't know, but I started to guess when I saw Thomas at the wedding. I had already received an anonymous tip at the news desk about your mother having an affair. So that was in the back of my mind. When Sean and Thomas were standing next to each other on the boat, they looked so much alike. With their shared middle name and the timing of the affair . . ."

"How could I have missed that? I'm an attorney, for heaven's sake," she said in a choked voice.

"So that's why he disappeared. Why he went dark," Jon reasoned aloud. "He had to think things through. His whole world got turned upside down."

"Oh." For the first time, Sarah realized the pain Sean must have gone through. Sorrow flooded over her. Her anger dissipated. "Jon, I really hammered him. And you. You tried to tell me about the affair, and I—"

"You didn't know," he said. "By the way, where are you?"

"Chautauqua." Unshed tears clogged her throat. "I need to go."

"No, you don't."

She hung up.

Creeping into her mother's green room, she sank onto the floor, hugging her knees.

"Why didn't you tell me, Mom?" she whispered.

Then the tears descended.

50

Sean's cell rang. It was Jon. He picked up immediately.

"Just talked to Sarah," Jon said.

"Is she all right?" Sean asked.

"I know about Thomas, and who he is to you. I've been putting together the pieces for a while now. We can talk about that later. Right now my concern is Sarah. She's at Chautauqua."

Sean blew out a breath. "Thank God. Then she's safe."

"Physically, yes. Emotionally, no. I'm on my way. Pushing the speed limit to get there as fast as possible."

"So she knows you're coming?"

"No, she hung up on me."

Sean sighed. "That sounds like my sister."

"But I'm still going. You know I love her, right?"

"Yes, I know." Sean couldn't resist adding, "As much as you tried to waffle on the subject."

"And you're good with it?"

"Couldn't be better."

"Then give me the code to the front door in case she won't let me in."

Sean laughed. "You got it."

Will sat in his living room, massaging the tension out of his neck. He hadn't been able to reach Sarah. He'd made a quick trip to her penthouse, but she wasn't there. The doorman said she'd asked for her car to be brought and had left with just her purse hours earlier. So where was she?

Will's cell rang. "Oh, Elizabeth. Have you—"

"She's at the summer house," Elizabeth declared. "Sean's talking with Thomas, but I wanted to let you know."

Will scowled. "She drove all the way there in that condition? What is she think—"

"Don't worry. She got there safely, and Jon's on his way."

"Jon?"

"Yes, Jon." There was a smile in Elizabeth's voice.

"I see," was all Will said before he hung up.

He shook his head. If Laura were there, he knew what she'd be doing. She'd be looking at him, hands on her hips, with a bemused expression that said, "Back off, buster. They've got things to discuss. More than just Sean."

Will knew better than to step into any womanly territory, especially with the Worthington women. Even if Laura was a world away in Malawi.

Thomas sat with Elizabeth and Sean at their dining room table for a belated dinner. "This is delicious," he said, savoring the last spoonful of Elizabeth's macaroni and cheese.

"Simple," Elizabeth replied, "but we love it."

It amazed Sean how comfortable Elizabeth was talking with a man who had just entered their lives and was the ex-president of the United States. Her relational ease and unpretentious ways had smoothed any tension. Sean was grateful.

"And now I owe you a story," Thomas said. "One long overdue." He looked at Sean. "But only if you want to hear it."

Elizabeth reached for Sean's hand and squeezed it.

"We both do," Sean replied.

"From the instant Ava and I met in college, we had a special connection. We quickly became good friends. Bill was a sophomore when we three had a class together. We hit it off and forged a friendship over three years of university, slogging it out over difficult subjects. Bill graduated a year earlier than Ava and me and plunged into work at Worthington Shares. But before he left, he asked Ava to marry him after she graduated. She was stunned, starstruck that someone like Bill wanted to marry her."

Thomas took a sip from his water glass. "Ava had no idea how much I cared for her. Our senior year, the two of us spent even more time together. She was lonely, missing Bill, who rarely visited. I told her he was just busy setting up a career. I came up with all kinds of excuses for his seeming lack of attention. I truly wanted the best for both of my friends, and I assumed that best meant each other. Still, I couldn't help my feelings. I loved and respected Ava. She was the only one who saw the potential in me. I chafed against regulations and what people told me I had to do, and dreamed of influencing the world in my own way."

Elizabeth smiled at Sean. "Sounds like somebody else I know."

Thomas went on. "It's because of Ava that I changed my path from law to politics and the presidential race. She believed in me—the immature boy I was then, and the man I could become. We graduated but kept in close contact. I was best man at their wedding. I flew in to town to see Will the day he was born. When I saw the love and joy in Ava's eyes as she held her baby and realized how I still felt about her, I knew I had to step away. I had to build my own life, separate from her and Bill.

"So I tried. I dated several eligible women. Because Victoria had the kind of breeding that made my mother happy, I married her. Life settled into a routine when my political career took off. Then I became president, and my moments were filled with different matters."

Thomas sighed. "Then one day I received a call from Bill. He said he and Ava missed seeing me and wondered if we could get together while our boys were still little. Victoria, Spencer, and I were heading soon for Camp David, so I invited Bill, Ava, and Will to come for a short vacation. We all looked forward to catching up."

Thomas cleared his throat. "I never intended for events to happen the way they did that night. But Bill had only been there a few hours when he received a business phone call. He said it was urgent and he needed to leave. I saw the hurt in Ava's eyes, and it reminded me of the pain she'd suffered from his lack of attention during university. Later that day Victoria decided she'd had enough of 'camping,' as she called it, and demanded that we leave immediately. I refused and said we had guests. I pleaded with her to stay for just a few days, at least until they were gone. But she left an hour later, taking Spencer with her and two of our Secret Service detail.

"When Victoria left in a huff, Ava looked at me and said, 'The only way to solve any of this is to breathe deeply and have a glass of wine.' We both laughed, and it broke the tension." Thomas smiled. "That was the best afternoon and evening I could remember since college. We walked comfortably around

Camp David, like we used to as friends at university, and caught up on the years in between. We both were lonely. Bill traveled a lot and seemed distracted when he was home. I knew that Victoria would not stay in our marriage once she was no longer first lady. The only things holding us together were Spencer and her desire for position."

Thomas shook his head, and his expression filled with regret. "Victoria ruined him. Made every wish come true. Gave him no boundaries. Raised his expectations until he became a spoiled bully, focused on himself. The power and status he gained as he climbed quickly in political circles made him even more of one. The worst thing is, I helped him get there." Thomas waved a hand. "But that is a story for another time."

"Would you like some coffee?" Elizabeth offered. "I've got some brewing, and I might be able to find some dessert in the freezer. We haven't been home long, so no grocery runs yet."

"Coffee sounds wonderful. No dessert, though. My waist-line has expanded enough over the years," Thomas replied, patting it.

51

"Sarah knows," Will informed Drew late that evening. "It wasn't the way any of us wanted her to find out, but it's a done deal."

"Is she okay?" Drew asked.

"Not yet, but she will be. Jon's already partway to Chautauqua to meet her."

"I see," Drew said. "Then she will be all right."

"You said the secrets would be revealed sometime. Now they are."

"And you're caught between being troubled and being relieved?" Drew asked.

"Yes. I can't help wondering how Mom and Dad, and Sarah, and Sean, are dealing with the secrets."

"Your parents are handling the news about the photos well. Bill said he told Ava, and she was furious someone was playing with the Worthington family like that."

Will pictured his mother's range of expressions when hearing that news. No one would want to go a round with Ava Worthington when she was in her protect-my-family mode. He and his mother were very similar in that way.

"On top of that, Thomas just flew in to meet with Sean and Elizabeth," Will added.

"Ah. No wonder you called. You've got a lot on your mind."

"Indeed."

"Will, there's nothing easy about any of these situations." Drew paused. "But easy isn't the route of a Worthington. Over the years you've faced numerous hurdles as you've each pursued your destinies. Your relationships with each other, forged by those hot fires, have strong, unbreakable bonds. The only things separating you—those secrets—are now on the table for all of you to examine. They've lost their power over you."

Will sighed. "As usual, you're right."

Drew laughed. "Of course I am. Just ask anyone except my wife. Because she's always right."

"Our wives share that in common," Will quipped back. "Mine's always right too."

They ended the call on that note.

Later, Laura interrupted his reverie with a Skype call. After he filled her in on the day's happenings thus far, she nodded. "That's why you're quieter than usual. You thinking about Sarah? Sean?"

He nodded back. "Yeah. Can't help that protective big brother urge. I just hate seeing either of them get hurt."

"You hate more that you can't do anything about it when they do," she added. "But that's life, Will. Good and bad come. You can't control everything about your own path or anyone else's. That's where faith comes in."

"Agreed." He shrugged. "Doesn't mean it's easy, though. I can handle the tough things when they happen to me, but when they happen to someone I love, that's another matter entirely."

She smiled. "In the business world, you're a force to be reckoned with. But deep inside, you're a softie. Don't worry, tough guy. Your secret is safe with me."

With those words, his burden became bearable.

Sean, Elizabeth, and Thomas cradled cups of steaming coffee with a dash of Kahlúa.

Thomas took a sip. "Wow, this is even better than dessert."

Elizabeth grinned. "Another of Sean's favorites. You two share a lot in common."

"I hope we can find out more about that," Thomas said. "Now, to continue with the most difficult part of the story." He looked purposefully at Sean. "You can stop me anytime you don't feel comfortable."

Sean gave a nod.

"That night at Camp David, after we'd tucked Will into bed, we opened another bottle of wine and reminisced over our meaningful senior year. As I looked into the eyes of the woman I had loved for years, my resolve crumbled. I told her what I'd longed to—how much I loved her and still loved her."

Sean flinched.

Elizabeth asked gently, "What did Ava say?"

Thomas's eyes misted. "She asked, 'Why didn't you tell me back then?' I told her I respected her and Bill too much. And that she had chosen him. I couldn't hurt either of my friends that way. 'But you didn't give me a choice,' she said, and started crying. I never could stand seeing her in pain. That moment was my undoing. Loneliness and pain washed over me. I took her in my arms and held her." He blinked as if to clear the memory. "I'll never forget the warmth and intensity of that love I'd desired for so long. Nor can I forgive myself for what happened next. I betrayed my two best friends in a time of weakness."

Sean held up a hand. "Those intimate details I don't want to know."

"The next morning Ava and Will left Camp David while I was in an early teleconference. Only her note remained in the room where she had stayed. I read it so many times, I still have it memorized." Thomas closed his eyes and quoted:

Thomas, my friend,
I loved you then, and I love you now. That hasn't changed.
Thank you for the reminder that we mattered back then,
and that I matter now.
But we can't turn back time, nor can we alter the course of
relationships set long ago. We have chosen different paths.
I must do what I know to be right. I must leave you
and return to Bill. He is my family, and the one who holds
my heart.

Ava

Sean closed his eyes. He'd heard what he needed to hear, as hard as it was. His mother had always loved Bill. Her heart wasn't torn between the two men then or now. But needing a reminder that she mattered told Sean volumes about the difficulty of her life at that time.

He felt a warm pressure on his hand and opened his eyes. Elizabeth's gaze was tender. She knew the confirmation he'd needed.

Thomas continued brokenly. "I wanted to call her, to beg her to come back, but I knew that would never happen. She had given her heart to Bill, and the woman I knew would never take it back."

CHAUTAUQUA INSTITUTION

As Sarah sat in her mother's green room, she recalled the day Ava had given her the heritage ring reserved for her. Sarah had wondered then about the timing. Laura had received a ring from Ava after she and Will were engaged. Sean had received a ring to give Elizabeth when he was making plans to propose. But Ava had given Sarah her heritage ring with no sign of a man in her life.

Sarah blinked. Was it because her mother had given up on her, still unmarried in her midthirties? Or something else?

Sarah recalled her mother's words: *"I want you to know how much I love you. How much your father loves you. You always have been, and will be, our princess. I hope the ring will be a reminder of that when you need it most."*

With Sarah's penchant for exact recall, she remembered her mother's face—the sadness, the regret.

So her mother had known this time was coming, and how much Sarah would need that precious tourmaline ring.

In the evening's darkness in the green room, Sarah couldn't see the heirloom she wore on her right index finger. But she felt its presence. The gem was indeed a reminder of her parents' love when she needed it most.

She simply needed to find her way out of the darkness back into the light.

52

NEW YORK CITY

"When did you know about me?" Sean asked. "Did she tell you?"

Thomas shook his head. "No, I didn't see Ava or talk with her after she left Camp David. I read about your birth in the society section of the *New York Times*. When I saw your picture, I knew. You had to be my son. Your baby picture had similarities to mine. And Ava had shared with me how much she longed for another child after Will but was unable to conceive. Her calling you 'Sean Thomas' confirmed my gut feeling. I somehow guessed it was her way of giving you a piece of our shared Irish heritage, and a bit of the father you would likely never know."

"Did you try to contact her after that?" Elizabeth asked.

"Yes. I tried. But she wouldn't respond." Thomas's eyes pleaded with Sean. "I will never be sorry for giving Ava what she wanted most—a child. That child of her heart and my heart was you. You were created out of an intense love between two best friends. For yours, Bill's, and Ava's sakes, though, my love had to be at a distance. I tried three times, out of desperation, to cross that line."

Sean tilted his head in question.

"The first was after I saw your baby picture in the paper. The second time, I watched from a boat on Lake Chautauqua as you, Bill, and Ava reunited after you'd realized the truth, fled, and then returned. In that moment, I understood the depth of Bill and Ava's love for you and the strength of the Worthington family. The third and last time, I phoned Ava at Chautauqua before your wedding."

Sean stiffened, and Elizabeth reached out a cautioning hand.

"But I will never cross that line again," Thomas assured Sean. "You need to know that Ava has never wavered from the words in her note to me—that her love would remain with Bill, the man she chose. The man who became your father."

Thomas tightened his trembling hands around his coffee cup. "Bill has shaped you into the man I wish I had been at your age. He's been more of a father to you than I could ever have been. Look at Spencer. Look at you. A vast gulf divides the two of you. Ava, in her wisdom, knew she had to protect you from my mistakes. Knew Bill was the steadier, better man. She was right. So she held the secret all these years. I didn't try to see her or you as you were growing up. I stayed away until she decided that it was time for you to know."

"But you still followed me," Sean said.

"Yes. All those years. You and your siblings. I saw the way Bill and Ava raised the three of you to do what's right, to stand your ground. To care about, help, and defend those with few resources." Thomas paused. "Sean, I'm so proud of you. So many times you could have caved under the pressure and temptations of being in the spotlight. But you never did."

Sean's mind flicked back to the night he'd been tempted. If it hadn't been for the voice calling him to stay on the right path, how easily he could have fallen—like his mother, like Thomas. Instead, he had entered his marriage with no regrets.

"No, I never did," Sean said.

"You are like Bill, even more than you think," Thomas explained. "Honorable men. Bill even shook my hand at your wedding, as hard as it must have been for him."

In that instant Sean realized how much he had underestimated his father—perhaps both his fathers.

"Someday," Thomas continued, "I will find a way to repay him. Nothing I could do will ever be enough, but I need to try. One action—my action—changed history. It altered the trajectory of all our lives. But it also brought you into this world."

"And without that, I wouldn't have you," Elizabeth told Sean. She got up from the table and circled behind Thomas. Then, without warning, she enveloped the ex-president of the United States in a hug. "Thank you for that gift, Thomas." She dropped a kiss on the top of his head.

CHAUTAUQUA INSTITUTION

Sarah had no idea what time it was—the middle of the night?—but a slight noise alerted her to look up from where she still sat on the floor of the green room. There, framed in the entry to the dark room, was a shadowy male figure. It moved slowly toward her.

"Sarah?" a quiet voice said.

Jon.

He stepped closer until she could see him clearly. Wearing rumpled light khakis and a wrinkled shirt, he gazed down at her.

An instant later, he was sitting on the floor beside her. His arm circled her and drew her closer until her head rested against his shoulder.

Then he simply held her while she cried.

A Secure Location

"We were able to secure the item," he told the man.

"So we have the extra leverage we need?" the man demanded.

"Yes, if it comes to that."

"And it contains the information we thought it did?"

"That, as well as direct links to the parties involved."

They would know shortly if they would have to play that highest card in their deck.

53

CHAUTAUQUA INSTITUTION

Sarah woke to bright sunlight late the next morning. Sensing a presence close to her, she opened one eye. She was lying on the sofa in the green room, her mother's favorite afghan over her. Jon was fast asleep with her across his lap, his arms still cradling her protectively.

She remembered talking long into the night, sorting out the details with Jon's help. His words had soothed her aching heart. "Sarah, they only wanted to protect you."

Finally, she had fallen asleep, exhausted, on the floor. He must have carried her to the couch.

Even after she'd basically thrown him out of her life twice, he hadn't left her side for long. He'd merely given her the respectful distance she'd asked for. Then, when she needed him most but hadn't known that herself, he had shown up.

She gazed up at him, his head tilted toward her as if still watching over her in sleep. Why hadn't she admitted it to herself before now? Jon was the most fascinating, intelligent, and loyal man Sarah knew. He didn't even orbit the same planet as the TV producer she'd dated, who was only about himself.

After she'd unleashed her anger and grief on Jon, he still moved closer to her. Not only that, he stayed. He had been straightforward and honest with her always. Darcy was right. Jon was a keeper. And, Sarah suddenly realized, their relationship was more than a deep friendship.

But did she love Jon? The kind of love that wanted only the best for him? That could sacrifice anything for him and weather any storm? She'd thought her parents had that kind of love until her mother's affair had surfaced.

Could I myself fall into an affair, given similar circumstances? The possibility nearly paralyzed her.

Then a memory stirred—or was it merely wishful thinking? During her exhausted sleep, a whisper had edged into her consciousness. "Sarah, I love you." She'd felt the gentle caress of a kiss on her cheek.

Her heart fluttered strangely. Had she finally found her true north? The person she wanted by her side for life? Like Will had found Laura, and Sean, Elizabeth?

At that moment, Jon slowly opened his eyes. The tenderness she saw in their blue depths both unsettled and calmed her.

NEW YORK CITY

Sean still felt groggy, even after a double shot of espresso. Thomas Rich had taken his leave late the previous night, though Elizabeth had kindly offered the use of their second bedroom. Sean's body ached from the intensity of the conversation with his birth father. Elizabeth hadn't pushed him for his thoughts. She had simply let him be until midmorning, when she'd brought him his first espresso.

His gaze lingered on Thomas's leather journal on the table.

He liked the plan he and Elizabeth had just discussed—to read it together, even a page at a time. Sean needed her insight. He couldn't think of anyone he trusted more to walk through this most personal book and its revelations.

This morning he'd asked her to read the first page to him. But he'd stopped her after just a few words. The emotion of reading how Thomas felt when he'd discovered he'd fathered Sean . . . well, Sean hadn't been able to handle it. He had wept uncontrollably within the safety of Elizabeth's arms. Now he felt exhausted, even with the caffeine.

On his own, he lacked the courage to follow the journal. But with Elizabeth, he could get through it.

Thomas had promised that Sean could ask any questions he wanted. They could meet again, as often as Sean wished, to sort out the answers. There was no pressure. Along the way, the two men would decide what kind of relationship they would have moving forward.

CHAUTAUQUA INSTITUTION

"Since we missed breakfast, I want to take you somewhere special for lunch," Jon said.

Sarah looked up at him, startled. "Like this? I'm a mess."

He swept a hand dramatically over his own wrinkled clothing and rubbed his unshaven chin. "And I'm any better? You're fine just the way you are. You never have to change for me."

"But I still have some pride. Give me a couple minutes and I'll be ready."

She washed her face, put her hair up in a ponytail, and changed her sweats to jeans. "So, where are we going?" she asked as they walked to his car.

Jon smiled. "You'll see."

While he drove, she closed her eyes and rested. She loved that about Jon. He didn't always have to talk. He could simply be with her. It was exactly what she needed right now.

At last she spoke. "I just realized I did the same thing Sean did. I fled. Didn't think about anything or anyone except myself."

He turned toward her. "Yes, you and your brother are more alike than you think. But Sean ran away from everything familiar. You ran *toward* what was familiar. That's a big difference."

It was a signature Jon statement—subtle but clarifying.

"You're right."

Several minutes later, they drew up to a little restaurant called The Springs in Maple Springs. It was almost directly across the lake from her family's home in Chautauqua Institution.

She sighed as soon as she saw it. "I love this place. Their crab cakes are homemade—to die for."

"I know. You told me a long time ago that this was your all-time favorite restaurant."

"And you remembered."

He winked. "Of course."

They entered to the tantalizing aroma of sizzling burgers and slid into a corner table.

Her father might love the Athenaeum, but this was Sarah's favorite—the kind of place where you could get a great burger with cheese for $6.95, and dinners for $10.95. Where the owner of the place went from table to table and talked with his customers. It was a place where she wasn't a Worthington. She was just Sarah.

They both ordered burgers with the full works, and crab cakes. Sarah was surprised how hungry she was as they awaited their food. When Jon excused himself for a moment to go out to his car, she was curious. But he didn't explain.

When the crab cakes arrived, Jon grinned. He took a birthday candle out of his shirt pocket, stuck it in one of the crab cakes, and then pulled out a small lighter. "Voilà—a candlelit lunch."

It was beautiful—a reminder of the simpler side of life.

"How on earth did you have a birthday candle and a lighter? You don't smoke."

"No, but I keep them both stashed in my car. I always find a way to celebrate my kids' birthdays, and it's often on the spot."

She smiled. The more of his heart he revealed, the more she was hooked.

54

Sean and Elizabeth were munching on pantry offerings for a belated lunch when she gave him a nudge.

"Think you should give your sister a call?"

He sighed. "Yes, but I'm wiped out. I'm not sure I can handle a lot more right now. And Sarah can be . . ."

She nodded. "I understand. But it may be easier than you think."

Sean eyed her. "And why is that?"

She grinned. "Jon's taking the brunt of her frustration on your behalf."

"Yes, that." He chuckled. "Brave guy." He reached for the phone and dialed Sarah's number.

Within the space of seconds, a masculine voice answered her phone.

"Jon?" Sean asked. "Is Sarah all right? I wasn't able—"

"We're working things out," Jon said calmly. "Give her a bit more time, and I'm certain she'll have plenty to say to you. In the meanwhile, don't worry. I'm here for however long I'm needed."

Sean didn't doubt it. With Jon, his sister was in the safest of hands.

Even with the abrupt end of the conversation, Sean breathed easier.

CHAUTAUQUA INSTITUTION

"Thanks for that," Sarah murmured as she and Jon strolled her mother's favorite cobblestone path. "I wasn't quite ready to talk to him. Want to process a bit more before I open my mouth." She didn't miss Jon's smirk and quickly added, "I know I can tend to be a bit spontaneous and—"

"Maybe hotheaded at times?"

"Yes, that." Sarah paused. "I still haven't apologized for hammering you twice, have I?" She looked down, fidgeting.

He clasped one of her hands and turned her toward him. "No need. I really do understand. The past is the past." Jon tugged her to begin walking again. "But as we were saying, those pictures with the Polar Bear Bomber will come to light eventually. No doubt of that. There will always be unscrupulous people who'll use anything to climb the ladder—politically or otherwise."

She lifted her chin. "So we don't let them win. We embrace the truth and tell it boldly at the next press conference."

"And turn it to your favor at a critical point in the election. Imagine, an honest politician." Jon laughed. "With nothing to hide."

She sighed. "Except the parentage of one of her brothers."

"That's something you and your family will have to work out." He frowned. "But I don't think revealing that private matter is the right way to go. Some things should stay private."

"And you think it will stay that way with me running for president? I'm amazed I have a couple of days to myself, with no media tracking me. Good thing too."

"Must be a novel experience for a Worthington." Jon grinned. "By the way, your father was right when he told you siblings it was time for a Worthington to be at the helm of America."

She looked at him in surprise. "You knew about that?"

"Yeah. Sean was pretty ticked when he left that family gathering. I got an earful afterward. But your father was right back then. He just didn't know the one running for president would be his *baby* daughter."

She whacked his arm, then grinned back.

Jon's belief in her meant everything. It gave her wings to fly. She rolled her eyes at herself. Even in her head, that thought sounded so cheesy, like a bad commercial. But it was the truth.

Jon had helped her see the strength of character in both Thomas and Ava. Yes, something had happened between them that was morally wrong. But afterward she had honored her husband, and he had honored his wife, and both had stayed away.

No, neither was perfect. *Neither am I,* Sarah thought ruefully. Her mother, the paragon of virtue and the perfect wife in Sarah's eyes, had fallen from her pedestal. With Jon's help, Sarah saw her mother's loneliness, her desperation to feel loved. She had always known her father was focused on his career, but she'd never considered the high price that had exacted on her mother.

And Bill? When had he discovered the truth about Sean and come to grips with it? Sarah wasn't sure. Yet now he and his wife were on a second honeymoon to Australia. The power of her father's love and his ability to forgive and move ahead had swamped her emotionally earlier that day. Once again, Jon had allowed her to cry it out, with no judgment.

For the first time, her perfect family had revealed their imperfections.

And what have I lost along the way because of my own drivenness in my career? she asked herself. That was a question she could wallow in for some time.

But Jon was right. The past was in the past and couldn't be changed. It was how they chose to handle what happened from here forward that would make the difference.

Her father's warning from long ago edged into her mind. *"Far more events than you could ever imagine are at play here."* Had he been trying back then to tell her to be careful? Because he knew or at least suspected that Sean wasn't his son by blood?

"We need to have a family conference," she announced suddenly to Jon.

He nodded, as if that was a foregone conclusion and he was just waiting for her to arrive at it.

"Drew too," she added. "But he likely knows everything anyway."

Jon squeezed her hand. "That man is a vault for secrets. And he is part of the family."

"We'll get everything out on the table between us. No more secrets. Without secrets, nothing can be held over our heads."

They stopped and sat for a minute on a bench overlooking the water of Lake Chautauqua.

"I refuse to have those photos revealed by surprise during my campaign. So I'm going to cut any potential gossip off at the knees," she determined.

"Sounds like a good plan. You going to run it by your family first?"

"Yes."

"What about Sean and Thomas?" He stared toward the water. "You think Thomas told his wife and son about their connection?"

She frowned. "Somehow I doubt it, with a woman like Victoria. If she knew, she would have used it for leverage. Though it is possible she and Spencer know. However, in my interactions with President Rich, there wasn't even a hint that he had any connections with my family. Of course, I wasn't looking for them then."

"Remember when I got that tip in the newsroom that your mother had had an affair?"

She swiveled toward him. "I never let you explain about that, did I?"

"Not really." He raised his eyes to hers, a twinkle in them. "You were, shall we say, a little combative."

She sighed. "I am sorry about that. So, what did it say?"

"The note was anonymous and addressed only to me. It said something like, 'If you like history and mysteries, try this one: Bill and Ava Worthington visited Camp David when Thomas Rich was president of the United States. Only Ava and Thomas stayed. What does that say to you?'"

Sarah narrowed her eyes in thought. "So it didn't say they had an affair, just largely hinted at it. But no hint toward a baby? Sounds to me like somebody was fishing."

"I agree. Tips are usually addressed to the *Times* in general, or sent multiple times with details to heighten their chances of getting through to someone who might be interested in checking them out. This was sent one time, straight to my attention."

"So whoever it was knows your reputation and your ability to uncover truth," she theorized.

"Possibly. Or the source wanted me to dig and clarify what had happened because they didn't know."

"Only one person makes sense," she mused.

He said it first. "Spencer Rich."

"You're right, because Victoria and Thomas are already settling their divorce. She has nothing else to gain. But Spencer? Maybe he's trying to find out if he has a brother so he has something to hold over his father's head. Or if he confirms his half brother is a Worthington, he'll try to force me out of the Republican race. He's already in so much trouble over the quid pro quo and funds from ISIS for his campaign, he may be grasping at anything to save him."

"Sounds reasonable," Jon agreed.

"Would you go with me to the family conference, Jon?"

He didn't seem surprised. "Anything you want."

"Okay. My parents will return to New York in a few days. I'll call them as soon as they're back. But I'll call Will right away."

New York City

Will was deep in conversation with Drew when he received a call from his sister.

"Sarah. You all right?"

"I am," she said with her usual determination. "But we need to talk. Is Drew there? If so, close your door and put me on speakerphone. He needs to know this too."

Once Will's office was secure, he told her, "Shoot."

He had expected an earful for not telling her the full truth about Sean. Surprisingly, she didn't even mention that. She was calm. He was impressed. Jon clearly had worked wonders in his little sister. Maybe with him in her life . . .

"You're listening to me, aren't you, Will?"

He refocused. "Of course."

"Jon," she directed, "tell Will and Drew about the note."

So, Jon was still there with her. Will and Drew exchanged a bemused glance.

After Jon had filled them in on the contents of the tip he'd received, they all agreed—it had to be Spencer Rich, and he was fishing for information.

"That means it's likely he doesn't know the full truth," Drew reasoned. "He may guess about the affair, but not about Sean."

"Exactly," Will said.

"So we hold our cards to our chest and don't let him see any of our next plays until they happen," Sarah added. "We're all good at that."

"So what's next?" Drew asked.

"After we announce the plans to Mom and Dad and Sean and Elizabeth, and get their agreement, I'll ask Sean to arrange for a press conference."

55

En Route to New York City

Darcy was known to be persistent, but she'd never call three times back to back unless it was important. Sarah phoned her from Jon's car as they drove back to the city. She'd left her car in Chautauqua.

"And just where have you been?" Darcy demanded.

"Later," Sarah answered swiftly. "Just tell me why you called."

"He finally cracked," Darcy announced.

"Carson, you mean?"

"Yep." Darcy seemed jubilant. "Felt the net closing in. Gave us details to show he's a good citizen."

"Don't leave me in suspense."

"It was Stapleton who directed Carson, but Sandstrom clearly agreed with it. However, Carson said Stapleton made it clear, without saying so directly, that he had orders from the highest possible source."

"Meaning, of course, Spencer Rich," Sarah interjected.

Jon raised a brow at the name and threw a questioning glance Sarah's way.

"There was no doubt of that in Carson's mind," Darcy explained. "Justin probably didn't even know he was being filmed. Carson just paid him an extra couple hundred bucks to show up at that certain bar and chat up the guy Carson gave him a picture of. He didn't ask why. He was just happy to have the money."

"Did Carson say how he met Justin?" Sarah asked.

"Yeah, and here's where it starts to get interesting. He says Stapleton told him exactly where to find the kid. Told him to offer Justin a job as a street actor for a day. Carson claims all he did was set up the deal. He told the kid he'd deliver a package to him at a specific time, and Justin met him on the subway to pick up the backpack. From there, he'd go straight to the American Frontier building."

"Did he tell Justin what was in the backpack?"

"No. At first, Carson claimed he didn't know himself." Darcy blew out a breath. "Then, after a little pushing and a nod from his lawyer, Carson said there was a lot of pressure on him coming from all directions—Sandstrom, Stapleton, and indirectly the president. All of those men said the Arctic situation needed to turn around in the media and that Will couldn't be elected, or it could blow their long-term plans of controlling the White House. It was just a little chunk off their building, and it would turn sympathy AF's way. Nobody would get hurt. It wasn't a big deal. So Carson agreed to do it."

"I'm sure it was tough to convince a man of his caliber," Sarah said sarcastically.

"Carson says Stapleton had given him an envelope to pay the kid a few days afterward, when things settled down. Carson told Justin to meet him on the first floor of the building in Times Square. But Carson claimed the kid didn't show. So he waited around until he saw cops arriving, then hightailed it out of there. He tried to reach Justin and then Stapleton but couldn't. He saw on the news that a guy had jumped off the top of the building, put two and two together, and panicked.

"Stapleton finally called Carson back, and they met. Stapleton calmed him down. 'You don't know the kid was the jumper. We'll just try to call him again in a day. Maybe he just got nervous,' he told Carson. He also asked Carson to scribble down the number of the burner cell he'd used with Justin. Then he told him to keep the pen and the envelope of money as a bonus for his work."

"Okay, stop right there," Sarah said. "If Stapleton delivered the backpack and all the goods to Carson, Stapleton would have bought the cell phone. Wouldn't he already have the burner phone number?"

"Ah, I knew you'd catch that." Darcy sounded triumphant. "But when I asked Carson that, he just looked blank. He said, 'Oh, I didn't think of that. Guess I must have been too upset to think straight.'"

"So Stapleton set Carson up to take the fall if anyone connected them with the bomber," Sarah reasoned. "The contacts, the payoffs, the backpack, the envelope of money he kept, his fingerprints on the pen that wrote the suicide note."

"Bingo. And I'm guessing Stapleton didn't take Carson's call right away because he was busy himself—likely entering Michael Vara's apartment and planting the suicide note. When we drew up this likely little scenario, Carson was more than eager to prove his story. Said he kept a backup of the video from the bar in a safe in his apartment and was willing to give it to us." She laughed. "Then he started claiming that he should be in the witness protection program because it wouldn't be safe for him anywhere."

"Bet you walked out after that request, huh?"

"I left him and his attorney to argue over the Cokes and donuts. But we still don't know what led Justin to the roof, much less to jump off it that night. And we still can't identify those fake cops. It's downright aggravating."

"But you will," Sarah said with confidence.

"Oh yes, we will."

A Secure Location

"Finally found one of them," he told the man. "Frederick Simms. The other fled to an unknown destination long ago and isn't likely to come back soon, if ever. Simms was more than willing to talk, once we connected some dots for him."

"Where is he now?"

"Writing up a statement after being asked some rather targeted questions. Then he'll be en route to DHS, with a couple of guys who mean business, to tell his story."

"Ah, to the legendary Ms. Darcy Wiggins?" The man gave a deep chuckle. "Don't envy him being in that interrogation seat."

"Impersonating a NYPD officer is the least of his worries."

"What was his story?" the man asked.

"Said a guy he only knows as 'Mr. F' by phone and has never met approached him about another job."

"So he'd done previous jobs for Stapleton," the man said.

"Looks that way. Stapleton said Simms would get half of the 10 grand up front and half when the job was done. Said he'd need a friend to carry it off. The job was simple. He'd be supplied with two uniforms. All the men had to do was go to the roof of a specific building in Times Square, wait for a call, and then do what they were told. Afterward they only had to keep their mouths shut. Simms says his friend got nervous when he saw the uniforms were NYPD and wanted to back out. He didn't want any trouble. But both needed the payday, so they went to the rooftop. Mr. F called them once they were there to say that their target was on his way to the roof."

"Were they supposed to kill him?"

"No, Stapleton said to detain him. He warned them that the guy was dangerous and needed to be off the streets. They were supposed to take him to a warehouse. Someone else would take it from there."

"But then things didn't go as planned," the man reasoned.

"No. Simms said the kid didn't look dangerous—just seemed off-kilter and scared. Before they could close in and grab him, he dove off the building. Simms said he and his partner stood there in shock for a minute, then realized they had to get out of there. They ran down the stairs and caught the first flight they could out of the country. Simms said Mr. F didn't seem like the kind of guy who would be forgiving if a job went bad."

"Why is Simms back in New York then?"

"Waited it out in South America for a while. Then his girl said she'd break up with him unless he returned home. He arrived last week. While talking with a friend at a bar, he came up with a lame excuse for why he'd been out of touch. One of our contacts heard him, put the pieces together, and called me."

"Wonder what Stapleton was going to do with the kid," the man said.

"Simms didn't know. But I have a hunch Stapleton knew Justin Eliot had psychological issues and was scared of being trapped."

"You're saying there was no way that kid was going to make it off that rooftop in one piece," the man replied.

"That's exactly what I'm saying. And since a suicide note was found, supposedly signed by Eliot but likely penned by

Stapleton, it's clear that at the end of the day, Stapleton was cleaning house."

"That kid never had a chance."

"No, he didn't."

New York City

Sean phoned Thomas. "I've read some of the journal. I'm beginning to understand what you did, and why."

Thomas was quiet. At last he said, "That's good. I wanted you to know why I stayed away for so long. But also why I watched over you."

"I didn't need you to do that," Sean shot back.

"Maybe not," Thomas replied. "But I didn't want you or your family hurt in any way, especially in connection with me. Now that you know the truth, you can choose what path you'd like me to follow in that regard. That's the least I can do for you."

Sean drew in a breath. "I'll need to think about it."

"Take all the time you need."

56

Will waited for his office door to shut, then made a private call.

"I need to know something," he said as soon as the phone was answered. "Awhile back, you made me a promise. Will you still do what I asked? Honor the request I made of you? Even if that means hurting someone dear to you?"

There was a pause on the other end, and then a solemn, "I will."

Will ended the call, then stood in front of the large glass window overlooking Madison Avenue. So it had been confirmed. But carrying the plan through might prove more difficult than any of them could imagine.

Will had been in business long enough to know that every outcome, even if promised, was not guaranteed.

The day after Bill and Ava returned from Australia, the family gathered at their place in New York City. Drew and Jon were also present.

Per Sarah's wish, now there were no more secrets among the group. Her parents knew about the way Carson, Stapleton, and

Spencer Rich had set up the photos with Sean and the Polar Bear Bomber to take care of Will's run and control all three of the Worthingtons. Ava had been predictably herself at her queenly best—flint-eyed, but with a spark that declared no one was going to mess with her family.

Bill was glowering. "Stapleton. The old fox. At times I wondered if I could trust him. Seemed too smooth. I heard of some of his dealings but dismissed them as gossip. After all, Will, he took you under his wing at American Frontier. But now I know. And Spencer Rich. I never did like that boy, even when he was young. I've liked him even less as president."

With Darcy's permission and Jon adding his notes, Sarah also filled in the group about the research they had done on the Polar Bear Bomber and who he was.

Bill looked incredulous. "So you think Justin Eliot is Stapleton's son?"

"No," Sarah said, "we know he is. A DNA test proved it."

Drew, who had at first seemed startled by the news, nodded slowly. "That makes sense. Stapleton's other son is bipolar, and he's kept him off the grid."

"And bipolar disorder has genetic connections," Jon added. "That, I know from research and from what Justin's friend Michael told us."

Bill's hands started to shake. "So, if we put together all the pieces, you're telling us that Stapleton had something to do with hiring his own son to bomb a building? Maybe even had something to do with his death?"

Sarah exchanged a glance with Jon. He nodded.

"Yes," she said. "That's what the facts point to. But to bring him to justice, we would have to prove that beyond the shadow of a doubt. We're missing a critical piece of evidence to tie his actions together. Will we find it? I don't know."

"Either way," Will said, "Stapleton has had to retire from the business world. City Capital decided they didn't need the bad press he was garnering. And I already had him removed from the AF board by vote."

"Mom, Dad, there's one last thing you should know," Sarah said. "Jon, would you explain?"

"There's no easy way to say this, so I'll just say it." Jon faced Ava. "Ava, I knew you potentially had an affair with Thomas Rich because of a note that arrived at the news office."

"But—" Ava interjected with a white face.

"Mom, let him finish," Sarah said.

Jon filled them all in on the note and his guesses as to why the note had landed on his desk.

"Spencer Rich doesn't know, but he's desperate and fishing," Bill said. "And he's determined to take my family down with him." He got up abruptly. "Excuse me. I have a call to make."

Ava waved him back into the seat. "No," she said quietly, "we will make that call together." She leaned toward him. "It's time."

Sarah frowned. "Time for what?"

"Time for an old friend to fulfill a promise," Ava stated.

Sean felt a prickle of concern at the back of his neck at his mother's words. He turned toward Will, who must have sensed the same thing, for both brothers shivered.

At that moment, Sarah said, "I have an announcement."

All eyes in the room focused on her.

Sarah lifted her chin with unflinching determination. "With throwing my hat into the ring, I can't afford to have secrets arise that could derail my campaign."

"Sarah," Bill began.

"Dad, are you going to tell me to stop now, that it's too dangerous, after we've already won so much—"

Bill held up a hand and pinned her with a fatherly glare. "No, that's not what I'm going to say." His voice boomed across the room. "I admit at first I wasn't crazy about the idea of you running for president. I wanted to protect you. You're my daughter." His tone softened. "But I know you are what this country needs. A balanced, forward-thinking president who stands on tradition but has a heart for the disadvantaged and those struggling. A person who is just as comfortable with those who are wealthy as she is helping an abused woman or a destitute family. I knew, once you decided to get serious about your life's work in college, that you were destined for something great. I have no doubt this is it."

Sarah blinked.

Ava's eyes glazed with tears. She looked back and forth between Bill and Sarah with pride and joy.

So much had changed in their family, Sean thought. The revealing of secrets had plunged them all into a terrible fire, but it also was a refining one. Through it, the Worthingtons and those they counted on had forged an even stronger bond.

At last Sarah spoke—directly to their father. "So you're really okay with your daughter being the first Worthington in six generations to make a run for the presidency? Instead of one of your sons? That no longer bothers you?"

Sean caught the plaintive longing in her tone. *Dad, just say it*, he thought. *Say it in front of all of us. She needs to hear it. As much as I needed to hear that I am truly your son, even though I don't carry Worthington genes.*

Bill got up from his chair. He moved toward his daughter and paused in front of her. "I'm not only okay with it, I'm enthusiastic about it. Princess, you will always be my baby girl, and I'll fiercely protect you no matter what. But perhaps I've done a little too much of that and not enough of telling you how much I believe in you." He took a deep breath. "So here goes. I believe you will not only finish the run for president well but be elected as the first female president of the United States. What's not to trust? What's not to love? You've charmed everyone and wrapped them around your little finger since you were little. You've fought for what's right as an attorney. You have never given up, even when the road was interminably long. You will make your mark on the planet—as the best president the United States has ever had."

Sarah blinked back tears. "Even when I'm running as a Republican and not a Democrat?"

Bill lifted a brow. "I'm still wrestling with that part of it."

Everyone in the room laughed.

At that moment, Sean was convinced the US presidency was indeed Sarah's destiny. She had the star qualities of charm, intelligence, and integrity that blazed into the hearts and minds of people of all ages. What America needed wasn't more politicians to blow smoke. The country needed transparency, honesty, a fresh approach. Someone gutsy who understood business and all echelons of society. Someone with strong moral and religious values who supported tradition and education but also the critical nature of new research. Someone who would never back away from the heat of a fire.

That was his sister.

Sarah Katherine Worthington, president of the United States.

It did indeed have a ring to it.

"Now that we're all on the same page, we need to make careful plans for how to cut off any third-party ideas at the knees," Sarah announced.

Sean focused immediately on the solution. "We can call a press conference. I'll set it up."

57

The media waited in record numbers in Tishman Auditorium, located in New York University's School of Law. Recently, the auditorium had hosted France's minister of justice. Reporters and cameramen were now stationed to capture a groundbreaking moment with a high-ranking Republican candidate poised for the presidency.

Will thought back to the day he'd been ready to announce his Senate run. Things had turned out differently than he'd planned, but in the end perhaps they had occurred just as they should have to allow for this day to happen. There was an interesting paradox in that.

He glanced around the crowd. From his right periphery, he spotted a figure that rocketed his blood pressure—one of Spencer Rich's top campaign staff. So the man was on hand, maybe to see how he could turn the political tide with some further dirty dealing. It didn't matter that Stapleton and Carson had lost their power and connections. Such men were merely spokes, easily replaced, in the wheel of a powerful man like Spencer Rich.

Such truths were why Will had placed the private phone call to his own powerful source. But now he wondered if the man was wavering in his long-ago promise. Would he truly uphold his end of the bargain?

Drew followed Will's intense glance to Rich's staff member. When Drew turned back toward Will, he whispered, "I see him too. But not here. Not now. Trust your sister. Trust Sean."

Not doing anything at this critical moment jangled Will's strong sense of justice and his innate urge to protect his family. However, he knew Drew was right. He nodded slowly and relaxed his stance.

But old habits die hard. He found his gaze still flicking to the campaign staffer. That man could be here for only one of two reasons, or maybe both.

Perhaps he was merely checking out the hottest competition. Or perhaps he had an ace card he planned on playing.

When the man slipped in behind reporter Ethan Miles, who was known for his outspoken brashness, and leaned toward him in a conspiratorial stance, Will knew exactly why he was there.

Will narrowed his eyes. So Spencer Rich was indeed trying to play his ace card at a critical juncture in the campaign. Rich hadn't yet figured out that if he went to war against the Worthingtons, he'd never win.

Sean scanned the crowd.

Jon was in the ranks of reporters, ready to cover the event. To ensure the best coverage for the *New York Times*, he'd brought along one of their lead cameramen.

Darcy was also on hand to watch how things rolled out with Sarah's surprise announcement.

Sean looked toward Elizabeth, who was still new to the Worthington life, sitting firmly entrenched next to Ava. He had no doubt his new wife could keep up with the whirl, or that the two of them would find plenty of ways to step out of it and escape to life outside the grid.

For now, though, both had agreed that he would remain as Sarah's campaign manager to the end. After that, he had plenty of time to figure out what was next. Sean had no doubt his sister would become the star he already knew she was. But just what would happen during the national conventions, with Sarah and Spencer Rich both still holding the ranks as the two strongest Republican candidates, was anyone's guess.

Spotting the intensity on Will's face, he followed his brother's gaze to Spencer Rich's campaign staffer and reporter Ethan Miles. At that moment, Will's head turned. The brothers' eyes met. The truth of the situation passed between them with a glance.

Sean touched Sarah's elbow and inclined his head slightly.

She too caught his meaning in an instant.

He handed her the folder they had prepared, and she gave a single nod.

They were armed and ready.

The first part of Sarah's speech about fine-tuning her running platform had gone splendidly. The crowd of political reporters had been eager to capture their own take on the story but had seemed, for the most part, very respectful and supportive of her announced positions. The first few minutes of the Q & A time had gone much as expected.

Then Ethan Miles pushed his way toward the front. "Ms. Worthington, your declarations about wanting to change America indeed seem admirable. However, I've just received some information that could alter the nature of the Republican campaign—your campaign in particular. I'd like your comment on these." With a flourish, he held up a couple large photos.

As reporters rushed forward for a peek at the photos, Miles pushed closer to Sarah on the platform. Sean stepped to the edge of the platform, leaned to take the photos from Miles, and briefly looked at them. Then he calmly passed them to Sarah.

In the light of flashing cameras, she looked at each of the photos. They were just as she and her family had expected— Spencer Rich's desperate ace card.

"Ms. Worthington, we're waiting for your answer," Miles said. "After all, these photos are pretty inflammatory. I think the American people have a right to know. These shouldn't remain hidden."

She lifted her head and pinned the reporter with an authoritative gaze. "Mr.—what is your name?"

"Miles," he said, his tone cocky.

"Mr. Miles, you mean these photos?" She reached under the shelf on the podium and withdrew a folder. "I believe these are an exact match for the ones you just handed me. I have no reason or inclination to hide these pictures. In fact, I brought them myself and will be addressing them later in this very press conference. For now, though, I will continue with questions that are relevant to my presidential bid and campaign platform."

"But Ms. Worthington, I insist—"

Sarah eyed him again. "Mr. Miles, you may insist all you

want. But I will follow proper protocol and answer relevant questions first before handling mere tabloid fodder. You are, of course, welcome to go or to stay until that moment arises in this press conference." She pointed to the next reporter with his hand up. "Yes?"

58

///

Will sat back in his seat, watching his take-charge sister with satisfaction. In one stroke, she'd completely deflated the aggressive young reporter of his "gotcha" moment by strategic planning, quick thinking, and above all, keeping her composure.

Will grinned. He was proud of her.

Drew caught his eye and smiled. "See?" his expression said. "I knew she could handle it, and she did."

Ethan Miles now slunk toward the back of the audience. His fellow reporters smirked at the spectacle of his debacle.

Will watched as the reporter passed Rich's campaign staffer, glared at him, then strode out the door.

The young buck who had gambled for a big win in his career had just lost any hopes he had of being hired by a reputable national network. Not one of them would touch him now. He'd be destined to live his reporting life in the shadows, scratching for tabloid news that he could only pray someone would take seriously.

Perhaps some things were as they should be for people who lacked principles, Will thought.

///

A few minutes into questions about her campaign, Sarah cast a glance at Sean. He nodded. It was time.

"Earlier, Mr. Miles, a reporter who has since left the building, handed me two photos," she stated. "As I said earlier, they match the ones in the folder I myself brought to this conference. Most of you are aware that my brother Will Worthington was prepared to announce his run for Senate last year. However, less than an hour before he was to do so, he was presented with these photos."

She held them up for the public to see, and cameras zeroed in on their contents. "I want to be completely clear on what these photos are. They portray two men sitting next to each other at a bar. One is the man who would shortly afterward become known as the Polar Bear Bomber."

The crowd started to buzz. Questions shot forth from the reporters.

Sarah held up a hand. "You will get your story—in fact, a much more intriguing one than you expected today. But in order to proceed, I ask for quiet and your cooperation."

A hush descended almost instantly in the room, with the remaining few talkers elbowed by their colleagues.

She smiled. "Thank you. I will soon reveal the name of the second man in the photos. First, however, I will give you details approved for release by DHS, the FBI, and the NYPD. These photos were taken when the second man was invited to meet a client at this specific bar. The client never showed. Instead, Mr. Eliot, the first man, was hired to go to the bar and chat with the second man. A hidden camera took pictures of the men in an effort to connect them to the upcoming bombing of American Frontier. I will not discuss the details of the bombing, as DHS, the FBI, and the NYPD will be releasing their own bulletins with those details.

"What is relevant to this press conference is how the photos came to be in my hands in the first place." Sarah addressed the audience with careful deliberation. "My brother Will was presented these photos by a man who worked with Eric Sandstrom, then still the CEO of American Frontier. Will was, of course, concerned, because the second man pictured in the photos is—"

The cameras and microphones were thrust farther forward.

"—Sean Worthington, my brother and now my campaign manager."

There was a stunned silence, then questions exploded. Sean stepped to his sister's side, calmly assessing the crowd as the media turned their attention toward him.

Sarah held up a hand again. She looked straight at Will in the audience, and he gave a slight nod. "Though Will knew that Sean could not be involved with a bombing—and that certainty has been confirmed—he had no wish to see our family dragged through the stress of the muckraking that would most certainly follow the release of the photos," she said. "So, with only a few minutes before his announcement, he did the only thing he could as a person who loves his family and wanted to protect them. He stepped down from the Senate bid.

"However, let me be perfectly clear. Neither Will nor anyone in the Worthington family has walked away from the fight behind the scenes. The photos were an underhanded attempt by powerful people to control the actions of the Worthington family. We could not let that stand. We have been at work with trusted colleagues, including those we highly respect in the FBI, NYPD, DHS, and DOJ, to put together the pieces about the parties responsible.

"Why did we not reveal this publicly before? you might ask. Because by doing so, we would have revealed information that was greatly needed to find the perpetrators. Some have now been brought to justice. Others are in process."

"Others?" a reporter called out. "How many others?"

"Specifics will be released in the timing of the governmental organizations involved," Sarah replied.

Sean now took over the podium. "A full story with the details we have given, as well as a few others, will be released within the hour online in the *New York Times*. Each of you will be provided with a briefing packet upon exiting the auditorium today so you can meet your deadlines. However, first, some final statements."

Sarah stepped back in front of the microphone. "As a Worthington, I grew up with two strong mantras: 'Family first' and 'Do the right thing always.' There will always be unscrupulous people who do despicable things in an attempt to get the upper hand on any who appear to be a threat to them. But why would those people be a threat? Because they won't back down from doing what is right. The Worthington family has never backed down from a fight. Nor have we ever backed down from doing what is right. As I proceed with this presidential bid, I make you all a promise."

As she spoke her next words, she looked directly at her father. "I will do the right thing always. I will embrace the truth, tell the truth boldly, and encourage everyone in America to do the same. Secrecy breeds gossip, mistrust, and even hatred. We've had enough of that in American politics. My campaign will be based on what the American people need and want, not on criticizing my colleagues on the other side of the fence. Yes, I am a member of a blue-blood family. But that same family has worked hard to support ventures that bring hope and better economic realities to millions of people in America and around the globe. *When* I am elected"—she smiled as her supporters in the crowd broke out in raucous cheers—"you will have a president who truly cares about the people of America. A president who treats each of you like a beloved family member."

A wave of applause cascaded over the auditorium.

But what warmed Sarah's heart the most was her business-like father clapping and the "well done" approval in his eyes.

A SECURE LOCATION

His call to the man was brief but informational. "Your gut feeling was correct. The president did try one last maneuver to sidetrack Sarah's campaign."

"The photos?" the man asked. "And?"

"The Worthingtons were prepared with a set of their own. The reporter's carefully constructed scheme—compliments of Spencer Rich—came crashing down around him." He chuckled. "That press conference will be the media highlight for a while."

"So Sarah emerged intact as a candidate?"

"Indeed. The misguided hit only increased her value in the public eye."

"I see." The man on the other end of the line seemed thoughtful. "But it still doesn't make her a complete shoo-in for president. Spencer's backing from Big Oil and Tobacco in general, and from those who can't entertain the thought of a woman ever as president, still remains strong. So that means—"

"Yes. We must reveal what we have in our hands—the power to destroy all he holds dear. And I must fulfill a promise from long ago, no matter who gets hurt in the process."

59

Two hours after the press conference, Sean's cell phone was besieged with further requests for information and heavy-hitter well-wishers. Elizabeth had waited quietly for him outside Tishman Auditorium instead of leaving with Ava and Bill. Now she drove toward their penthouse while he answered phone calls and googled news story headlines and percentages.

At last he sat back, sighing in satisfaction. Sarah's initial percentages of voter trust were through the roof. The revelation of the photos hadn't hurt her in the least. That was a big relief, as the responsibility had weighed heavily on him.

"So?" Elizabeth asked.

"All is good. Listen to these headlines and social media:

"At last, an honest politician. Is there really such a thing? It sure looks like it.

"A female president? It didn't seem likely until Sarah Worthington decided to run. Now? Just prepare the pink carpet in the Oval Office. It's a done deal, folks.

"About time. Somebody with brains and business sense.

"She used to work for the DOJ. She'll be tough on crime. That's what our big cities especially need.

"The best-looking president we'll ever have!"

That one prompted laughter from both Sean and Elizabeth. When they were safely inside their penthouse, Elizabeth snaked an arm around him. "Well, look at that. No one else is home. Since you're done now, I've got some plans of my own," she whispered in his ear.

He never could resist her.

———— /// ————

Sarah kicked off her pumps as soon as she entered her apartment. Wriggling her bare toes over the coolness of the wood floor felt wonderful.

The July day had been hot and a little sticky. What she wouldn't give right now for—

Her cell rang. She rolled her eyes. No rest for the weary.

Upon checking the number, though, she answered immediately. "Jon."

"Hey, I'm at the door downstairs. But the substitute bellman is doing his duty well, protecting you from my reporter credentials." Jon laughed.

"I'll ring him and straighten it out," she said.

"Just do it quickly. I've got something for you that won't wait long."

She raised a brow. "What on earth?"

He laughed again. "It'll be explained as soon as you open the door."

A few minutes later Jon was at her door. He extended a bag to her. "It's hot. Thought you might be up for a treat, so I stopped for a carton of your favorite ice cream." He tilted his head. "By the way, I'm inviting myself in to eat it with you."

She grabbed the bag. "You got a deal there, buster. Bet we can make fast work of it."

Less than a minute later both were seated on the wood floor, with two plastic spoons stuck in the quart of chocolate cherry ice cream that sat between them. Jon had rolled up his shirt-sleeves and shed his jacket, socks, and shoes.

"Wow, I needed this," she said.

"Me too." Jon was quiet for a minute. Then he said, "Sarah, life is going to change a lot if you get elected. You sure you're ready for all of it?"

She turned slowly to look at him. Strange how when Jon asked the question, it didn't bother her like it did when her brothers or father asked. "I know it will. But yes. I have thought about it long and hard. I never dared voice this dream aloud to anybody." She chuckled. "Darcy is the first one who guessed I might even be interested. It surprised me when she didn't think I was crazy for even considering it."

"I've never thought you were crazy." He waved a spoon of ice cream at her. "Maybe a bit melodramatic at times."

"Hey!" She waved a spoon back. "Okay, I deserved that."

"No, you deserve the best of everything. Always." His eyes were warm, sincere.

Sarah tilted her head. "Could that best ever . . ."

She couldn't speak the words, yet Jon understood. "I'm not going anywhere," he said simply.

"Even when I become the first female president of the United States?" she asked.

"You're that certain, are you?" he teased. "Well, I'm sure too. But I have this philosophy."

"And that is?"

"Everything worthwhile is worth waiting for."

A Secure Location

"Has the object been secured in its location?" he asked the man.

"Indeed. I made certain of that before I made the call to Spencer. He was, shall we say, startled."

"I can imagine. I doubt he expected enemy fire to come from the source it did. But you made it clear—"

"Yes," the man said in a solemn tone. "He is to announce within 48 hours that he is dropping out of the presidential race. Otherwise, the phone that connects him, Stapleton, the Polar Bear Bomber, and the ISIS funds will be delivered to DHS."

The line was quiet for a moment.

"Any regrets?" he asked.

The man sighed. "Of course. That this situation was created in the first place."

"And if Spencer doesn't step out?"

"His complicated world will get much messier very quickly."

The call ended.

He couldn't see Spencer Rich choosing that option. Though it was highly unlikely that he would be impeached, Spencer was smart enough to know not to go down that road. If he did, his reputation would be tarnished far worse than Richard Nixon's, and present-day Americans were far less forgiving than those during the Watergate scandal. Spencer was already busy trying to keep himself from being too deeply singed from the fire of connections with American Frontier and from the even hotter fire of the allegations of ISIS funding for his presidential campaign.

Spencer Rich had been cornered and bagged. If he was a smart fox, he'd know it and take the easy way out of that bag.

Either way, they would know within 48 hours.

60

The day after the press conference, Sarah met Michael, Justin's friend, for coffee at a small diner. He'd just flown in from London to do a theater clinic for a group of troubled youth in New York.

Michael had already snagged a corner booth. He smiled when he saw her and got up to shake her hand.

"Thanks so much for all you've been doing on Justin's behalf. I appreciate you and Jon keeping me in the loop before the official press hits."

"I only wish we could do more," Sarah said as they sat. "Like nailing Stapleton for what he really did. But the evidence just isn't forthcoming."

Michael nodded. "Even if Stapleton could be arrested for murder, that act wouldn't accomplish what I want most—my friend Justin back. But there is peace in knowing that Stapleton will no longer be in positions of authority." He shook his head. "I wouldn't want to be in that man's shoes, living with the knowledge of what he did for a lifetime—to his own son."

Sarah studied him. There were so few good guys like Michael and Jon in the world. People who genuinely cared about others. "Will you be all right, Michael?"

He sighed. "Sure. Of course. I just wish I could have gotten to him sooner, before he got swept into all of this." He straightened his shoulders. "It makes me even more determined to catch some of the troubled kids I work with and steer them onto the right path. Not all of them have loving moms like Rebecca. Most have MIA or toxic dads. As for Stapleton, I'm not sure what he is—terribly misguided, egotistical, evil? Only God knows."

"I'm sorry," Sarah said. "Truly sorry for Justin and the way his life ended."

He smiled at her. "At least now, thanks to you, Jon, and Darcy, the world knows the truth about Justin. That he would never have harmed anyone. That he never would have placed that backpack by the building if he'd known what was in it. For that, I am in your debt. If I can ever help you in any way, all you have to do is ask. I'll be on the next plane from London or Ireland, wherever I happen to be at the moment." He checked his watch. "But for now I need to depart. I promised I'd meet Mrs. Chesterton for a quick walk in the park before my session."

"And how is that dear lady?" Sarah asked. She was glad to hear he was still in contact with Marie Chesterton, who had cared so much about the children in her charge at St. Mark's.

"Still taking children who need it under her wing—just in a less official capacity," Michael said. "Says while she has time on this earth, she wants to do all the good she can."

With those words, Michael got up, doffed his Irish fisherman's cap in farewell, and strode out of the diner, melding into the crowd of New Yorkers.

Sean's social network notified him of the announcement before he saw it in the press. He immediately searched network sites to get the fuller story. The news was so recent it was still bare-bones in details, but it was already sending shock waves to multiple interested parties. Those in the Republican camp were startled and vitriolic, to say the least. Those in the Democratic camp were celebrating, since a heavy-hitter rival had been cleared from the ranks.

Spencer Rich had withdrawn from the presidential race in the height of the action. He had merely cited that he felt it was time for him to take a break after the intensity of the presidency, and allow some fresh blood to enter the presidential office. With his fairly high rankings, in spite of his recent controversies, the move made no sense to political strategists. Why withdraw in July, when he'd already weathered so much, and right before the Republican National Convention? Especially since he had clearly been going for Sarah Worthington's throat in the Republican campaign debates?

But Sean knew the real reason. The attempt to reveal the photos at the press conference had been Spencer Rich's highest ace to play against Sarah. When he was trumped by her quick action, Rich could have fought harder if he'd had any other cards to play.

Sean nearly sagged in relief. Spencer didn't know the truth—that Sean was his half brother. Otherwise, he would have circled back, even for a private round with the Worthingtons.

That meant their family secret rested only in the hands of those who would safeguard it—the Worthingtons, Drew, Jon, and Thomas Rich.

Yet the fact that Spencer had given up so easily was still a bit troubling.

Almost as if someone forced his hand, Sean thought.

He reached for his cell and dialed his father.

Will stared at the headlines Drew had thrust in front of him. "Rich withdrew."

Drew nodded.

"Interesting timing," Will said simply.

"Indeed."

The two men's eyes met. Drew's gaze was knowing.

Will thought of his private phone call to Thomas Rich and his urgent question: "Will you still do what I asked? Honor the request I made of you? Even if that means hurting someone dear to you?"

Will had had his doubts that the man would back a Worthington over his own blood. Now, though, Will had proof of the answer. But how exactly had Thomas managed to pull those strings so quickly?

"So Spencer is out of the race," Bill said as soon as Sean called.

"Was that the phone call you needed to make?" Sean asked. "To Thomas?"

"Yes, son, it was. It was time for us to protect our family." Bill paused. "Thomas agreed it was only right. He didn't explain how, but he said he'd take care of it."

Sean's thoughts whirled. Spencer wasn't the kind of man who would back down easily, nor would he simply do his father's wishes if asked.

That means Thomas has something Spencer doesn't want known.

Sean blew out a breath. Could it have anything to do with the bombing? The ISIS funds? Or was it something else?

At this juncture, Sean wasn't sure he wanted to know. Sometimes it was best just to let sleeping dogs lie.

A Secure Location

"I can imagine how angry Spencer was," he told the man. "But he acted more swiftly than either of us expected."

"Too much was at stake for him not to pay attention," the man said brusquely.

That was the crux of the issue. If the cell phone was released, it would mean more than the end of Spencer Rich's political career. He could have been the first president tried for treason for using foreign funds—terrorist money—in a campaign and thus removed from office. Instead, Spencer had clearly decided to weather out the rest of his presidential career until the next president was elected.

"Sarah Worthington is now the only clear Republican candidate. With the recent press conference, her ratings have rocketed. That she'll win the Republican National Convention is a given. It wouldn't surprise me if the other candidates drop out as well."

"And no one on the Democratic side is even close to her rankings," the man said. "That means, with a united Republican effort behind one beloved candidate—"

"Yes. Shortly a Worthington will be at the helm of the most powerful country in the world."

61

The Republican National Convention convened in Cleveland, Ohio, on July 18–21. The Democratic National Convention would be held July 25 in Philadelphia. Both would undertake their traditional work in not only selecting their party's majority nominee for president but fine-tuning their party platforms.

Sean and Sarah had barely taken a breath since the press conference. Sean had fielded some very angry calls from Kiki Estrada after Spencer Rich withdrew. Yet Kiki clearly knew the Democratic Party didn't have a leg to stand on in the race to the White House. No one could go up against a candidate like Sarah Worthington and win now. Even some of those who didn't usually vote Republican had swung to the Republican side during the primaries. But that didn't mean the Democrats were ready to back down.

When the voting was held in the evening at the Republican National Convention, Sarah won the nomination by a wide margin.

On the final day of the convention, her acceptance speech was received with thundering applause.

"I stand here tonight," she concluded, "because of a rock-solid mantra I've grown up with—'Do the right thing always.' America is faced with significant challenges, and we must choose to do the right thing for our nation, for our world, and for each other. We must also ensure that the generations to come can pursue their dreams. We must have the courage to make needed changes to strengthen the stance of America, to bring about a stable economy that honors the dignity of work and rewards self-enterprise. No one person can do it. We all are needed. Together we can restore America's standing not only as the most powerful nation in the world, but as a country that truly cares for and provides for individual Americans." She raised her hand in a fist. "Those are my commitments to you. Commitments that I *will fulfill* as the next president of the United States."

The wave of cheering was deafening.

NEW YORK CITY

Will watched Sarah's RNC speech on the large monitor in his office. He'd had no doubt she'd emerge as the majority nominee, and now it was a done deal.

He nodded in satisfaction. Choosing the high road and staying on the path didn't always garner short-term gains, but such strategy won in the long term, whether in business or in politics.

Spencer Rich still remained in office. The impeachment proceedings continued, almost as a backdrop to his presidential work and as a formality now that he'd announced he wouldn't run for another term. Therefore, he wouldn't likely be removed from office until a new president was inaugurated.

Stapleton's public life and Spencer Rich's private life were both playing out as sad dramas of what riches and power did to those who didn't deserve them—those who didn't follow the "much is required" mantra that Bill Worthington held so dear and had passed on as an enduring legacy to his children. Both had fallen hard for the false ideas that only they mattered and that they could do whatever it took to get the things they wanted.

Every step in Stapleton's life had led to a slow slide of morals. The truth of how low the man had gone was likely buried in so many layers over the years that it could never be proved. Had Stapleton had anything to do with Rebecca's parents' sudden deaths, so she'd have to become dependent on him? Will hoped not, but his gut told him otherwise.

Then, after Rebecca died, Stapleton had likely watched Justin come unhinged. Yet he had not stepped in to help his own son. Instead, to bring financial gain to the company where he was board chairman, he had arranged to hire his own son to bomb AF's headquarters. Had he been so callous as to think he could also get rid of any connection to an out-of-wedlock son in the same action? Had he known what might happen when Justin was herded to the edge of that building?

The very thought was sickening, and such a contrast to Bill Worthington's sacrificial love. Even after suspecting for years that Sean wasn't his biological son, and that his wife had had an affair with his best friend, he had given Sean the Worthington name and treated him as his son, even when their relationship wasn't easy.

Will's eyes flicked back to the screen. His gaze settled on the two Worthington men who now stood together. Bill's hand was planted firmly on his son's shoulder. A camera panned his face. He was looking proudly toward his daughter, smiling.

Life had its days where things turned out exactly as they should. Today was one of them.

CLEVELAND, OHIO

Sean crossed his arms in satisfaction. They'd achieved the next stage in the process. The fight was far from over, though. Now the election campaign would begin, with the top candidates from each side going head-to-head with each other in what usually became heated debates.

Sarah's strong stance on the issues Americans cared about and her interaction with voters and policy makers was critical in the intervening months. Americans would cast their ballots in November. Those ballots, contrary to public opinion, weren't votes for a chosen candidate. Instead, the ballots selected groups of electors in the electoral college who actually cast the votes for president in December. That was why a candidate could win literally millions of popular votes but still no electoral votes.

Sarah's election campaign had to focus on every strata of America, showing equal interest and concern.

It was a big job. Some would call it impossible, especially for a female candidate without a lot of years in politics behind her.

Sean grinned. As a Worthington, he didn't believe in the word *impossible*. Neither did Sarah.

No, their fight wasn't over. They still had a long road ahead. But Sean and Sarah were both determined that on January 20 of the following year, Sarah Worthington would be the one inaugurated as president of the United States.

62

NEW YORK CITY

Sarah had adjusted to the election campaign trail in the last three months as if she'd been born to do just that. Hugging the elderly, getting on eye level with children, talking with blue-collar workers, discussing the needs of the middle class, listening to corporate executives about their concerns—all were realms in which she was comfortable. Her margin in the important states of Iowa, New York, and others was widely increasing.

Several outspoken political analysts had announced there was no longer any contest in the race. Even powerful Democrats, disgruntled with their own weak choice for president, admitted they'd vote for her.

Sarah had won the trust of Americans by her honesty, integrity, humility, sense of humor, and straightforward, take-charge attitude.

At last she had a few quiet hours back in New York at her penthouse. She would relish them.

Glancing toward her dining room table, she smiled at the

vase of white daisies that adorned it. The card read, *A reminder of the simple things.*

In her refrigerator was a carton of her favorite spicy Indian curry, with another note: *Because I know how much you love this . . . and how little time you've had to eat.*

Only an investigative reporter like Jon could manage to wangle his way past the by-the-book bellman downstairs to deliver both of those items.

He was on assignment, or she knew he'd be there himself. He'd been true to his promise to always be there and not go far.

Sarah propped her feet up on the coffee table and threw an afghan over her toes. *Life truly is a work in progress, constantly unfolding,* she reflected. Just as her mother had claimed, Sarah's revealed destiny was an assortment of experiences and choices that built upon each other—like the individual shells on her mother's sea chest—instead of a perfect, distinguishable masterpiece from the beginning.

Sean was so glad to be landed. He glanced around his One Madison penthouse and grinned. It was no longer the cold, sterile environment of a bachelor. Now it was bursting with bits of color and patterned fabrics from Elizabeth's travels around the world.

With Sean's attentions distracted, Elizabeth had taken a three-month research project with her father on board a ship in the Indian Ocean. The ol' coot needed some company, she'd said. It was like old times, when she did everything with her father.

But Sean had missed her. She'd fly in tomorrow, and Sean couldn't wait.

In the meanwhile, in the quiet, he decided it was time. Elizabeth had suggested he read the last entry in Thomas's leather journal when he was by himself. Then they could process it together, after he'd had time to reflect.

He picked up the journal and caressed the soft leather. The book had been a wealth of information in helping him understand his birth father. It was with both anticipation and regret that he opened to the last page.

And now, Sean, our story may end here or continue. That is up to you. I will no longer follow you without your permission. I will not contact you unless you wish it so. Although I long to be in your life and to be called "family" again among the Worthingtons, that is not my decision. It is yours. It is your father's and mother's. I will never again take control over something that is not my right to control.

But no matter what decision you make, my feelings for you, Ava, and Bill will not change. To me, you will always be family. I love you, Sean.

If I can ever earn the right to address you as my beloved son, I would be honored and grateful.

Forever,
Thomas

Sean stared at the final page. So many emotions had vied for expression since he'd discovered his true parentage. After realizing his own weaknesses, he had forgiven his mother. Through the journal, he had begun to understand Thomas Rich. Compassion for his birth father flooded over Sean.

Thomas. I forgive you. And I will work toward accepting you as a part of my life.

It was all Sean could give at the moment. But for now, it was enough to know that their destinies as father and son would continue to be intertwined.

A Secure Location

He remembered the scene as if it were yesterday, even though it was decades ago.

Hearing crying, he'd sought out the source. He found Ava Worthington searching through an old trunk of her grandmother's. He rushed to her side. "Are you all right?"

She extended some baby shoes toward him in a pleading gesture. "What am I to do with them?"

Confused, he took them gently from her. *Did she lose a baby I didn't know about?*

"Turn them over," she whispered.

He did. On the backs of those shoes was a message in feminine script: "To Sean Thomas. A Gift of Love." But when separated, the left shoe read "To Sean" and "A Gift." The right shoe had the words "Thomas" and "of Love."

"Sean's shoes?" he asked.

Her tears didn't make sense until she explained that after Sean's birth, Thomas Rich, the president of the United States and a dear university friend, had seen his baby picture in the news. Thomas had called to talk to her, but she had refused the call. Now she regretted that action.

"With that single move, I cut my son off from his birth father—part of his heritage," she said.

He'd never forget the shock he'd felt at that moment as the truth registered.

"You're the only one I can trust," Ava said brokenly. "Bill doesn't know." She handed him a slip of paper with a phone number. "Call Thomas," she begged. "Tell him the truth. He needs to know for sure that Sean is his son. He will understand why I can't contact him. But wait—" She rummaged frantically through the old trunk. "Meet him. Give these to him. Tell him I sent them. They are all I have left to give."

She held up the right baby shoe and a tiny white shirt embroidered with pink and purple flowers. "He will understand why I'm sending these items." She extracted some tissue and lovingly wrapped the items, then handed them to him.

"Any message?" he asked.

"Tell him . . ." She hesitated. "Sometime he may be called upon to watch over Sean, and to help his old friends Ava and Bill. When that time comes, I trust him to do the right thing."

He did her bidding exactly as she wished.

Two days later, while Bill was on a business trip, the man flew to Langley with the package and delivered it directly to Thomas Rich, the now former president of the United States, in his home.

He had returned with both Thomas's promise and a secret assignment.

One that remained to this day.

63

After months of hard work on the election campaign, Sean knew the next few hours would be the toughest ones. It was November 4, the day the votes would be tallied. As the results rolled in from each state, Sean and Sarah stood side by side in her campaign headquarters.

The entire Worthington family, plus Jon and Drew, would gather there later for the final countdown. Whether Sarah won or lost, they would be together.

Laura greeted Will with a kiss at the door. "I figured you might come home early today," she teased.

"Couldn't focus," he told her.

"I understand. I'll leave you to your thoughts."

His mind had been on his sister all day. Was it indeed her destiny to become the next president of the United States? And not only that, but the first female president?

He replayed the conversation he'd had earlier that day with his father.

"When I told you it was about time a Worthington turned this country around," Bill said, "I didn't think the first Worthington in six generations to make a bid for the presidency would be your sister."

"Neither did I," Will said, "but even before she told me, I had this feeling she'd run. And I didn't question it. I knew it was right."

"Well, I was wrong. It wasn't your place, or Sean's. It was Sarah's all the while. I'm so proud of you, Will—for the way you have relentlessly and passionately pursued growing Worthington Shares, and also for your integrity in doing the right thing for American Frontier. I know it hasn't been easy, and it won't be easy going forward. But you will wake up every morning knowing what it feels like to change the world, and tackle it again. The same goes for Sean, who is changing the world every day in a very different way that is perfectly suited to him. I'm so proud of him. And Sarah, who chose to defend the defenseless in law school, tackled the tough jobs at the DOJ and then as AG, and had the courage to pursue her dream. You have all fulfilled the 'much is required' mantra."

Will was stunned. It was the longest speech his father had ever given, and the most affectionate one Will had ever heard him utter.

As he reviewed his father's words now, he realized anew that more than just an election hung in the balance. Principalities and powers were watching all around them. The fate of a nation—and those of the nations America touched—hovered.

The still, small voice spoke. *It is well, Will.*

Suddenly he knew. There was only one possible outcome of this primary decision.

Six generations had waited for this night. And they would not be disappointed.

⸻

Sarah waited, eyes transfixed on the monitors that announced the results from the final few states that could swing the balance.

Her father stepped up next to her. His arm circled her shoulders protectively. "I believe in you, princess," he whispered. "I've always believed in you." As the last tallies came in, he stood with her—an island in the sea of election-day tumult.

Twenty minutes later, champagne corks popped around the room. A happy chaos reigned.

Sarah's mom hugged her with joyful tears.

"You knew we'd do it," Sean threw at her before he was off networking and celebrating with the campaign volunteers.

Will, Bill, and Drew were all uncharacteristically grinning.

Jon stayed back as she was besieged by well-wishers, but his warm gaze enveloped her with a "well done."

"Later," she mouthed.

He winked. She knew that meant he wasn't going anywhere.

Jon was right. Everything worthwhile was worth waiting for—as long as it took.

Even if it meant waiting for at least four years while she carried out her duties as the next president of the United States.

64

Drew Simons was ushered into Thomas Rich's mansion. The two men shook hands warmly, then entered Thomas's study. He nodded, dismissing his Secret Service detail. Drew smiled and lifted a hand toward the two men. By now they were all old friends.

"So, it is done," Thomas said. "The assignment you agreed to all those years ago—to protect Sean and his family from harm and to see to their welfare in all ways."

Drew nodded.

"So what will you do now?" Thomas asked.

"Exactly what I've been doing." Drew cocked his head toward Thomas. "At first it was just a job to work my way into the financial district of New York, as I'd hoped." He grinned. "It also pleased my father. After all, you, he, and Bill all hung out in the same circles at university. To Dad, there was nothing better than aiding an old friend and helping his son get to where he wanted to go in life."

"But something changed after your father passed away so suddenly."

Drew nodded. "Yes. With him gone, and my mother's death while I was in university, I found myself without family. Bill and Ava took me in—made me part of theirs."

Thomas chuckled. "The Worthingtons have a way of doing that. Bill and Ava adopted me in university when I was feeling disgruntled and casting about for direction." He sobered. "You returned the favor when Ava was feeling lost."

Drew nodded. Yes, he had seen her sorrow in keeping her secret from her husband. He'd seen her loneliness when Bill was on the road and the brave façade she wore. Drew had been drawn to be Will, Sean, and Sarah's father while Bill was away. He'd grown to fiercely protect them from a world that judged them harshly just because they were wealthy. He also respected Bill and agreed with his life philosophies, with one difference. Drew vowed that when he had his own family, he would be there to walk alongside them, even if his business suffered. After their marriage, Jean too had seen to that.

Aloud, he told Thomas, "By then I was loyal to the Worthington family. Your assignment gave me the resources and financial backing to protect them and ensure their welfare at any cost, wherever they traveled in the world. For that, I thank you."

For over three decades, the Worthingtons hadn't known Thomas was watching over them. Then Thomas had given the journal to Sean. But even he hadn't known the extent of Thomas's involvement until yesterday.

"And the meeting?" Thomas asked.

With Thomas's agreement, Drew had gathered Bill, Ava, Will, Sean, and Sarah at his home. It was only the second time in the history of his relationship with the Worthingtons that Drew had called a family meeting. There, with Jean's support, he had told them the full story of Thomas's involvement over the years, and his own actions behind the scenes to ensure the safety and welfare of the Worthington family. It was time, he and Jean agreed, to reveal the depth of their love and care for the family. Then it was up to the Worthingtons to decide what to do next.

"They were stunned," Drew said simply.

"You gave them details?"

"Yes, I fully explained. I told them I would answer any questions they might have. That you would also answer any questions."

"What did Sean say?" Thomas asked.

"'All these years, I had two fathers and a beloved mentor watching over me.'"

Thomas's eyes welled. "You're all right with the Worthingtons? They know you're in their court? That you carried out an additional assignment from me simply because you cared so deeply about them? Because you considered them family and wanted to protect them?"

"Yes, I'm all right. And yes, they know. Long ago I chose to step into that unseen role. Now, with their permission, I will remain in that role."

Yes, he would continue to walk alongside the Worthingtons. It was his destiny. Drew was confident of that.

Thomas Rich, former president of the United States, stood in the lavish richness of his study after Drew departed. Quiet descended, and with it an unbearable emptiness. His eyes flitted to the secret drawer that had once contained the journal and Sean's baby items. It now contained only one item—the cell phone that had convinced Spencer to withdraw from the race. It was the record of texts and calls between his son and Frank Stapleton, as well as confirmation of their dealings with ISIS to garner election funds. It also proved that Stapleton had contacted Justin Eliot to change the location of their meeting to the top of the high-rise.

The fact Spencer had morally sunk so low shamed Thomas to the core. Yet because Spencer was his son, Thomas couldn't bring himself to release the proof publicly. Perhaps it was because Thomas himself had done so much wrong in his life. But he had used that proof privately to remove Spencer from the presidential race. He would use it again, if needed, so Spencer would never hold another public office.

Life certainly hadn't turned out the way Thomas thought it would. As he absently scanned his office shelves, his attention landed on the book Sean had left behind in Corvo. Thomas scooped it up from where it nestled among the hundreds of books in his voluminous library. Someday he would return it to its rightful owner. Yet he felt strangely reticent to do so, as if he would be losing something precious. Lately an unexplainable force had drawn him again and again toward the book, as if it had the trajectory of a burning arrow.

He flipped to the inscription.

To Sean. Light for your path. Love you to the moon and back. Sarah.

Thomas didn't even have to read the words anymore. He knew them by heart, because they had burned into his heart and mind. He needed light for his path, and somehow just the presence of that book in his library had provided that in his darkest hours in the last few months. Still, he couldn't escape the niggling thought that he was being pursued by something much greater than himself. Perhaps someday he'd make his peace with that.

"One day I hope you will," Sean had told him. In the meanwhile, Thomas had decided that the secret drawer would never hold any secrets other than the cell phone he needed to keep for now. The only other secret would remain privately between himself and the Worthington family—that of Sean's parentage.

One night of moral weakness had altered his friendship with Bill and Ava Worthington. It had torn the fabric of trust they'd had at the university. Thomas had once thought that trust irreparable. But now he stood united with Ava and Bill again as their friend, their history swept aside in an act of forgiveness that had shaken him to the core.

He'd never forget the day Bill and Ava had called him after their family meeting, when they knew that the photos of Sean with the Polar Bear Bomber could be released to the media.

"You were my best friend," Bill had said.

"And mine," Ava added.

They had missed him, they said.

"Forgive me," Bill said in a broken voice. "For not staying at Camp David. For putting the two of you in that situation. For wasting so many years because I guessed but was afraid to confront the truth. Afraid to lose Ava's love."

"And forgive me," Ava whispered, "for not being courageous enough to tell Bill the truth. You should have been a part of Sean's growing up."

Thomas was overwhelmed. His throat tightened. "I was so needy. Lonely. Lacking for love. Missing friendship."

"We forgive you," Bill said. "Will you forgive us? Can we start over?"

Tears trickled unheeded down Thomas's cheeks. "Yes." Silence reigned for a moment before he added, "But there is something I must do first. Ava, do you remember the promise you asked me to make when you sent Sean's baby shoe and shirt to me?"

"Yes," she said softly.

"It's time for me to do what is right. I must sacrifice one son to save another—and to pave the way for our new relationship."

So Thomas had done what was right, and lost the only family he had on paper. His wife, Victoria, had been the easier of the two. She was already cut off from him, enamored with her new lover. She had been surprised when he granted her 50 percent of his wealth without a fight. Their divorce was already finalized.

His son Spencer was another matter. When Thomas had entered the White House for a private conversation with his son, he didn't tell Spencer he knew about the note sent to Jon. All he said, with deep regret, was how disappointed he was in the man Spencer had become.

When Spencer flung Thomas's words back in his face, blaming his father for everything that had gone wrong in his own life, Thomas simply said, "You're right. I should have been there for you in your childhood. I wasn't. And I accept the blame for that. But what you have done since—that is on your head."

Then he had turned on his heel and walked out of the Oval Office, leaving a for once speechless Spencer staring after him.

The single greatest mistake he'd ever made, Thomas noted, was the way he'd reared Spencer—to believe that he was the center of the universe. It brought Thomas no joy to take down his own son. In fact, his heart was weighed with grief. But he knew it was the right thing to do.

Thomas looked now at the new but old photo that graced his desk. A university photo of three best friends, heads together, laughing and exchanging heartfelt dreams with each other. A photo he thought he'd never see again, after letting it slip below the waters of Lake Chautauqua. Bill and Ava had sent him the old photo in a new frame the week after the three friends had made their peace.

Thomas picked up the photo and read the inscription on the back.

To Thomas. Old friends, new beginnings. Love always, Bill and Ava.

Thomas squared his shoulders. For the first time since that night so long ago, he was stepping into the future again without trepidation.

The worst had been faced. The best, he was convinced, was yet to come.

Epilogue

On a blustery January 20, Sarah Katherine Worthington took the presidential oath: "I do solemnly affirm that I will faithfully execute the Office of the President of the United States, and will to the best of my ability, preserve, protect, and defend the Constitution of the United States."

Afterward, as the new president of the United States, she scanned the enthusiastically clapping crowd.

Sean and Elizabeth grinned and gave her a thumbs-up. Ex-president Thomas Rich sat comfortably next to Sean, nodding in satisfaction. The press could talk all they wanted, but they would only gather that Thomas was an old friend of the Worthingtons, and he was showing his support.

Even the stoic Will stepped out of character and winked at her.

Drew smiled. "Well done," his keen blue-gray eyes said. "I knew you could do it."

Sarah's mother sat primly in her suit purchased just for the occasion. She wiped away a tear.

Her father beamed at Sarah. "I believe in you," that proud expression said. "You are one of us. A Worthington."

In that moment, Sarah's heart overflowed, her desire for acceptance and respect from her father met at last. But this time it wasn't based on what she did but on who she was.

Her gaze moved next to Jon, and her eyes misted.

He was signing, "I love you."

BIRTH ORDER SECRETS

Have you ever felt compelled to act a certain way, as if you've been programmed?

The Worthington siblings—Will, Sean, and Sarah—grew up side by side in the same family, yet each sees life through a completely different lens. As a result, they respond to events differently.

Have you wondered why your sister or your brother is so polar opposite to you in lifestyle, behavior, and everything else? Why you're a neat freak and your sibling is messy? Why you're a procrastinator and your sibling is a finisher? Why you pick the friends you do? Why you're driven to succeed? Why you're less comfortable around your peers and more at ease around people older than you? Why you're attracted to a certain type of person, or to a specific occupation? Why you struggle day to day with never being good enough? Why you're always the one mediating between warring family members or co-workers?

The answers to these questions have everything to do with birth order secrets. Your place in the family has a lot to say about why you do what you do. It gives you important clues about your personality, your relationships, the kind of job you seek, and how you handle problem solving.

This Birth Order Secrets bonus feature highlights key traits of firstborns, onlyborns, middleborns, and lastborns. You don't have to meet all the criteria in a certain list to be a specific birth order. In fact, if you don't, there are reasons for that too. (For more intrigue, read *The Birth Order Book*.)

Discovering and understanding the secrets of birth order can powerfully change your life and revolutionize your relationships at home and at work.

Millions of people have already seen the results. You can too. I guarantee it.

Dr. Kevin Leman

FIRSTBORN

First on the scene.
Held to a higher standard.
Star of the show.

If you're a firstborn:

- You are a natural-born leader. People look up to you.
- You have a strong sense of what is right and just.
- You love details and facts.
- You like to know what's expected of you and have high expectations for yourself and everyone else.
- You love rules . . . well, you call them "guidelines." In fact, you may have a few too many.
- You always feel under pressure to perform.
- You don't like surprises because you're a planner and organizer.
- Books are some of your best friends.

ONLYBORN

Goal-oriented.
Self-motivated.
High-flying achiever.

If you're an onlyborn:

- You are a planner and an organizer and work well independently.
- You have high expectations for yourself and others. The word *failure* is not in your vocabulary.
- You were your parents' first and only guinea pig in child rearing.
- You were a little adult by age seven, comfortable with those older than you but not always at ease with your peers.
- You find yourself saying *always* and *never* a lot.
- Add *very* or *really* in front of any firstborn trait, and that describes you.
- You are extremely conscientious and reliable.
- Books are your best friends.

MIDDLEBORN

Navigator.
Negotiator.
Relational genius.

If you're a middleborn:

- You're determined to choose your own path.
- You're pretty good at avoiding conflict.
- You're even-keeled, the mediator, the peacekeeper. You see all sides of an argument.
- You sail through life with calm and a sense of balance.
- You thrive on relationships.
- Friends are your lifeline.
- No one in the family ever asked you, "What do you think we should do?"
- You navigate life's seas in your own subtle way—although you may be the only one who realizes you're the peanut butter and jelly of the family sandwich.

LASTBORN

Winsome.
Natural entertainer.
Rule breaker.

If you're a lastborn:

- You're great at reading people.
- You've never met a stranger.
- You can be very persuasive.
- Admit it—you like to be the center of attention.
- You're good at getting other people to do what you want them to.
- You're a natural salesperson.
- Many people still call you by your pet name, even if you're an adult.
- You love surprises!
- Although you don't like to admit it, you were just a little bit spoiled.

Acknowledgments

Grateful thanks to:

- All who read our books, enjoy the journey, and find their own "aha moments." You make writing worthwhile.
- Our family members, who each relentlessly pursue making a difference in the world in their own unique ways.
- The Revell team, especially Lonnie Hull DuPont and Jessica English, for their enthusiastic support of this publishing dream.
- Our longtime editor Ramona Cramer Tucker, who is the peanut butter and jelly of our sandwich.

About Dr. Kevin Leman

An internationally known psychologist, radio and television personality, speaker, educator, and humorist, **Dr. Kevin Leman** has taught and entertained audiences worldwide with his wit and commonsense psychology.

The *New York Times* bestselling and award-winning author of over 50 titles, including *The Birth Order Book*, *Have a New Kid by Friday*, and *Sheet Music*, has made thousands of house calls through radio and television programs, including *Fox & Friends*, *The Real Story*, *The View*, Fox's *The Morning Show*, *Today*, *Morning in America*, *The 700 Club*, CBS's *The Early Show*, *Janet Parshall*, CNN, and *Focus on the Family*. Dr. Leman has served as a contributing family psychologist to *Good Morning America* and frequently speaks to schools and businesses, including Fortune 500 companies such as YPO, Million Dollar Round Table, Top of the Table, and other CEO groups.

Dr. Leman's professional affiliations include the American Psychological Association, SAG-AFTRA, and the North American Society of Adlerian Psychology. He received the Distinguished Alumnus Award (1993) and an honorary Doctor of Humane

Letters degree (2010) from North Park University; and a bachelor's degree in psychology, and later his master's and doctorate degrees, as well as the Alumni Achievement Award (2003), from the University of Arizona. Dr. Leman is also the founder and chairman of the board of the Leman Academy of Excellence (www.lemanacademy.com).

Originally from Williamsville, New York, Dr. Leman and his wife, Sande, live in Tucson, Arizona, and have five children and four grandchildren.

For information regarding speaking availability, business consultations, seminars, webinars, or the annual "Wit and Wisdom" cruise, please contact:

Dr. Kevin Leman
P.O. Box 35370
Tucson, Arizona 85740
Phone: (520) 797-3830
Fax: (520) 797-3809
www.birthorderguy.com
www.drleman.com

Follow Dr. Kevin Leman on Facebook (facebook.com/DrKevinLeman) and on Twitter (@DrKevinLeman). Check out the free podcasts at birthorderguy.com/podcast.

About Jeff Nesbit

Formerly Vice President Dan Quayle's communications director at the White House, **Jeff Nesbit** was a national journalist with Knight-Ridder (now the McClatchy Company), ABC News's Satellite News Channels, and others, and the director of public affairs for two prominent federal science agencies: the National Science Foundation and the Food and Drug Administration.

For nearly 15 years, Jeff managed Shiloh Media Group, a successful strategic communications business whose projects represented more than 100 national clients, such as the Discovery Channel networks, Yale University, the American Heart Association, the Robert Wood Johnson Foundation, and the American Red Cross. Shiloh Media Group helped create and launch three unique television networks for Discovery Communications, Encyclopedia Britannica, and Lockheed Martin. They developed programming and a new cable television network concept for the Britannica Channel; global programming partnerships for the successful launch of the Discovery Health Channel, including a novel CME programming initiative and the Medical Honors live broadcast from Constitution Hall; and programming strategies for the creation of the first-ever IPTV network developed by Lockheed Martin.

Jeff was the co-creator of the *Science of the Olympic Winter Games* and the *Science of NFL Football* video series with NBC Sports, which won the 2010 Sports Emmy for best original sports programming, as well as *The Science of Speed*, a novel video series partnership with the NASCAR Media Group.

Jeff has also written more than 25 inspirational and commercially successful novels—including his latest blockbusters, *Jude*, *Peace*, *Oil*, and *The Books of El*—for publishing houses such as David C. Cook, Tyndale, Zondervan/Thomas Nelson/HarperCollins, WaterBrook/Random House, Victor Books, Hodder & Stoughton, Guideposts, and others. He is the author of the critically acclaimed *Poison Tea* (Thomas Dunne Books, 2016).

Jeff is executive director of Climate Nexus and writes a weekly science column for *U.S. News & World Report* called At the Edge (www.usnews.com/news/blogs/at-the-edge).

Resources by Dr. Kevin Leman

Books for Adults

The Birth Order Book
Have a New Kid by Friday
Have a New Husband by Friday
Have a New Teenager by Friday
Have a New You by Friday
Have a New Sex Life by Friday
Have a Happy Family by Friday
Planet Middle School
The Way of the Wise
Be the Dad She Needs You to Be
What a Difference a Mom Makes
Parenting the Powerful Child
Under the Sheets
Sheet Music
Making Children Mind without Losing Yours
It's Your Kid, Not a Gerbil!

Born to Win

Sex Begins in the Kitchen

7 Things He'll Never Tell You . . . But You Need to Know

What Your Childhood Memories Say about You

Running the Rapids

The Way of the Shepherd (written with William Pentak)

Becoming the Parent God Wants You to Be

Becoming a Couple of Promise

A Chicken's Guide to Talking Turkey with Your Kids about Sex (written with Kathy Flores Bell)

First-Time Mom

Step-Parenting 101

Living in a Stepfamily without Getting Stepped On

The Perfect Match

Be Your Own Shrink

Stopping Stress before It Stops You

Single Parenting That Works

Why Your Best Is Good Enough

Smart Women Know When to Say No

Books for Children, with Kevin Leman II

My Firstborn, There's No One Like You

My Middle Child, There's No One Like You

My Youngest, There's No One Like You

My Only Child, There's No One Like You

My Adopted Child, There's No One Like You

My Grandchild, There's No One Like You

DVD/Video Series for Group Use

Have a New Kid by Friday

Making Children Mind without Losing Yours (parenting edition)

Making Children Mind without Losing Yours (public school teacher edition)

Value-Packed Parenting

Making the Most of Marriage

Running the Rapids

Single Parenting That Works

Bringing Peace and Harmony to the Blended Family

DVDs for Home Use

Straight Talk on Parenting

Why You Are the Way You Are

Have a New Husband by Friday

Have a New You by Friday

Have a New Kid by Friday

Available at 1-800-770-3830 • www.birthorderguy.com • www .drleman.com

Connect with the Authors

DR. KEVIN LEMAN
DrLeman.com

Follow Dr. Leman on
Dr Kevin Leman | drleman

• • •

JEFF NESBIT
JeffNesbit.net

Follow Jeff on
jeffnesbit

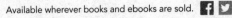

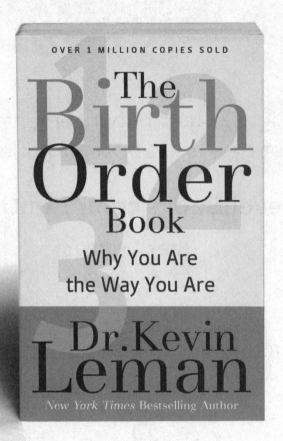